CONFIDENTIAL MEMO

Badge No. 1113: Grace McCall-Fox

Rank: Sergeant

Skill/Expertise: Cool-headed while working under cover, and possesses an innate (and useful) ability to charm.

Reason Chosen for Assignment: Her serene, angelic appearance inspires trust in targeted suspects—but may also awaken the passion of her partner and ex-lover, the FBI special agent in charge of the case.

Mark Santini—Federal Bureau of Investigation

Rank: Special Agent

Skill/Expertise: Top hunter in the Bureau's Crimes Against Children Unit, a cause near to his heart.

Reason Chosen for Assignment: Legendary for his captures of child abusers and killers, and for keeping himself closed to emotion. Will partnering with his old flame lead to a change of heart?

Dear Reader,

Once again, we invite you to experience the romantic excitement that is the hallmark of Silhouette Intimate Moments. And what better way to begin than with *Downright Dangerous,* the newest of THE PROTECTORS, the must-read miniseries by Beverly Barton? Bad-boy-turned-bodyguard Rafe Devlin is a hero guaranteed to win heroine Elsa Leone's heart—and yours.

We have more miniseries excitement for you with Marie Ferrarella's newest CAVANAUGH JUSTICE title, *Dangerous Games,* about a detective heroine joining forces with the hero to prove his younger brother's innocence, and *The Cradle Will Fall,* Maggie Price's newest LINE OF DUTY title, featuring ex-lovers brought back together to find a missing child. And that's not all, of course. Reader favorite Jenna Mills returns with *Crossfire,* about a case of personal protection that's very personal indeed. Nina Bruhns is back with a taste of *Sweet Suspicion.* This FBI agent hero doesn't want to fall for the one witness who can make or break his case, but his heart just isn't listening to his head. Finally, meet the *Undercover Virgin* who's the heroine of Becky Barker's newest novel. When a mission goes wrong and she's on the run with the hero, she may stay under cover, but as for the rest…!

Enjoy them all, and be sure to come back next month for six more of the best and most exciting romance novels around, right here in Silhouette Intimate Moments.

Yours,

Leslie J. Wainger
Executive Editor

Please address questions and book requests to:
Silhouette Reader Service
U.S.: 3010 Walden Ave., P.O. Box 1325, Buffalo, NY 14269
Canadian: P.O. Box 609, Fort Erie, Ont. L2A 5X3

The Cradle Will Fall

MAGGIE PRICE

Silhouette®

INTIMATE MOMENTS™

Published by Silhouette Books

America's Publisher of Contemporary Romance

SILHOUETTE BOOKS

ISBN 0-373-27346-0

THE CRADLE WILL FALL

This edition published by arrangement with Harlequin Books S.A.

® and TM are trademarks of Harlequin Books S.A., used under license.
Trademarks indicated with ® are registered in the United States Patent
and Trademark Office, the Canadian Trade Marks Office and in other
countries.

Visit Silhouette at www.eHarlequin.com

Printed in U.S.A.

Books by Maggie Price

Silhouette Intimate Moments

Prime Suspect #816
The Man She Almost Married #838
Most Wanted #948
On Dangerous Ground #989
Dangerous Liaisons #1043
Special Report #1045
  "Midnight Seduction"
Moment of Truth #1143
*Sure Bet #1263
*Hidden Agenda #1269
*The Cradle Will Fall #1276

*Line of Duty

Silhouette Books

The Coltons

Protecting Peggy

MAGGIE PRICE

turned to crime at the age of twenty-two. That's when she went to work at the Oklahoma City Police Department. As a civilian crime analyst, she evaluated suspects methods of operation during the commission of robberies and sex crimes, and developed profiles on those suspects. During her tenure at OCPD, Maggie stood in lineups, snagged special assignments to homicide task forces, established procedures for evidence submittal, even posed as the wife of an undercover officer in the investigation of a fortune-teller.

While at OCPD, Maggie stored up enough tales of intrigue, murder and mayhem to keep her at the keyboard for years. The first of those tales won the Romance Writers of America's Golden Heart Award for Romantic Suspense.

Maggie invites her readers to contact her at 5208 W. Reno, Suite 350, Oklahoma City, OK 73127-6317, or on the Web at http://members.aol.com/magprice.

To white knights…

Chapter 1

At five minutes to five, Sergeant Grace McCall-Fox limped into the Oklahoma City PD's Youth and Family Services squad room, feeling as old as her undercover disguise made her look. She had a jagged hole in her right support stocking, put there during the day's last arrest when she used her knee to force an uncooperative juvie to kiss pavement while she cuffed him. One pocket on the tan wool coat she'd scored at a thrift store sale had gotten ripped in the struggle and small pebbles had somehow wedged into both toes of the prison-matron-looking lace-ups she'd borrowed from her grandmother's closet. Her cheeks were chapped from the hours she'd spent trolling the frigid shopping mall parking lot; the gray streaks she'd sprayed on her raven-black hair had turned sticky the minute snow had begun falling. Her right arm ached from having been nearly jerked from its socket by several wanna-be purse snatchers who thought they'd make easy prey of an elderly woman out doing her Christmas shopping.

Instead of a fragile senior citizen, they'd encountered a slim, petite, thirty-year-old cop who'd dropped them on their collective butts in one smooth move.

"McCall!"

The booming voice pulled Grace's gaze across the squad room to the tall, gray-haired man leaning out an office door.

"Sir?"

"I need to see you," Lieutenant David Kelson said. "Now," he added, before stepping back into his office.

Grace dropped her vinyl decoy purse on her desk, pulled off her coat and gold wire-rims with nonprescription lenses. Thinking Kelson might want to review the plan on her current undercover op, she snagged the file, then wove her way around the scattering of city-issue metal desks, mostly vacant this late in the day.

Through the wedge of the open door she saw that Kelson was now seated at his desk, his attention focused on the paper in his hand.

Gripping the file, Grace smoothed a palm down the baggy gray dress she'd bought at the same time as her coat.

"Sir?" she asked.

Kelson glanced up. "Come in, McCall." Like everyone, he used the shortened version of her hyphenated last name. "How'd things go today at the mall?"

"The team took down four juvie purse snatchers and three auto burglars. We're hoping to nab more tomorrow."

"That happens, it'll be without you. The FBI has asked for your assistance on a case. Consider yourself on special assignment."

"Yes, sir." She arched a brow. "What sort of assignment?"

Kelson rose. "I'll let the agent in charge brief you."

The drift of her lieutenant's gaze across her shoulder gave her the first indication of another presence in the office. "I understand you two have worked together?"

"I'm looking forward to teaming with you again, Grace."

She went utterly still at the sound of Mark Santini's deep, rich voice coming from behind her. A voice from her past. A voice whose owner had continued to haunt her over the span of six years, even though she'd loved and married another man during that time.

Spine stiff, she forced herself to turn. And felt everything slip out of focus when her gaze met familiar eyes so deeply brown it was impossible to see a boundary between pupil and iris.

Oblivious that the earth had just tilted beneath her feet, Kelson retrieved his overcoat, then moved around the desk. "Sorry I can't stick around, Agent Santini," he said, offering Mark his hand. "Like I said, I'm due to meet my wife at a Christmas party."

"No problem. I had hoped to get here earlier, but cutting through red tape to get that court order held me up. I'll brief Sergeant McCall on the case so she and I can hit the ground running in the morning."

"Use my office as long as you need." The lieutenant turned to Grace. "Agent Santini has cleared your assignment through the chief's office." Kelson snagged the paper he'd been reading when she walked in, handed it to her. "Here's a memo to you from the chief that makes your assignment official. Keep me updated."

"Yes, sir." Tucking the paper into the file folder, Grace watched her boss cross the office and walk out, closing the door behind him. Wishing she was also on the other side of that barrier, she pulled in a breath and glanced back at Mark. A good head taller than herself, he looked down at her, his gaze slowly traveling the length of her—from gray-sprayed hair to prison-matron shoes—with a few lay-overs.

"Elderly is an interesting look for you, Grace."

"It fools a lot of juvie purse snatchers," she said, and struggled for additional words that wouldn't come.

Physically, Special Agent Mark Santini had changed some in six years. His hair, as thick and black as her own, was still combed straight back, but it was cut shorter now, and silver had begun to salt the temples. The planes and angles of his face were leaner, sharper, and circles under his eyes evidenced lost sleep, yet the man was still down-to-the-ground gorgeous. Always a consummate clothes-horse, his black silk suit was tailored and expensive. But the coat hung somewhat loose off his broad shoulders, and the pants were a little baggy, as though he'd lost weight. Instead of making him look gaunt, however, the effect created an approachable, relaxed appearance.

Grace was anything but relaxed as she clenched the file folder against her breasts. Mark stood so close she could have reached out and touched him. Touched the man who'd swept into her life with a startling magnetism that soon had her considering giving up her cozy, settled world. And even though she hadn't, he had remained a ghostly presence that had nearly destroyed her relationship with Ryan Fox.

She had loved Ryan with all her heart. To the depths of her soul. Just the thought of the doubts he had suffered because of her reckless behavior over Mark had her heart shattering all over again.

She did her best to shove away the quick, instinctive tug of resentment that accompanied the thought. What had happened years ago had been her doing, not Mark's. He had no idea she'd gone temporarily insane and made the decision to toss away her lifelong dream and meld her life with his. No idea that the history they'd shared had shaken the foundation of her subsequent marriage.

"How are you, Grace?" His voice was all business, devoid of emotion.

"Fine," she said, using the same impersonal tone. "And you?" Strange, she thought, that two people who had been such passionate lovers could transform into nothing more than polite acquaintances.

"Busy. Eternally busy." He studied her with calm observation, his expression unreadable. "I was sorry to hear about your husband's death. I sent a card. I hope you got it."

"I did. Thank you." She stood perfectly still, picturing the masses of flowers and mountains of cards that had filled their home after Ryan died in the line of duty.

Deliberately she shifted to settle the file folder in a nearby visitor chair. She used the moment, a much-needed moment, while her back was to Mark to steady herself. She had no desire to revisit that time three years ago when she'd lost so much.

Schooling her expression, she turned to face him. A whiff of the familiar spicy male tang of his aftershave reached her. A quick clutching in her belly came and went. Dammit, what man wore the same aftershave six years running?

Lifting a hand to her throat, she settled her fingers against the point where her pulse hammered as if she'd just chased down a fleeing felon. Her body was simply reacting to a known stimulus, she told herself. Nothing more.

Wanting to steer the subject away from herself, she said, "I don't doubt you're busy, considering all the positive publicity you've garnered for the Bureau the past couple of years. Clearing the Boston Baby case must have made you the star of the Crimes Against Children Unit.''

He slid one hand into the pocket of his trousers. As always, he looked as though he could emerge from a mass murder crime scene with an incredibly relaxed air. ''Several other CACU agents also had a hand in solving that case. I'm just the one they chose to put out front at the press conferences.''

No kidding, Grace thought. She felt sure he'd been assigned the spot in the limelight on that case because he fit the profile of what the media thought an FBI Special Agent should look like: tall and athletic, with a coolly handsome face and dark hair. Perfectly groomed. Santini possessed the totally centered grace of a natural-born hunter, who looked dashing both on television and in print.

And in person, she admitted grudgingly. His compelling looks had attracted her like iron filings to a magnet when she'd first laid eyes on him six years ago. Then Mark had worked at the Bureau's Oklahoma City office. She'd just been promoted to detective and had been assigned to the same multi-agency task force as he. The respect they developed for each other's professional abilities quickly broadened to friendship, and they became lovers, drawn together by a passion that Grace had often sensed seemed stronger than both of them.

Soon after that, Mark snagged the transfer he'd coveted to the CACU, based at Quantico, Virginia. And then he was gone—a man with no roots, no ties, infinitely comfortable with his lone-wolf existence. How different her life with Ryan would have been if she'd stuck to her guns after declining Mark's offer to move to Virginia with him.

Now here was Santini, intending to work with her again. He'd do whatever job he'd come to do, then be gone. And never once look back. Like before.

This time, though, experience had taught her the value of keeping her priorities straight.

She gave her watch a meaningful look. "Mark, if you could give me a quick rundown on your case, I'd appreciate it. I have family business to take care of this evening that I can't put off."

A look crossed his face, a quick shadow that disappeared in one hammer beat of her heart. "How is your family, Grace?"

"Everyone's fine." She paused, wondering if his reaction was displeasure over her refusal to drop everything and give him more time tonight. "Josh, Nate and Bran have all received promotions over the past two years. Morgan and Carrie are on the force now. Engaged to OCPD cops."

His mouth curved. "Is there any member of the McCall clan who isn't in law enforcement?"

"Mom and Gran are the holdouts."

"They get points for marrying cops."

"Yes." Even as her lover, Mark had shared next to nothing about his past, saying only that his childhood had been wretched. He had never spoken of his parents. As far as she knew, he had no other family so there was no point in asking about the Santini clan. Still, things might have changed. She glanced at his left hand, saw he wore no ring. "What about you?"

He arched a dark brow. "I haven't married a cop."

And because she couldn't stop herself, she countered, "Brenda wasn't a cop."

"Brenda." He narrowed his eyes, as if trying to recall the blond, gorgeous, long-stemmed White House staffer Grace could still picture perfectly. "I haven't married anyone. The job doesn't allow much time for a personal life."

The job, Grace thought, that he was bound to the way

he would never be bound to a woman. Mark had made no secret that as far as he was concerned, his priorities lay with whatever case he was working at the time. Always the case. Because of that mind-set, she was relatively sure he considered what had happened between them water under the bridge, but for her it had meant much more.

Just then his pager chirped. He pulled it off his belt, checked the display, then pressed his fingers to his eyes.

"Problem?" Grace asked.

"A call about a child-abduction case I'm working in California," he said, clipping the unit back on his belt. "My gut tells me it just turned into a homicide."

"If you're working it, why aren't you there?"

"Because my boss called late last night to tell me the director wanted me here. I hopped a plane from California first thing this morning." He lifted a shoulder. "You know how it is, Grace. In law enforcement, you do what you're told. Go where you're sent."

"That's why I spent the day cruising a mall parking lot in granny garb," she commented, then wrapped her arms around her waist. "So, why don't you brief me on the case that prompted the director of the FBI to send you back to Oklahoma City? And why you went to my chief and specifically requested I work with you?"

"The case is a political hot potato that involves a young woman's death. Her father has a lot of power, and he's throwing his weight around, so here I am." Mark eased back the starched cuff of his shirt to check his watch. "Since I need to call California and you don't have a lot of time right now, I'll hold off briefing you until morning. There's nothing we can do on the case tonight, anyway. As for your other question, I contacted OCPD because I learned long ago it smoothes things considerably to attach someone from local law enforcement to any investigation

I work. The reason I requested you is simple. I need a local cop who's not only good but smart. Someone I can trust not to muck up a sensitive case.''

''Nice to know you have such faith in my abilities.''

''I've always had faith in you, Grace. Personally and professionally.''

Since he had never opened up enough to tell her how he felt about her, that was news.

''We have a subpoena to serve at eight in the morning,'' he added. ''We need to get together earlier so I can bring you up to speed. You can meet me at my hotel at seven, or I'll come by your place and pick you up. Your choice.''

Grace slicked the tip of her tongue over her dry lips. She was a great believer that the home team held the advantage. Considering that her stomach was grinding and her nerves had settled into perpetual vibration mode, meeting in the morning on her turf was preferable.

''My home.'' She gave him the address, then retrieved her file folder off the chair. When she straightened and turned, Mark took a step toward her. Up close, the shadows under his eyes seemed more pronounced.

''I meant what I said, Grace.''

His voice had gone as soft as a whisper on the still air. A whisper that had her pulse thudding hard and thick at the base of her throat. ''About?''

''I'm looking forward to working with you again.''

She drew in a deep breath. The longer she spent in his presence, the more her unease heightened. He'd hit the target when he said cops took on whatever assignment came their way—she had no choice but to work with him.

So she would do her job. Period. Even though time had not seemed to dull the physical attraction she felt for Mark, she couldn't let that matter. Couldn't let him get to her again. He would be here and gone. As soon as they dealt with his case, he'd be gone.

She had once been close to falling in love with Mark Santini. Had spent years dealing with the endless cycle of guilt tied inescapably to that relationship. She'd paid her dues and wasn't going down the same road again. The man standing only inches away was past history, and she was a completely different woman—one who was making a determined effort to get on with her life.

She would do better tomorrow, she assured herself. The shock at seeing Mark again would have worn off and she'd be back on level ground. Right now she needed to get away from him, needed time to deal with the fragments of a hundred memories she'd locked away that were now rushing to the surface.

"I'll see you in the morning," she said.

"Yes."

Turning her back on him, she headed toward the door. As she moved, she felt his eyes on her, tracking her.

Time passed, she thought. When it did, events and people became larger than they were or smaller. She wanted to believe that this man who'd stepped so unexpectedly from her past into her present had become so small that he was next to invisible. A mere blip on her radar screen. Wanted to believe that Mark Santini was so inconsequential that his presence would have no effect on her future.

The way her heart was pounding had Grace very, very afraid that wouldn't be the case.

Chapter 2

Her face had been an open book, Mark mused the following morning as he steered his rental car through Oklahoma City's snowy streets. Grace had been shocked to find him standing in her boss's office. Stunned was more like it. Understandable, considering it had been nearly six years since they'd laid eyes on each other.

Since they'd been lovers.

He tightened his jaw as the wipers slapped a steady cadence back and forth, clearing two fans on the snow-covered windshield. What bothered him—what had eaten at him most of the night—was knowing that when they faced each other, *she* should have been the only one caught off guard. The only one wrestling with emotion. That hadn't been the case. Hadn't at all been what he had expected.

Dammit, he had *known* she would walk through the door of her lieutenant's office at any minute. Had anticipated her arrival.

Yet the instant she stepped into view, he'd been hit with a jolt of electricity. He had spent a lifetime moderating his emotions, had built up a level of control so rigid that nothing or no one ever caught him off guard.

Grace McCall-Fox had. Big-time.

Knowing that just the sight of her had made his mouth go dry and his gut clench into knots did not sit well. Granted, she was the one woman—the *only* woman—for whom he had felt a pull of something far beyond physical attraction. While they were lovers he had chosen not to analyze the intense, mindless emotion that had drawn him to her. It had been a huge enough step for him to acknowledge that his relationship with Grace had been the first from which he couldn't seem to make a clean break and walk away. So, when the transfer he'd coveted to the Bureau's Crimes Against Children Unit came through, he'd asked her to move back east with him.

She'd said no. Understandable, seeing as how her world revolved around her large, rowdy family. Then there had been tradition to consider—almost every McCall had served on the Oklahoma City PD. Doing so had been Grace's lifelong dream, one she found impossible to give up.

He had coolly accepted her decision. Made no effort to change her mind. Logically he knew his promotion to the CACU meant he would spend most of his time traveling, leaving Grace behind in an unfamiliar city. She'd have gotten the raw end of the deal, and he hadn't blamed her for turning him down.

So, he had walled off the regret that had washed over him, just as he had taught himself to block out all other emotion. He had put the memory of Grace McCall into the far reaches of his mind and immersed himself in his work.

It was only natural she'd crept into his thoughts now and again over the years, but he and Grace had parted on good terms and what was done was done. He wasn't the only one who had moved on, either. Grace had married a cop—then buried him three years later.

For himself, Mark had spent the past years building his reputation in the law enforcement community, along with unused leave time. He had no roots, no family, no woman waiting for him to return. It was the lifestyle he wanted. He traveled wherever the job took him, primarily from one crime scene to another. He worked case after case, dealing with an endless cycle of abused, kidnapped and murdered children. Child after child, body after body, one malicious crime after another.

The horror he encountered in his work never surprised him. He'd grown up knowing firsthand that the devil walked the face of the earth. Knew too well the terror suffered by a child at the mercy of a monster. Years later he had learned that most of the people in the small town where he'd grown up had known about the beatings he'd endured, but had chosen to look the other way. He'd joined the FBI, vowing to hunt down as many child-preying deviants as possible.

Without warning, the fatigue that now held him constantly in its grip shuddered through him. He tightened his gloved hands on the steering wheel and attempted to twitch the weariness out of his shoulders. What he needed was a good night's sleep, but he'd long ago given up hope for that.

Over the past year—or was it two now?—he'd had a recurring dream that replayed the images of the bruised and battered victims in every case he'd worked while in the CACU. An unending parade of child after child. Monster after monster. The dream was like acid, slowly eating away the hours he slept each night.

Now, if he got any rest at all, it was fitful. He had forgotten the last time he'd slept through an entire night. Forgotten what is was like to eat a meal and not have the lining of his stomach ignite like a blowtorch. He had dropped weight. When he ate now, it was because he had to. He moved from crime scene to crime scene, hotel room to hotel room, lying awake and alone in strange beds, sweating from the dream that plagued him.

Exhaling a curse, he reached down deep inside for the strength to fight off the draining fatigue. He couldn't stop. Couldn't back off. He had monsters to catch.

He checked the notepad on which he'd jotted the address Grace had given him, drove two more blocks and made a right turn. Dammit, he should be in California, working the kidnap case that he'd correctly guessed had turned into a homicide last night when the little girl's body had been found. Or maybe he was needed worse in New Orleans where three preteen boys had disappeared in the past month. Then there was the small town in Alaska where a killer currently preyed on young female victims.

Mark felt another tremor of fatigue. Each one of those cases had first priority; in each, time was critical. Just wanting—*needing*—to be somewhere else aggravated his frustration and exhaustion.

And maybe, just maybe, he wasn't totally sure he felt up to dealing with Sergeant Grace McCall-Fox. Not after the way he'd reacted to her yesterday. He was pointedly aware that her elderly lady look had done nothing to quell the jolt he'd felt when she walked into the office. No one had to remind him about the truly fascinating body concealed beneath that baggy gray dress. Or point out it had been years since he'd felt that kind of warmth surge in his blood. He'd reacted to Grace's presence yesterday the same way he had the day he met her. Instant attraction. A burning, immediate desire to get his hands on her. Searing lust.

Now, though, he didn't feel either physically or emotionally up to dealing with that kind of response. Chances were, he'd made a huge mistake by requesting to use Grace as his contact with the OCPD. What was done was done, however, and there was no changing that.

He spotted the address, then pulled the car up to the curb in front of a two-story house painted a cool blue with gleaming white trim. Through the veil of snow, the small porch with slender ivy-wrapped columns looked inviting, with a white wicker table and chair snugged into one corner. A garland of evergreen framed the front door; a wreath adorned with a gigantic plaid bow and loaded with shiny red balls hung in its center. Four cars crowded the driveway, including an OCPD black-and-white. With so many cops in the McCall family, Mark didn't even hazard a guess on who had driven the cruiser there.

Instead of climbing out of the rental car, he left its engine idling while he gazed at the house and conjured up a picture of Grace.

He had always found a certain fascination with her face—those carved cheekbones that rose high and taut against skin the color of gold dust, her thinly bridged nose and angular chin. Then there was her mouth—full and rich and moist. A mouth that had taken him over the edge to heaven countless times.

That was it, he reasoned, and closed his eyes against a remembered kick of lust. His response to her yesterday had been totally physical. She was, after all, a beautiful woman with whom he'd engaged in uncountable bouts of hot, steamy sex. He hadn't been with a woman at all for some time, so it was only natural he would respond to one who had once had the power to stir his blood with just a look. A touch. A moan that slid, raw and ragged, up her throat.

"Christ," he muttered when a quiet ache of longing for that part of his past rose inside him. He didn't know what the hell was going on, but whatever it was, he damn well didn't need it.

He snapped off the ignition, jerked off one glove and scrubbed a hand over his face. Judging from what he knew right now about the case he and Grace would be working, he probably wouldn't be in town long enough to do anything about this unexpected stirring in his blood. They would deal with what needed to be done, then, as always, he would move on. Which he figured was best for everyone involved.

Mark snagged a file folder off the passenger seat and stepped out of the car into the swirling snow. The frigid air stung his cheeks, scraped his throat like little bits of ice. The cold wind blew back the flaps of his black wool coat; frozen crystals crunched beneath his shoes as he made his way up the walk and ascended the small flight of stairs.

Stamping his feet on the welcome mat, he rang the bell. When the door swung open, it took him a second to realize the sandy-haired uniformed cop whose broad shoulders nearly blocked the entire doorway was Brandon McCall.

"Well, well, the Great Santini. I hate like hell to admit it, but it's damn good to see you."

Mark grinned. Of Grace's three brothers, he had taken a special liking to Bran. "Damn good to see you, too, McCall. As much as I hate to admit it."

Chuckling, Bran swung the door open wider and Mark stepped inside. He was instantly hit with the warm aroma of cinnamon and baking bread.

"Smells good, doesn't it?" Bran asked.

"Like heaven." Mark tucked the file folder under one arm and pulled off his gloves. He realized with a start that his mouth had begun to water, a sensation he barely remembered. Too bad his stomach could no longer deal with anything but the blandest food.

"I about fell over when Grace mentioned you were in town." Bran took a sip of coffee from the thick-handled mug he carried. "Didn't think I'd ever lay eyes on your ugly face again."

"I had to come back to Oklahoma City to see if you still lose every game of touch football you play," Mark countered as he shrugged out of his coat.

"Typical Fed. Got nothing stored in your head but useless information." A smirk tipped up the right corner of Bran's mouth as he examined Mark's gray silk suit. "I see you're still wearing those pretty-boy suits and ties."

Mark sent a pointed look at Bran's sharply pressed gray uniform shirt and navy pants. His leather gun belt had a polished gleam, and the silver lieutenant bars on his collar points shone like beacons beneath the light. "At least one of us looks good while fighting crime."

Bran barked a laugh at the insult. "I would never try to compete with you in the clothing department, pal. Grace has coffee ready. We'll drop off your coat in the living room on our way to the kitchen."

"Thanks."

Mark trailed Bran down the wood-planked hallway, noting the rooms they passed were typical of an older house—small, with high ceilings and plenty of tall, narrow windows that let in the hazy winter light.

Bran paused at an arched doorway. "Just toss your coat over the couch."

Mark stepped into the room filled with furniture upholstered in calming neutral tones. The wood was dark and polished, the accent pieces in shades of deep rose and smoky gray. Lush green plants speared out of colorful pots that sat on tables and the floor. Across the room a towering Christmas tree wrapped with twinkling white lights and tinsel filled one corner. Packages tied with red and gold satin ribbons pooled beneath its branches.

Mark stared at the tree. His mother had never bothered with Christmas decorations. Or presents. Not when buying them would cut into the money she spent on her precious booze. Even after he bought his condo in Virginia, he'd never once considered putting up a tree. No reason to, since he spent most Christmases at locations where crimes had occurred.

Mark laid his coat over the couch's back. Nearly a year ago, Bran had e-mailed him with news that he had eloped with a private investigator. Mark was about to ask Bran how married life was treating him when he noted the folded quilt and bed pillow sitting on one of the cushions. A paperback by an author whose books he remembered Bran liked lay on the coffee table in front of the couch. Mark narrowed his eyes, thinking back to the cars he'd seen parked in the driveway. The OCPD black-and-white had the same amount of snow covering it as the other three cars. Which meant it had been parked there all night. Since it looked as though Bran had sacked out on the couch, asking about his wife probably wasn't the smartest thing to do.

"Nice house," Mark commented instead.

"Yeah," Bran agreed. "Looking at it now, it's hard to believe it was a dump when Carrie and Morgan bought it."

"I thought this was Grace's place, too."

"Not originally. Carrie and Morgan bought it the day

before Ry got killed.'' Bran angled his chin. ''You ever meet Ryan Fox while you worked here?''

''No. I understand he was a good cop.''

''One of the best.'' Bran's expression darkened, his mouth tightening into a thin line. ''Grace found him just seconds after that drugged-up car thief shot him. It about killed her when she lost Ry and…'' He closed his eyes. ''Anyway, Grace sold the house they owned, and bought into this one. Renovating the place turned into a project for the entire family. Did us all good to spend that time together.''

Family. Mark had never fully understood the depths of that kind of bond, but he'd witnessed the strength of the link that existed between the McCalls.

Bran checked his watch. ''Wish I wasn't in a rush, but I have to make lineup at eight. I want to grab one of Morgan's cinnamon rolls to take with me.''

He led Mark past a small dining room, turned left when they reached a steep wooden staircase at the end of the hall, then stepped into the kitchen where copper pots and pans hung on a rack over a small butcher-block island. Gray slate topped the counters; small pots of what Mark guessed were herbs lined the windowsill. Beyond the wide pane of glass, powdery flakes swirled in the gray morning light.

He caught movement out of the corner of his eye and turned just as Grace stepped through a doorway on the opposite wall. She wore a snug cherry-red sweater, pegged black trousers and practical low-heeled boots. A gold badge and holstered Smith & Wesson 9mm automatic were clipped to her waistband. Her sleek, shoulder-length hair, now devoid of yesterday's gray streaks, looked as black and shiny as the satin lapel of a tuxedo.

''Morning, Mark.'' Her voice sounded the way he knew

her flesh felt—warm and comforting, like water over a smooth stone.

"Morning."

"Make yourself comfortable." She gestured toward the long-legged stools on one side of the island where an over-size poinsettia bloomed in a brightly painted pot. He noted that her stunned look of yesterday was gone; now she gazed at him with dark eyes as calm as a convent.

"Thanks." He settled onto a stool while Bran drained his coffee mug, then reached into a wicker basket and pulled out a cinnamon roll the size of a manhole cover.

"Want one?" he asked Mark. "They're fresh out of the oven."

"I'll pass."

"Your loss." Bran dropped a kiss on the top of Grace's head. "Thanks, sis. Tell Carrie and Morgan I'll see them later."

"Sure." When Grace looked up at her brother, Mark saw the quick shadow that passed across her face. "You'll take care of yourself?"

Bran tweaked her chin. "I promise to eat my vegetables, Mom."

"You're a good son," she said sweetly even as she jabbed an elbow into his ribs.

Grinning, Bran turned and gripped Mark's hand. "How long you planning to be here?"

"That depends on what Grace and I find out today. I'm just not sure."

"Let's try to squeeze in time to grab a beer while you're here."

"You're on," Mark said, then watched Bran head out of the kitchen. He looked back at Grace. The shadow that had crossed her face had settled in her eyes. "I get the distinct impression you're worried about your brother."

"I am. He and Tory split up before Thanksgiving. Bran puts up a good front, but inside he isn't handling things too well."

"I'm sorry to hear that. Bran sent me an e-mail to let me know he'd remarried." Mark paused, thinking about Bran's shy, unassuming first wife who'd died suddenly from a brain aneurysm. "Is Tory anything like Patience?"

"The exact opposite. Which I suspect is one of the problems with the marriage." Grace picked up a dish towel, laid it back down. "Bran rented this god-awful apartment. Has electric-blue paint on the walls, green wall-to-wall shag and day-glo orange countertops. He wakes up in that place with a hangover, the glare will kill him. The only furniture he has is a bed, a ratty recliner and a TV."

"Maybe he's hoping it's all temporary. That he and Tory will get back together soon."

"That's what we're all hoping." Grace raised a shoulder. "I keep an eye on him, try to make sure he eats right, but it's a losing battle."

Mark rested his forearms on the counter. "I see you're still looking out for everyone."

Her mouth tightened as she stared at the door through which Bran had disappeared. "Not the easiest thing to do when you're dealing with a man who's a blockhead." She pulled a mug out of one of the cabinets, then looked back at Mark. "Coffee?"

"Actually, I'm more into tea these days," he said as he reached into the inside pocket of his suit coat.

"Tea?" Grace stared at the teabag now dangling from a string clenched between his fingers as if it were an alien life form. "This coming from the man I've seen consume a gallon of task-force coffee without a wince."

"I've turned over a new leaf. If you could nuke some water, I'd appreciate it."

"No problem." In minutes his tea sat steeping in front of him.

Grace refilled her coffee mug. "In addition to the cinnamon rolls, we've got croissants and poppy-seed muffins."

"All baked by Morgan, I suppose."

"Correct." Grace carried her mug around the island and slid onto the stool beside his. "I'm going to miss her when she gets married and moves out."

"When's the big event?"

"Valentine's Day. She's marrying Alex Blade. Do you know him?"

"Blade." Mark sipped his tea while reaching into his memory. "When I worked here, he teamed up on a couple of undercover assignments with Sara Rackowitz, one of our female agents." Mark paused, his mouth curving. "Are you sure Morgan's old enough to get married? Last time I saw her, she had just gotten her driver's license. She had a mouthful of braces."

Grace's eyes met his over the rim of her mug. "You've been gone a long time, Mark."

"True." So long that he couldn't remember anymore what it felt like to go into the same office each day. Sleep in the same bed every night. He took another sip of the tea that was touted to be mild on the stomach, all the time wishing it were coffee.

Leaning in, Grace pinched an anemic-looking leaf off the otherwise thriving poinsettia.

Watching her, Mark felt memories flood over him. At the beginning of their affair, Grace had visited his apartment and been appalled at its bare-bones look. Since he spent most of his time at the office, he'd rented only the basic amount of furniture needed for one person who was rarely home. It sure as hell had never occurred to him to add accessories. Before long, Grace had brought over scented candles, woven throws and colorful pillows. Several potted plants from the landscape business her mother owned had soon followed. He could picture her in that apartment now, clipping leaves off those plants. For the first time, he understood that Grace had created a nest of contentment for him. The only one he'd ever had.

When she shifted back on her stool, the movement sent her light, subtle scent drifting over Mark like a gentle stroke of hands. Soothing. Inviting. He closed his eyes for an instant, wishing he could lose himself in that scent. In that soft voice. In the woman.

"So, Agent Santini, ready to tell me about the case we'll be working?"

"Ready." He could wish for a hell of a lot of things, he thought as he opened the cover on the file folder he'd brought with him. Problem was, he'd learned a long time ago that wishes were futile. "Does the name Landon Grayson ring a bell?"

Grace's brows shot up. "Slightly. He's only about the most powerful man in the U.S. Senate."

"*The* most powerful. Which is why I'm here. The Bureau's annual budget is at Grayson's mercy."

"What would law enforcement be without politics?" Grace asked dryly. She paused. "How is he involved in this case?"

Mark flipped up a page in the file. "Grayson's daughter died here not long after she'd given birth at a state-run medical clinic. She apparently died of complications associated with the birth."

Grace narrowed her eyes. "If she wasn't a victim of a violent crime, why are *you* here? Why not use an agent from the local office if Grayson wants the death looked into by the FBI?"

"The Bureau did that to begin with." Mark took a minute to decide the best way to explain things. "I need to back up and walk you through this from the beginning."

"All right."

"From all accounts, Grayson's daughter, Andrea, was a headstrong and stubborn kid. One who apparently gave new meaning to the word *rebel*. She and the senator never got along."

"What about her mother?"

"Died when Andrea was an infant. Over the years Andrea ran off a couple of times. The cops always found her and brought her home. By the time she was fifteen she'd figured out how not to get caught. She had a fake ID made in the name of A'lynn Jackson, her mother's maiden name. The next time Andrea and the senator fought, she walked out of the house and vanished."

"How long ago was that?"

"About three years."

"And now she's dead."

Nodding, Mark pulled a photo from the file of a smiling girl, full of eager youth. Andrea had a pretty face framed by long auburn hair, and a tall well-shaped build. "This is the most recent picture the senator had of Andrea, taken just before she left home the last time."

Grace studied the photo. "She looks a lot older than fifteen."

"She drifted around the country, using her mature looks and the above-average singing voice she inherited from her mother to score gigs with bands in country-western bars. If anyone questioned her age, she had the fake ID that upped her age to legal. She also worked as a waitress in those bars, and gave dance lessons."

"Did she have any contact with her father during that time?"

"Twice. Right after Andrea left home, Grayson hired a private investigator to find her. Somehow the P.I. figured out she was using her mother's maiden name, and he picked up her trail in Kansas City. The report in the file doesn't say how, but Andrea got wind the guy worked for the senator. She called Daddy, told him if he didn't call off his P.I. she'd disappear from his life forever and never have anything to do with him."

"I take it the senator is the one who backed down?"

"Yes. Andrea was his only child, and he blamed himself for her rebellious streak."

"Why?"

"When his wife died, the senator dealt with his grief by burying himself in his work. He hired a series of nannies to raise Andrea."

"So she basically lost both her mother and father at the same time."

"That's the size of it," Mark agreed. "Fast forward to a month ago. The senator returned from an overseas trip to find a message from Andrea on his private answering machine. She acknowledged they'd had their differences and a lot of what she called 'bad stuff' had happened between them. Said she wanted to call a truce, then added she was pregnant and due any day. After asking if she could bring her baby home, she assured her father she would call back in two days to find out his answer." Mark took a sip of tea. "Apparently being pregnant changed the way she looked at things."

"Knowing a baby is on the way can do that."

Mark glanced up. Grace's voice had gone soft, taking on an almost elusive sadness. As had her dark eyes. "Something wrong?"

Her eyes cleared as she handed the photo back to him.

"Nothing more than the fact that a young girl is dead. In the message, did Andrea say where she was?"

"No, but Grayson got the number off his phone's caller ID. She didn't call back when she said she would, so he contacted the Bureau's assistant director and asked for help in finding out where she'd called from. The number checked to a place called Usher House in Oklahoma City."

"I know it well." Grace sat her coffee mug aside. "A woman named Millie Usher established the shelter about five years ago for homeless, pregnant girls. I've dealt with several runaway juvies who've stayed there."

"The home is church funded, right?"

"Right, but Millie opens the door to girls from all faiths. Her rules are simple—no drugs, no alcohol, no men allowed." Grace propped an elbow on the counter. "I take it that's where the agent from the Bureau's local office comes in? He went to Usher House to see if Andrea was still there?"

"Yes. The agent didn't find a record of Andrea Grayson. But when he showed her picture around, several people identified her as A'lynn Jackson and said she'd lived there a short time. When our agent asked about the baby's father, two girls staying at Usher House told him Andrea didn't know the guy's name. Just that he was some trucker passing through the city." Mark flipped through a few pages in the file. "Millie Usher claimed that when Andrea showed up, she told Millie she had decided to give up her baby for adoption. Andrea's decision on that was so firm, she'd already had someone at the clinic help her fill out the paperwork to legalize things."

"She had an ID under a fake name showing she was of legal age," Grace said. "She probably claimed she had no next of kin and signed an affidavit swearing she didn't know the identity of the baby's father."

"All correct," Mark said. "Which, according to Oklahoma's parental consent laws, cleared the way for the state to handle the child's adoption."

Grace frowned. "But between the time Andrea arrived at Usher House and when she called her father, she'd changed her mind about giving up her baby."

"That's the logical assumption."

"Did your agent find out what changed her mind?"

"No. Not long after Andrea phoned her father, she showed up at the clinic in labor. According to our agent, she didn't tell anyone she'd decided to keep the child. Andrea gave birth a couple hours later to a healthy girl, then began hemorrhaging and died of the sudden blood loss."

"What happened to the baby?"

"Per the papers Andrea had previously signed, the infant was turned over to Loving Arms Adoptions, one of the agencies that has a contract with the state. Since A'lynn Jackson had failed to give the clinic the name and contact information for a next of kin, her body was donated to the state medical school's cadaver program."

Grace winced. "How did the senator take that news?"

"Reportedly with a lot of anger fueled by his grief."

"I can imagine." Grace pursed her mouth. "So how did Agent Santini wind up with this case in his lap?"

"Through no doing of my own," Mark returned dryly. "Grayson knew my name because I testified before a committee he chairs. He demanded the assistant director assign me to secure the release of his daughter's body and investigate the legalities of the adoption."

"He wants to raise his granddaughter?"

"Yes." Mark sent Grace a sardonic look. "Probably hoping to make up to Andrea for the crummy job he did with her."

"You don't think he's sincere?"

"Maybe he never laid a hand on Andrea, but he kept his distance for years. Abused her emotionally. That can do as much harm as repeated beatings. The damage just doesn't show on the outside. Who's to say he won't treat his granddaughter the same way?"

Without warning, Mark felt an old hurt and vicious bitterness close in on him. He tightened his grip on the mug. He made a point to keep what happened to him as a child where it belonged—in the past. Always the past. That those old emotions had just risen to the surface left him feeling exposed, a sensation totally foreign to him.

"Mark, did you know Andrea Grayson?"

He looked up to find Grace's eyes probing his face. She was the only person with whom he'd ever been tempted to share the details of his past. It was just as well that he'd held back. They were colleagues now, with only their jobs in common.

"No, I never met her," he said evenly. "Why do you ask?"

"Because you sound like there's something personal about this case."

His jaw tightened. "I always take it personal when a young person dies. Andrea is dead, and try as he might, the senator can't take a step back and make things right." Mark rubbed the back of his neck in an attempt to ease the tension that had settled there. "What Grayson can do is get strings pulled and red tape cut on his behalf. Which is where I come in. And why I spent most of yesterday getting a court order for the release of his daughter's body from the medical school's cadaver program."

"I hope for everyone's sake you managed to do that."

"Yes. The med students are out for the holidays, so the body is in the same shape now as it was when the school received it. Grayson had a private plane pick up Andrea's body last night and fly it to D.C. Since she died with one of the clinic's doctors in attendance, no autopsy was required. The senator wants to make sure he's being told the truth about her death, so he hired a private company to perform an autopsy.''

''If there is something suspicious about the death, the fact the body's already embalmed won't help.''

Mark nodded. ''I understand they'll have to compare samples of clean embalming fluids with that in the body. Check to see if any foreign elements or compounds are present.'' He glanced at the clock over the stove. ''The autopsy should just now be getting underway.''

''I take it you and I will be serving the subpoena you mentioned yesterday to Loving Arms Adoptions so we can try to find Andrea's baby?''

''That's first on our list.''

''Suppose the autopsy doesn't turn up anything nefarious? If the adoption records are sealed by the court, they won't be available to us, despite your subpoena.''

''True, and it's possible we'll run into that kind of road block. But it's also possible the adoption isn't finalized and Loving Arms isn't yet under any order by the court. If that's the case, our subpoena requires them to let us see the records they have on Andrea Grayson's daughter. If the infant is still under the agency's care, the senator can send a pack of lawyers to get his granddaughter turned over to him.''

Grace stood, walked around the island and dumped the remainder of her coffee in the sink. Turning, she shook back her hair.

The gesture was so familiar that Mark felt his throat close. A picture rose inside his head of her lying in his bed, her body slick with sweat from their lovemaking, her warm, silky legs tangled with his. They had shared some light comment that had prompted her to prop herself up on one elbow and smile down at him with a smugness that mirrored the same sated contentment he'd felt. Then she'd laughed and shaken back all that glorious hair. He'd slid his fingers into the dark fall, tumbled her onto her back and lost himself in her again.

"So," Grace began, "if everything goes smooth, your work here might not take long."

He kept his eyes steady on hers, fighting back both the vision and the erotic sweep of memories that accompanied it. He had been with other women since her, but the relationships had been scattershot with no emotional bonds forged. No other woman had brought him the same sense of completeness as Grace. Had never even gotten close.

"Right," he agreed, shifting gears smoothly even as remnants of an age-old need clawed in his stomach. "With luck, we could have everything tied up fast."

He noted her fingers fisting against her thighs, then flexing. "And then you'll be gone."

"That's my plan."

"Well, Santini, you always did have a plan. And the willpower to stick to it."

"Things work better that way, McCall."

"Don't I know it," she agreed as she turned and flipped off the light over the sink.

He rose off the stool. "Ready to serve that subpoena?"

"I'll get my purse and coat, then meet you at the front door."

"Fine." Standing there with warm, homey scents hanging in the air, Mark watched her go. As he listened to her footsteps tap against the hallway's wooden floor, he realized he still wanted her. Mindlessly.

Which was his tough luck.

Chapter 3

Grace didn't want to think about how natural it had felt to have Mark Santini in her kitchen again. Of how just sitting on the stool beside his had seemed so achingly familiar. Of how empty she'd felt when he acknowledged he would leave.

Again.

Of course Mark would leave. That was what he did. He jumped from city to city, case to case, then he moved on.

She had spent most of the previous night tossing and turning, reminding herself of his gypsy lifestyle. Reminding herself that no matter where he was, Special Agent Santini was on the road to somewhere else. His whereabouts were at the whim of the FBI, and that's the way he liked things.

Now, as she walked beside him through fluffy, spiraling snowflakes toward the building that housed Loving Arms Adoptions, Grace shoved her gloved hands into the pockets of her coat, then fisted them. She was *not* going to do this again. Not going to let her crazy hormonal reaction to this hotshot cop with a killer face and fancy suits guide her like she had six years ago. She was smarter, wiser and had received enough hard knocks to know she couldn't have everything she wanted.

Which didn't really matter, since she no longer *wanted* Mark Santini.

Didn't want any man at the moment. She readily admitted that the black, vicious grief she'd felt over losing Ryan—and later the child she carried—had sent her burrowing into a numbing emotional cocoon. If she ever got brave enough to peel off the protective layers and look for another man, she would set her sights on someone like Ryan. Her husband had been easygoing, as dependable as the sunrise. Mr. White Picket Fence who'd wanted to settle down and raise a bushel of kids. Again, she felt the bitter, dragging regret. She had never once thought of Ryan as a rebound love. Yet, when he overheard a conversation after he and Grace married about the reason she'd made the visit to Virginia to see Mark, that's exactly how Ryan had viewed himself—as the man she'd turned to on the rebound. The man she'd *settled* for.

She and Ryan had barely started dating when she'd made that trip. She'd recognized something special about him, yet even then she'd known she couldn't move on until she resolved things with Mark. So she'd gone to Virginia on the chance she and Mark might somehow be able to meld their lifestyles. There she discovered he'd already moved on with the leggy White House staffer.

She would regret for the rest of her life Ryan's overhearing that conversation. Regret how deeply he'd been hurt. He had been dead nearly three years, yet the regret continued to hang over her like clogging, black smoke.

What she did not need—did not intend to create—were additional regrets over Mark Santini.

So she would ignore the unrelenting, maddening chemistry that pulled her toward him, and do her job. Then watch him leave.

Again.

"Here's hoping this goes smooth," Mark said as he pulled the building's front door open for her.

Nodding, Grace stepped past him into the lobby, an arty rectangle decorated in soft hues. She knew he wanted things to go without a hitch because the smoother they went, the sooner he could head to his next assignment. Unbuttoning her coat, she blamed the dry ache that settled in her throat on the sudden transition between the frigid outdoors and the warmth inside.

Loving Arms Adoptions was located in a multiroom suite with coral carpets and leather furnishings. A thin, fortyish woman in a gray suit sat at a well-organized desk, typing on a computer. She looked up when Mark and Grace walked in, turned from her computer and gave them a mild smile.

"Can I help you?"

They displayed their badges, then Mark asked to speak to the agency's director.

"Do you have an appointment with Mrs. Quinton?"

"No, we have a subpoena," he said politely. "If your boss is too busy to see us, we'll serve the subpoena to you."

"Wait here." The woman popped out of her chair like a cork from a champagne bottle and hustled down a carpeted hallway.

Grace slid Mark a look. "You always did have a knack for getting a woman's attention, Santini."

He gave her a quick, smug grin. "It's a gift."

Grace tried to ignore the instant hot ball of awareness that all-too-familiar grin lodged in her belly. Dammit, the man was like a force field, hauling her closer, when all she wanted was to keep her distance.

Just then the receptionist reappeared and escorted them into a large office. Centered in the room was a dark wooden desk behind which a gray-haired woman with vivid blue eyes sat, taking them in.

"I'm Patsy Quinton," she said, gesturing them to chairs in front of the desk. "Now that you've put my secretary in a tizzy, officers, what can I do for you?"

"We're looking for a baby," Mark said.

The woman nodded. "Most people who come to Loving Arms are."

"A girl," he continued, then gave the date Andrea Grayson had given birth. While he explained the facts of the case, Grace handed Mrs. Quinton a copy of the form Andrea had signed at the clinic authorizing her daughter's adoption. "If the infant has already been adopted, we'd like to know by whom," Mark finished.

The woman studied the form, her eyes sharpening after a moment. "I need to check something," she said, then turned to her computer and began tapping keys. After a moment she eased out a breath. "I can't help you."

"We have a subpoena for your records on the child," Mark said. "Also the written approval of the infant's natural grandfather to view those records. If necessary, Sergeant McCall can contact a judge who will authorize a warrant for us to search your files for the information we need."

Mrs. Quinton didn't look impressed. "You and Sergeant McCall can serve me with a hundred legal documents, Agent Santini, but they won't get you the information you're looking for. We simply have no record on that infant.''

Grace leaned forward. "You mean the adoption is finalized and the record is sealed?"

"I mean we don't have a record. That particular adoption was not handled by Loving Arms."

Mark gestured to the copy of the form Quinton had previously scanned. "The form filled out at the clinic where the child was born states the adoption was handled by your agency."

"Their paperwork is in error," Mrs. Quinton said, concern clouding her blue eyes. "In more than one area, I'm afraid."

Grace felt her shoulders tighten as her cop instinct clicked in. Something was wrong. Very wrong. "What areas?" she asked quietly.

"As I stated, Loving Arms did not handle the placement of this child. And there's a problem with the signature at the bottom of the form. It can't be right."

Shifting forward, Mark studied the woman, his eyes giving nothing away. "There are two signatures on the bottom of the form," he said. "The doctor who treated Andrea Grayson and the social worker from children's services who picked up the infant from the clinic. Which signature can't be right?"

"The social worker's," Patsy Quinton replied. "The woman whose signature is on that form quit her job about two years ago and moved out of state."

Hours later Mark sat beside Grace in yet another office while warning blips pinged in his brain. He had learned long ago to listen to his instincts. They were currently sending the message that it wasn't a paperwork snafu that had caused Andrea Grayson's baby to seemingly disappear off the face of the earth.

The infant was gone.

Her mother dead.

Coincidence?

Mark checked the clock that hung on the wall of the small, cramped office. He needed to call D.C. to find out if the autopsy on Andrea Grayson's body had been performed as scheduled. If so, he had some pointed questions for the pathologist. Right now, though, he wanted some answers from the doctor who'd delivered Andrea's child.

"I don't know how this could be." Dr. Thomas Odgers sat behind a desk inches deep in paper, staring down in disbelief at the contents of a file folder. He was a balding, bearded man in his sixties with a baritone voice and wire-rim glasses.

At present, his face was as pale as his starched white lab coat. "I just… I simply don't understand."

Mark started to speak, but held back when Grace rose and moved to the desk. "How about I tell you what *I* understand, Dr. Odgers?" she asked in a mild voice. "You delivered a baby girl at this clinic whose mother subsequently died under your care. This clinic—of which you are the director—has paperwork stating the baby was picked up by a caseworker from children's services for an adoption to be handled by the Loving Arms Agency."

"Yes." Adjusting his glasses, Odgers glanced down at the paperwork, then looked back up. "That's correct."

"One thing that is not correct is the caseworker's signature," Grace continued, gesturing at the form.

"Are you sure of that, Detective McCall?"

"*Sergeant* McCall, and I'm positive. Agent Santini and I spent quite a lot of time this morning at the adoption agency and then at the state's children's services office.

Someone at this clinic forged the name of a caseworker who quit her job two years ago.''

''Dear God.''

''Another thing that isn't correct on your form is the name of the agency slated to handle the adoption. Loving Arms has no record of this infant.''

His fingers steepled in front of his chin, Mark kept his eyes on Grace. They'd met while working on the Midnight Slasher task force, investigating the murders of a series of teenage prostitutes. He and Grace had teamed up to conduct interviews with several subjects. Mark had been impressed with her intuitive, no-nonsense interrogation skills and an intense passion to get to the truth. He was still impressed.

Just as he still felt the pull that had always existed between them. Would forever feel it, he supposed.

Six years was a long time, and he knew there was no sense in dredging up the past when the present demanded all his energy and attention. Yet, watching Grace, he wondered what their lives would be like now if she had moved to Virginia with him. If he'd had something more to offer her than just shreds of time.

''The state has contracts with three different adoption agencies,'' Odgers pointed out nervously. ''I feel certain our listing Loving Arms on the form was a clerical error. We named the wrong agency, that's all.''

''That's not all,'' Grace persisted. ''Agent Santini and I have checked with the other two adoption agencies that have contracts with the state. None of them handled this child.''

''I...don't know what to think.'' Odgers slicked a palm over his nearly bald head, now glistening with sweat. ''I don't know.''

Mark rose and moved to the side of the desk opposite

Grace, a symbolic closing in on their quarry. "I suggest you come up with something, Doctor," he said quietly. "As Sergeant McCall pointed out, the trail to Andrea Grayson's infant starts and ends here."

"I can only tell you what I know. I delivered the baby, then examined her again just before the social worker was due to pick her up." Odgers looked back at the file, and Mark saw the face of a man whose mind was racing to find an explanation. "That's the last time I laid eyes on that infant. I swear."

Grace gazed down at him. "Did you see who picked up the baby?"

"No, but it's rare I ever see the social workers. I'm either in exam rooms with patients or in here dealing with paperwork." He held out a hand, palm up. "I'm sure there's some logical explanation for the child's whereabouts."

Mark leaned in. "I hope so, Doctor." He waited a beat, watching the man sweat. "If a social worker walked into the clinic right now to pick up a baby, who would that person deal with?"

"Today it would be Yolanda."

"Today?" Grace asked.

"That's because Iris is off. Iris Davenport. Her sister had surgery, so she's staying with her during her recuperation. Iris usually deals with paperwork on all adoptions." Odgers rechecked the form. "I remember now. Iris assisted with the birth of the child in question."

Grace frowned. "You had a clerk assist you during a delivery?"

"No." Odgers blinked several times. "Heavens, no. Iris is an RN, a very good one. The office staff is buried in Medicare, insurance and numerous other forms, not to mention patient records. Iris takes care of the adoption forms, and the office staff is glad to have her help.''

Wanting a clear view of the man's face, Mark returned to his chair. ''Doctor, if you know what happened to Andrea Grayson's child, you'd better tell us now.''

''I don't know.'' The man's hands fisted. ''I felt awful when the mother died. The delivery had been an easy one, and she seemed fine. Minutes later, she began hemorrhaging. I tried to save her. I've been a doctor for forty years. I'm in the business of keeping people alive.'' He pulled off his glasses, his eyes locked on Mark's as if he were his only lifeline. ''I don't know what happened to the infant, but it's crucial she be found. You have my full cooperation in this matter.''

Mark intended to run a thorough background check on the doctor, even though his gut told him the man was telling the truth. And his instincts were usually on target. He exchanged a look with Grace, and he could tell she agreed with him. He shifted his attention back to Odgers.

''Doctor, have there been similar deaths here?''

Odgers's already-pale face turned gray. ''Surely you're not suggesting…''

''I'm not suggesting anything,'' Mark said. ''I'm asking a question, one of many you'll have to answer. Have any other women hemorrhaged to death after giving birth here?''

''One. Nearly a year ago, I think. The young woman wasn't my patient, so I'm hazy on details. I do know she'd been seeing Dr. Normandy. Frank Normandy. The patient delivered a healthy baby, then later bled to death.''

''What happened to her baby?'' Grace asked.

''I…have no idea. I'll have to pull the file.''

''Do that,'' Mark said. ''We'll want to see Dr. Normandy.''

"He quit some time ago. Took a hospital job in Chicago to be closer to his wife's family."

"We need his personnel file." Mark paused. "What nurse assisted Normandy when the woman died after delivery?"

"I'll have to check." Odgers swiveled in his chair toward his computer. Using his index fingers, he tapped on the keyboard. A moment later, he closed his eyes. "Iris," he said quietly. "Iris Davenport assisted during that birth, too."

"You didn't get your wish," Grace said as Mark followed her across her house's shadowy front porch. The early-evening gloom was quickly transforming into a frigid darkness, so she had to squint to get her key into the lock. Neither Morgan nor Carrie had made it home yet, so no one had turned on the porch light.

"What wish?" Mark asked, his breath a gray puff on the freezing air.

"This morning you said you hoped things went smooth." She caught the fresh pine scent of the Christmas wreath as she pushed open the door and stepped into the warm, inviting hallway.

"We definitely didn't get smooth," he agreed, his voice grave as he closed the door behind him.

The sense of dread that Grace had first felt during their interview at the adoption agency had intensified throughout the day and now felt like an anvil in her chest. "What we got were too many questions that no one seems to have the answers to."

"Someone always has the answers." Mark slid his gloves into the pockets of his black wool coat. "We just have to figure out who that someone is, then go after them."

"You're right." She pulled off her gloves and coat, then opened the door to the small closet near the front door. "I've worked child abduction cases, but they were mostly one parent snatching a child from the other. Even though the child was missing, I was pretty sure he or she was safe. Being cared for."

Mark gazed down at her, his face somber. "That's not the type of child abduction case I get called to. There are a lot of sick scum out there."

Saying nothing, Grace hung up their coats. She and Mark had been cops a long time and they'd seen too much evil. Still, she always hoped for a happy ending. Considering the nature of his job, she doubted Mark ever expected a rosy outcome.

When she turned, she saw he had moved a few steps down the hall and now stood at the arched entrance to the living room, the file folder he'd carried in from the car clutched in his hand.

"Is this where you want us to work?" he asked.

Stepping beside him, she reached for a wall switch, flipped it on. The lights on the Christmas tree winked on, looking like tiny white stars trapped in its limbs. What they'd found out today had left her in no mood for holiday cheer.

"No, not here."

"Where, then?"

"Until the information we requested starts coming in, all we can do is brainstorm. Right?"

"Right."

"Let's do that in the kitchen while we eat. I'm starving and you should be, too, since you hardly ate anything at lunch."

"I had soup."

"Broth. You had broth, Santini." She headed down the

hallway, crooking a finger at him. "Follow me, and I'll show you the difference between broth and soup."

Twenty minutes later they sat side by side at the butcher-block island, steaming bowls in front of them.

Mark slid her a look. "So, this is soup," he said, spooning up another bite.

"Didn't take long for a sharp guy like you to spot the homemade noodles, chunks of chicken and other nutritious stuff."

He nodded gravely. "I'm a professional investigator. I sleuthed out the nutritious stuff right off."

"'Atta boy, Santini."

He'd taken off his suit coat, loosened his crimson tie and unbuttoned the neck of his starched white shirt. Grace knew this was the first time she'd let herself relax since they walked into the adoption agency that morning, and she sensed the same went for Mark.

Sensed, too, that she had probably been nuts to bring him back to her house since she intended to keep their relationship on a professional level. The smart thing would have been to go along with Mark's suggestion to wait at her office for the information they'd requested. It was just that the more time she'd spent in his presence, the deeper the lines of exhaustion in his face seemed to be etched.

So, why did she care if he looked tired? she wondered. Why give special consideration to a man who'd walked away so effortlessly six years ago?

With no answers to those questions forthcoming, she slid a hand into the wicker basket next to her plate, tore off two pieces of the crusty French bread she'd heated and handed one to Mark. "Butter?"

"No, thanks." His gaze swept the kitchen. "Bran mentioned the remodeling of this place was a McCall family project. From what I've seen, you did a great job."

"We think so."

"How long did the entire project take?"

"A couple of months," Grace answered. "Granddad and Gran oversaw things. They doled out assignments like they were drill sergeants. Everyone pitched in, carried their weight, except for…"

Mark gave her a puzzled look when her voice trailed off. "Except for?"

"It was right after Ryan died. Then I got sick…the flu." And with her system so vulnerable, her resistance so weakened, she'd lost their baby, her final physical link with Ryan.

"Grace—"

"Anyway, I love this house," she said, determined to force back the memories. "So do Carrie and Morgan. Having had the family's help in breathing life back into the place makes it even more special."

Her appetite gone, Grace set her bowl aside and squared her shoulders. "Ready to brainstorm our case?"

Mark watched her for a beat, then pushed his bowl out of the way. "Ready," he said, while opening the file folder. "Here's what we know so far. Nearly a year ago a fifteen-year-old girl named DeeDee Wyman gave birth to a son. The birth was without complications, the baby healthy. Wyman suddenly began hemorrhaging and died. Six months later, Andrea Grayson walked into the same clinic and became a carbon copy of Wyman, with the exception that she had a different doctor and gave birth to a daughter."

Grace nodded. "From our checks with all three adoption agencies that have contracts with the clinic, we know none of them handled either infant, although the clinic's records show differently."

"Records filled out by Iris Davenport, the nurse in attendance during both births,'' Mark added. ''Records with the same forged signature of a former child services caseworker.''

''At this point, Iris Davenport—presently in Kansas City taking care of her ill sister—seems to be the solid link between both deaths,'' Grace said. ''And the two babies who have seemingly dropped off the face of the earth.''

''They're somewhere,'' Mark stated, checking his watch. ''The background checks we requested on Davenport and Dr. Odgers should come through on your fax soon. And I ought to hear back anytime from the pathologist with the tox results of Grayson's autopsy.''

''So we wait.'' Grace gathered up their dishes, then headed to the sink. She rinsed the bowls, turned and ran into a wall of solid muscle.

''Sorry,'' Mark said, gripping her upper arm to steady her.

''I...didn't hear you behind me.''

''Just doing my part to help clean up.'' He sat the wicker bread basket beside the sink, but made no move to put space between them.

Grace caught the faint whiff of his familiar spicy cologne, and felt her insides tighten. ''Always...nice to have a helper in the kitchen,'' she managed. Knowing she was between two seemingly immovable forces of granite-topped counter and muscled male had her skin heating.

Mark gazed down at her with concerned intensity. ''Grace, I didn't mean to upset you before. Mentioning the house. Bran told me Morgan and Carrie bought it about the same time Ryan was killed. I just didn't think before I brought up the subject. I'm sorry.''

''It's...okay.''

''From the look I saw in your eyes, it clearly isn't okay. Ryan Fox was a lucky man to have found you.''

''I'm the lucky one,'' she said, her voice an unsteady whisper. She had forgotten how easily Mark's voice could take on that soft intimate tone. They were talking about her husband's death, yet her blood was heating over her ex-lover's voice.

The knowledge of how quickly memories of the way she used to feel for Mark consumed her had panic flaring in her stomach. It was almost as if they weren't memories at all.

That jolting revelation had her taking a step sideways. Then another. Good Lord, what if he touched her? Was she sure—absolutely sure—she could resist him?

His eyes stayed locked with hers. ''I'm sure the past three years have been hard for you. There's nothing more difficult than to lose people you love and need.''

As she stared up at him, it occurred to her she had no idea if he was speaking in generalities or making a personal observation. How *could* she know? They'd been lovers for months, yet Mark Santini had never opened up enough to tell her about his background. His family. Never once told her how he felt about her. About them.

Which, she conceded, hadn't mattered at the time. Mark hadn't needed to tell her anything in order to keep her in his bed.

But now, for some reason she couldn't explain, it mattered very much.

She wrapped her arms around her waist. ''Tell me something, Mark. How do you know losing someone is difficult?''

His dark eyes narrowed on her face. ''What?''

''Have you lost someone? Someone you loved and needed? I have to ask, since you've never mentioned your family to me. I don't know anything about you. I never knew *anything* about you.''

"You're wrong, Grace. You knew me better than anyone."

What she *knew* was that his first and only love was, and always would be, the job. She didn't bother to point that out. Pointing it out wouldn't change the past, alter the present or impact the future.

Just then a telephone rang in the distance.

"The fax machine," Grace said, glancing toward the hallway. "That should be the background information on Odgers and Davenport." She'd no sooner gotten the words out than Mark's cell phone chimed.

He unclipped the phone off his belt as Grace headed out of the kitchen into the hallway. She stepped into the small, cozy room she and her sisters had converted into an office. The fax machine was humming, rolling out pages.

When she returned to the kitchen, Mark was still on the phone. She knew instantly from his comments and questions that his caller was the pathologist who'd performed the autopsy on Andrea Grayson. Grace slid onto a stool at the island and separated the pages on Dr. Odgers's background from those on Iris Davenport. While Grace scanned the info on the nurse, she was aware that Mark's expression grew grimmer with each passing minute.

When he clicked off the phone, his shoulders were stiff beneath his white dress shirt.

"Bad news?" she asked.

"The pathologist found traces of an anticoagulant drug in tissue samples taken from Andrea Grayson. It wasn't a fluke she bled to death. Someone wanted her dead."

"So they could take her baby," Grace theorized. "Mark, I've got a bad feeling DeeDee Wyman was injected with the same drug. Murdered for her child."

"I'm thinking the same, which solidly makes Davenport our prime suspect since she was present at both births."

Mark moved to peer over her shoulder. "Anything interesting on her?"

"She got a parking-trespass violation for leaving her car in a fire zone."

"How is that interesting?"

"The address on the citation is Remington Park Racetrack."

"Okay, so Davenport likes to play the ponies. That takes money."

Grace continued to scan the pages. "She lied to Dr. Odgers when she told him she'd be in Kansas City taking care of her ill sister. That would be hard to do, since Iris doesn't have a sister."

"Did the credit card trace get a hit on where she is?"

"Las Vegas," Grace answered, thumbing through the pages. "Iris checked into the Gold Palace a couple of days ago. Looks like she's planning to stay at least another week."

"The Gold Palace is one of the high-dollar places on the strip. Betting on horses," Mark murmured. "Casino gambling. All takes money."

"Interesting that a nurse working at a state-run clinic has the means to fund a ritzy vacation." Grace continued shuffling the faxed pages. "It's going to take us time to go through this, but it looks like she was drowning in debt up until about a year ago. Then she came into some money. She took a trip to Tahoe. Stayed at a resort hotel-casino."

"That was right after DeeDee Wyman died and her baby went missing. Then Andrea Grayson dies, her baby disappears, and Nurse Nancy takes another trip to a city where she can gamble."

Grace looked up. "I imagine we're thinking the same

thing. Davenport kills pregnant runaways no one is likely to miss, then sells their babies to fund those trips.''

Mark settled onto the stool beside Grace's. "Too bad we can't prove any of that. Dr. Odgers said all clinic personnel have access to the delivery room. And the newborns.''

"And where the paperwork's concerned, Davenport can say someone using the name of the former social worker showed up with the right credentials and took each baby. That's stretching it, but it'll be up to us to prove otherwise. Right now we can't.''

"First thing we need to do is find out what happened to DeeDee Wyman," Mark said. "If her body wasn't cremated or donated to the cadaver program like Andrea Grayson's, we'll need an exhumation order and a fast autopsy. If we get the body, I have a feeling we'll find traces of the same anticoagulant drug in her.''

"Even if we can't get Davenport on the murders, she'd be nuts to confess to taking the infants. Each kidnap would be a long-term felony charge. If she keeps her mouth shut, we might never find those babies. Or Davenport's accomplices, if they exist.''

"You're right." Mark pursed his mouth. "So, at this point, we don't approach Davenport as cops.''

Grace frowned. "Too bad that's what we are.''

"Davenport doesn't know that. And it's the last thing she'd suspect if we meet her by chance in Vegas.''

"In Vegas?" Grace asked carefully. She could almost see Mark's mind working in the dark depths of his eyes.

"We hook up with Davenport, presenting ourselves as a well-to-do married couple. A couple desperate to have a child.''

Just the thought of parading as Mark's wife, sharing a

hotel room with him, tightened the knots already in Grace's stomach.

"Aren't you a little too high profile to work undercover?"

"I'm known in law enforcement circles. But as a precaution, I'll change my hair color. Make my brows straighter."

"Since you prefer to work with local law enforcement, maybe you'd better contact the Las Vegas PD," Grace persisted. "Make arrangements for one of their female cops to work with you while you're there. Meantime, I can stay here, dig through the background info on Odgers and Davenport."

"No. If we charge either of them, they'll be filed on and tried here, the jurisdiction where the crimes were committed." Mark paused. He might as well have been sitting at a poker table for all Grace could tell from his expression. "You have a problem working with me, say so. I'll arrange to have another female OCPD cop assigned to the case."

"I like to finish what I start." With stubbornness stiffening her neck, Grace stared at the faxed pages. "I want to find those babies. They were kidnapped out of the womb. I want to make sure they're safe."

"Then you'll have to work the case, start to finish. Your choice, Grace. In or out?"

The fist of tension she didn't want to acknowledge held firm in the pit of her stomach. She had thought she was over him. Over the hurt she had harbored over his keeping a part of his life closed off to her. The way she'd reacted a few minutes ago proved that was still an issue. She hated knowing that, despite the passage of six years, this man could make her feel like a jumbled mess on the inside.

And now she was going to Vegas to parade as his wife!

It was the goal that was important, she reminded herself. Find the babies. She had worked undercover numerous times. It was all pretense. Acting. This assignment would be no different. As long as she kept her mind on the job, *the goal,* she could handle working with Mark.

Handle it when he walked away.

Again.

''I'm in,'' she said quietly.

Chapter 4

Rarely had Mark seen an investigation involving multiple law enforcement agencies, shifts in geographical locations and the planning and financing of an elaborate undercover op move with such smooth swiftness.

He knew the efficient slicing of red tape by all involved parties was not because traces of the same anticoagulant drug discovered in Andrea Grayson's body had been found in DeeDee Wyman's hurriedly exhumed remains. Granted, two young women murdered right after giving birth at the same state-run clinic was cause for an intense investigation. As was the fact the infant born to each young woman had seemingly disappeared off the face of the earth. Further, the prime suspect was the nurse who assisted in both deliveries. Those basic details, however, were not the reason the case had been tagged a *red ball*—cop lingo for the homicide of a prominent official or celebrity. This time, one of the victims was the *daughter* of a rich, powerful man.

Mark could almost feel the strings being pulled all the way from Washington, D.C., by Senator Landon Grayson. His only child had been murdered, his granddaughter kidnapped. Grayson chaired the committee that controlled the Bureau's funding. Every citizen was deemed to be equal under the law; in truth, though, due process came swifter to the rich and powerful.

Which was why, barely two days after Mark and Grace got their first whiff that their case was a homicide and their prime suspect was in Las Vegas, they were on a plane. A short limo ride later, they checked in to the luxury suite that had been reserved in their undercover names.

Now, standing in the living room of that elegant suite, Mark slipped a folded bill to the bellman who had overseen the delivery of their luggage.

"Thank you, Mr. Calhoun." The fifty-something attendant, dressed in the Gold Palace's spotless amber-colored uniform coat and black trousers, was too experienced to even glance at the bill before pocketing it.

Mark settled his briefcase on an end table polished to a mirrorlike finish. He knew that gamblers on hot streaks gave heart-stopping tips to staff members of the hotels in which they stayed. But the undercover persona the FBI had created for him was not one of a high-rolling risk taker. Anyone running a background check on Mark Calhoun would discover the Houston, Texas, native held major interests in a number of profitable oil and gas companies and the burgeoning field of wind energy production.

Despite his substantial wealth, the fictional Mark Calhoun was not a man who tossed chips into the center of a green felt-covered table, crossed his fingers, then rolled the dice. When he did splurge, it was on homes, vehicles and vacations that provided diversions from the stresses and disappointments of everyday life. This trip was intended to be one of those diversions to help buoy up the fictional Calhouns who had received word that their third attempt at in-vitro fertilization had failed.

"There's an ice machine in the minibar," the bellman said, nodding toward the glossy black wet bar on the far side of the suite. "We've stocked the refrigerator and cabinets according to the preferences your assistant faxed to our concierge."

"Good." In truth, Grace had compiled the list, which, Mark had noted, contained several boxes of the stomach-soothing tea he habitually consumed. Even in undercover mode, she saw to the comfort of those around her.

As if checking for any small detail left undone, the bellman swept his circumspect gaze around the spacious living room done in sapphires and emeralds, accented with mahogany wood and lush arrangements of flowers. "Is there anything else you or Mrs. Calhoun require at the moment?"

"Where is the safe?"

The bellman inclined his head toward the alcove arranged into an office area with a dark wood desk inlaid with intricate marquetry. Behind the desk sat a trim, matching console. "The safe is in the closet beside the console. You create the combination you desire, then clear it on your final use."

"Fine." Mark slipped his key card into the inside pocket of his black suit coat. The safe would be used to store his and Grace's law enforcement credentials and weapons during their stay. As an extra level of security, Mark would attach a small device that required the entering of three separate combinations before the safe's door would open.

Catching movement out of the corner of his eye, he

glanced sideways as Grace stepped out of the double-wide doors that led to the bedroom.

"Darling," he said. Sending her a husband's intimate smile, he extended a hand her way. "Do the other rooms meet with your satisfaction?"

Mark studied Grace as she crossed the ocean of Oriental carpet that separated them. Just as he had done by a subtle change to his hair color and brows, she, too, had altered her appearance. Instead of the sweaters and man-tailored slacks she favored, she now wore a figure-skimming silver silk pantsuit and matching high-heeled boots. Her hair, usually clipped back, hung loose, falling like soft, black rain to her shoulders. She'd shaded her brown eyes with copper highlights that lent them a slightly exotic look and applied a darker blush, emphasizing her fine-boned cheeks. A slick of coral covered her lips, making her mouth look glossy and luminous and far too tempting to a man who knew exactly how that mouth tasted.

A man who was well aware that her new look in no way made her a different person from the woman he'd known so intimately. She had merely transformed herself into a different *type* of person on the surface.

Just as he had the day he watched her walk into her boss's office after a separation of six years, Mark felt something stir deep inside him. Something no other woman had ever been able to touch.

Even as her hand slid into his, he reminded himself that, although he and Grace had shared something special, they had chosen to walk away and let it die. The logical part of Mark's brain theorized that whatever it was that now moved inside him was merely an echo of the searing need and passion he had once felt for Grace.

And regret, he conceded.

How many times over the years had he replayed their

relationship in his mind, adjusting the elemental needs and desires they both felt in order to get a different outcome? More times than he would like to admit.

Since it appeared their basic needs had not changed, Mark knew he should have the good sense to leave well enough alone. But at this instant, standing beside her with his hand circling hers and the warmth of her flesh seeping into his, temptation lured him like a seductive smile. And the force of the regret he still carried for what might have been nudged him from behind.

"The bedroom and bath are fine." Grace gave the bellman a polite, polished smile. "I had asked for a schedule for the health spa."

"Yes, Mrs. Calhoun, it's on the desk. Once you decide when you want to visit the spa, the concierge will take care of the scheduling."

"Thank you," Grace said. "I think that's all for now."

"Yes, ma'am."

Mark breathed in Grace's soft, subtle scent while they stood side by side, tracking the bellman's progress across the suite. When the door clicked closed behind the man, Mark sensed her shoulders stiffening, felt the tenseness settle into her fingers, still wrapped in his hand. He knew he should ease his grip, release her. Yet, he held on while memories he'd locked away rushed to the surface. Memories of the feel of her soft hands against his heated flesh. The warmth of her body, the comfort she had offered that no one else had ever given him.

When she tugged her hand from his, he felt the scrape of the stunning diamond she now wore in the guise of Mrs. Mark Calhoun.

With his mind snapping back to thoughts of the job, Mark turned to the table where he'd left his briefcase. While he input the combination and unsnapped the locks, he felt the familiar shudder of the fatigue that lately seemed to reach to the marrow of his bones. That sense of weariness reminded him Grace McCall-Fox wasn't the only thing he had to regret. There were the cases he had failed to solve, the trials lost. The child molesters and killers who had slipped through his fingers, the dream that almost nightly had him seeing again each of those victims, reliving every failure. He carried each regret like a stone around his shoulders. With all that weight, he shouldn't feel so hollow on the inside, but he did.

"Mark?"

He looked up, met Grace's waiting gaze and saw the puzzlement in her dark eyes. They'd spent the past two days formulating their ops plan for this assignment, and he knew what she was waiting for. Knew, too, she was wondering if there was some reason he'd stood staring like an idiot into his briefcase.

He bit back a curse, disgusted with himself. This was not the time to try to delve into the dark recesses of his own mind. He and Grace were there to cozy up to Iris Davenport, the nurse suspected of murdering Grayson and Wyman, then kidnapping their newborn infants. This was just another assignment. When it wrapped up, he would move to the next case and lose himself in it. Then the next.

Refocusing his thoughts, Mark retrieved two small black devices from his briefcase. As planned, Grace switched hers on, angled it to show him its glowing green light, then turned and headed for the bedroom. Striding across the living room, Mark activated his own unit, checked its light, then placed the unit on the console behind the desk. The boxes looked like cell phone chargers. In actuality they detected electronic radio waves emitted by eavesdropping devices. As long as the green light glowed, he and Grace could talk and be reasonably sure they wouldn't be overheard and recorded. Although on the surface they had no reason to think Iris Davenport would bug their suite, they had no idea who might have aided and abetted her in the murders and kidnappings. Or whether Davenport in fact was the guilty party.

Mark shook his head. The case was riddled with unknowns and a distinct lack of evidence. But he and Grace had to start somewhere. Their instincts had pointed to the nurse who drew a salary from the state yet had somehow managed to pay off mountainous debts. Added to that were Davenport's occasional stays at posh hotels that sported casinos. She was getting her money from somewhere, and the background checks conducted on her had found no legitimate source.

"The bedroom and bath got a green light, too," Grace said when she returned to the living room, carrying a file folder.

"So far, so good." Mark picked up the health spa information off the desk and began flipping through the pink, floral-scented pages. "Looks like this is the same schedule for spa activities the agent from our local office faxed us."

Settling into the chair behind the desk, Grace opened the folder then checked her watch. "According to the info your agent sent, Iris has a spin class in about an hour."

"Spin." Mark raised a brow. "What exactly is that? Some sort of dance class?"

Grace slid him a look from behind her dark lashes. "Not up on spa lingo, are you, Agent Santini?"

"Guilty, Sergeant McCall. When I find time to work out, I hit a police gym. I don't hear a lot of spa lingo getting batted around in those places."

"In this instance, spin refers to stationary bikes. Guess it's the concept of spinning your wheels and getting nowhere." Grace gave him a pained look. "Do you know how long it's been since I've ridden a bike, Santini? I can already feel my lungs heaving and muscles locking up.''

''All in the line of duty.'' Mouth curving, Mark leaned against the edge of the desk and checked his watch. ''If you hustle, you can make that spin class. As your very accommodating husband, I'll be happy to call the concierge and set it up while you change.''

''Gee, thanks,'' she said with a smirk. ''When I get back, make sure you have my bath ready. Vanilla-scented candles lining the tub's rim would be good. And a glass of merlot to help ease my aches and pains should do the trick.''

''How about I make myself available to wash your back?''

Mark hadn't thought before asking the question. Had it been a different woman in any other situation, his offer would most likely have been dealt with by a flippant refusal or welcoming acceptance. But this wasn't any woman. This was Grace, and he happened to have glided his soapy fingers along the tempting hollow of her spine on numerous occasions.

He saw by the darkening of her eyes that the question had conjured up the same memories for her. Memories of the times they'd soaked together in an oversize tub while soft music drifted on the air and candlelight flickered in clouds of steam. Of the times their bodies had joined beneath the water's sensual warmth. Of the times his hands had explored her gentle curves and sleek planes while his mouth suckled her breasts, wet with perfumed water.

Just as it had so long ago, need pumped like heat into his body. He laid a hand over hers. ''Grace.''

''Don't, Mark.'' She began to pull away, but he tightened his fingers on hers.

"Don't what? Don't remember the life we shared? You want to tell me how to do that?"

When she said nothing, he studied their joined hands. "There have been times over the past years when I couldn't do anything but think of you. Of the time we spent together. Of what we had—"

"It was a long time ago." She pulled her hand from under his and rose.

"It was," he agreed. "But right this minute it seems like it all happened yesterday." His gaze conducted a slow, measured journey of her. "Maybe because you look the same."

"I'm not the same." She faced him across the span of the desk. Her cheeks were flushed, her mouth set. "We agreed to keep this business. *All* business. To concentrate on finding out what happened to those two mothers and their babies. We have to find those babies."

"We will," he said quietly. "And I remember our agreement. Problem is, it doesn't wipe away the past. Not for me, anyway." He dipped his head. "That flush in your cheeks tells me it isn't working for you, either."

"I haven't forgotten." She wrapped her arms around her waist. "The good times, or the bad. The worst being when we went our separate ways. We'll do that again, just as soon as we solve this case. I've had to say goodbye to too many people I've cared about. You. Ryan." She closed her eyes, opened them. "I'm not the same person, Mark. I know now that I'm not good at saying goodbye. So I choose not to get involved with a man when I know up front that's what I'll have to do."

"Saying goodbye is one of the things I excel at."

"It seems you're the one who hasn't changed."

"True."

"If you can't work with me on a nonpersonal level, then

you'd best find another partner. It's not too late, since we have yet to make contact with Iris Davenport.''

''I have the partner I want,'' he said levelly. ''We're both professionals, Grace. The job comes first.''

''Always has,'' she murmured while rechecking her watch. ''So, I suggest we get started. I'll go change while you call the concierge.''

''You got it,'' Mark said and reached for the phone.

Instead of picking up the receiver, he watched her walk away, her movements as graceful as a dancer. With each step she took, the hollowness inside him deepened. He had spent years on his own, needing no one. But always, always he had thought of her, and those thoughts had given him a sense of comfort.

It wasn't comfort he felt now as he watched her walk away, but a pulsing sense of loss.

Nearly an hour later Grace shut the door on the pristine locker the spa attendant had assigned her, thinking how idiotic her advice to Mark had been.

Don't remember.

How could she expect him to forget their past when she had tossed a part of it in his face?

Looping a snowy-white hand towel around her neck, she decided she must have lost her mind to suggest he have a steamy bath waiting for her when she returned to their suite. Surely her subconscious had been inspired by her seeing the elegant bathroom with its huge tub, fashioned for lounging. Soaking in hot, steamy water had always been her favorite way to relax, a routine she'd turned Mark on to during the months they'd been lovers.

Turned him on in more ways than one, she thought wryly while easing out a slow breath.

His offer to wash her back had, in the blink of an eye,

tumbled her into the past. She had no problem picturing Mark with the heated water lapping at his broad chest. Hadn't forgotten the sight of his muscled shoulders and, visible through the clear water, his narrow hips and sinewy thighs. Remembered well the glint of passion that had shone in his dark eyes while his hands moved in slow circles under the water to caress her breasts…then the rest of her.

Grace buried her face in one end of the hand towel. Only to herself would she admit that spending the last three days with Mark had been agony. Not because she hadn't wanted to be with him. Because she *had*.

She was only human, after all. She had physical needs, needs that had long been neglected. Needs that she *knew* this one particular man could satisfy quite exquisitely. Needs that seemed to double and triple when she was in the same room with him. But she couldn't allow herself to take that step. Not when it was just a matter of time before Special Agent Santini walked out of her life again.

When she looked at the whole picture, she saw full well that Mark was not the right man for her. He hadn't been six years ago, and he wasn't now. They had far different lives, incompatible priorities. Nothing had changed.

"Mrs. Calhoun, are you okay?"

The attendant's voice snapped Grace back to the present, reminding her of the reason she was standing in the health club's locker room, clad in turquoise spandex. She had already begun her role as the wife of a rich man, capable of buying her anything her heart desired. Including a baby.

She waited a beat, then let the towel drop from her eyes. Around her, the white, spotless tile gleamed and walls of mirrors sparkled. She could hear the sound of showers running somewhere out of sight behind her. Women in various states of undress milled in the background.

"Yes, thank you. I'm fine." Grace gave the blond attendant wearing the spa's distinctive skintight gold unitard a repentant smile. The woman was so young and vibrant that Grace pictured her prancing through a grueling aerobics routine without a drop of sweat marring her perfect skin.

"I'm just not looking forward to all the exercise I've booked for myself." Grace didn't add that she'd stocked up on ibuprofen after seeing Iris Davenport's aggressive workout schedule.

"We'll take good care of you, Mrs. Calhoun," the attendant assured Grace while ushering her out the locker room door. "We've got you booked for a massage at the end of each day's session. Trust me, you'll be totally relaxed when you leave here."

Totally dead, you mean, Grace thought.

"Let's get you to the spin class."

"Can't wait," Grace commented as her escort led her through a maze of high-tech weight machines, glitzy personal trainers and clients clad in varying shapes, sizes and colors of spandex. Befitting the Gold Palace's ambiance, the floors were Italian marble, and the walls were lined with mirrors that glittered like icy diamonds. Painted art-deco figures gazed down from the high ceiling.

Having spent time studying the picture in Iris Davenport's employee file from the clinic and her driver's license, Grace spotted her prey instantly. Even if the nurse hadn't resembled her photos, there was no way to overlook the pleasant fine-boned face framed by tumbling red hair. Iris stood beside one of the spin bikes, wearing snug black exercise shorts, a yellow tank top and workout shoes that had an expensive look about them.

The bikes were set in a half-moon around the instructor's; when her attendant headed for a bike in the front row, Grace stopped her. "I'll take one in the back," she said, moving casually to the bike beside Iris. "That way if I fall off, the entire class won't see me."

The attendant smiled. "You'll do fine, Mrs. Calhoun. I'm Keely, just ask for me if you need anything."

"Like a wheelchair?" Grace ventured, making sure her voice was loud enough to carry to the woman now perched on the bike beside hers.

As Grace had hoped, Iris chuckled while tucking a hand towel over the handlebar. "Don't worry. I'm a nurse, so if you fall off your bike I'll tend to you."

"Thanks." Grace sent Iris a sardonic smile. "I'll hold you to that."

"These classes *are* killer, so I know what you mean about the wheelchair," Iris said, then tilted her head. "I don't remember seeing you in the spa before. Is this your first time here?"

"My husband and I just checked in," Grace said as she slid onto her bike. She and Mark had spent hours practicing their cover story, and now the words came easily. "I'm Grace Calhoun."

"Iris Davenport."

"My husband and I are here on a sort of second honeymoon," Grace continued. "Mark's on the golf course already. Since I don't play, I decided I'd better spend time here every day to balance out all the desserts I plan to splurge on during this trip."

"I'm doing the same."

"You're on your second honeymoon?" Grace kept her expression warm and friendly while she asked the question. So far they'd been unable to link Iris with a man. Any man.

"No, I'm not married." Iris raised a shoulder. "Haven't found the right guy yet. I'm here to splurge on myself." With what appeared to be a genuine smile, Iris skimmed a glance over Grace. "Doesn't look like you need to worry about those desserts. You've got a great figure."

"So do you," Grace said. It was true—Iris was tall and slim, with curves in all the right places.

"Thanks." Iris leaned in. "I used to be twenty-five pounds heavier, but I've taken it off in the past year. No way am I going to put it back on."

The past year. Grace focused on those words just as their sylph-like instructor with glossy black hair held back by a headband perched on a bike and keyed her mike that transmitted to the twenty riders who now surrounded her. As instructed, Grace started a slow pedal while surveiling the woman beside her out of the corner of her eye.

Nearly a year ago, DeeDee Wyman had given birth to a son, then died. The infant boy had disappeared. According to the credit report on Iris Davenport, it hadn't been long after that she'd begun paying off the staggering gambling debts she'd owed.

Silently Grace acknowledged she and Mark had no proof Iris had found other avenues where her nursing skills might bring in larger profits. Even so, every cop instinct Grace had developed after years on the job told her Davenport was guilty of snatching newborns for sale later on the black market.

Grace had done her research—she knew that couples desperate to have a child were often told by adoption agencies the average wait was more than five years. Even then there were no guarantees a child would be found for them. No promises that the child would be healthy and of the same race as the adoptive parents. It was no mystery why couples with adequate funds—sometimes in the range of five figures—often chose to enter into what was usually referred to as a private adoption.

While their instructor gave orders to pedal faster, and rivulets of perspiration trickled between Grace's breasts, she gave Iris another long look. For someone drowning in debt, selling an infant born to a homeless teenager for a cool five-figure sum must have been a very tempting solution.

Even if murder was involved.

Grace agreed with Mark's theory—the operation was too complicated for Iris to run things alone. Working at a state-run clinic didn't put her in contact with couples who had the money to purchase an infant. So far the FBI had been unable to tie Iris to anyone who looked like good accomplice material. Grace's cozying up to Iris was intended to not only get the goods on the nurse, but also unearth her accomplice.

Lungs heaving, Grace gave her moist forehead a quick swipe with her towel. "Want to help me dropkick our instructor's cute little butt?" Grace asked, gritting her teeth against the burn in her thighs.

"Can't." Iris panted out a breath. "I have to conserve my energy. I've got weight training after this."

"Really?" Grace asked, giving her a surprised look. "So do I."

At Iris's suggestion, they suffered through grueling dumbbell lunges and biceps curls together. Their spa session ended with a massage.

"So, I've told you what I do for a living," Iris said. She lay facedown on a padded table, naked except for the towel draped across her bottom. "How about you? What do you do?"

"I was a landscape designer in Houston," Grace replied from the table beside Iris's. "That's where Mark and I live.

I quit my job about six months ago.'' Grace almost moaned as her masseuse's nimble fingers spread warm oil across her bare back. ''Now I'm not sure that was the smartest thing, considering.''

''Considering?''

Grace paused as if trying to pull in strength to discuss a painful subject. ''Mark and I have been trying to have a baby for a couple of years. We've had no luck. I quit my job, thinking maybe concentrating on my career was having a negative effect on things. That doesn't seem to have been the problem.''

''I'm sure you're frustrated.''

''We both are, although Mark does a good job of not showing it in front of me.'' Grace felt the warm massage oil seep into her skin, scenting the air with the delicate aroma of roses. ''I know I could be a good mother and he will make a great father. He's so warm and loving. And a wonderful provider.'' Grace felt a ping of satisfaction when Iris let her gaze rest on the gold band with its enormous diamond Grace had purposely kept on while exercising.

''What does your husband do?''

''He's in oil and gas,'' Grace said vaguely. ''And owns holdings in other energy concerns.''

''I see.''

''Actually our second honeymoon is only one reason we're in Vegas,'' Grace continued. She hadn't expected to have a chance to impart so much information to Iris during their first meeting, but since the opportunity had arisen, Grace intended to gain as much mileage as possible. ''Our third attempt at in-vitro fertilization failed last week. Mark thought we both could use some getaway time to help take the edge off our disappointment.''

"It must be so difficult for you," Iris said. "To want a baby so badly."

"Yes." Without warning, a swell of grief for the child she'd lost hit Grace. A fist closed around her heart when she thought of how overjoyed Ryan had been when she'd told him she was pregnant. And then, barely an hour later, Ryan lay dead. And weeks later she'd miscarried...

The tears stinging her eyes left Grace shaken. It was strange how grief could hide inside you, laying low like a virus, then surge back to life without warning.

"Hey, I didn't mean to upset you." Iris stretched her arm between the tables to squeeze Grace's wrist. Iris's smile remained sympathetic and her eyes friendly, but Grace could almost *feel* the possibilities clicking in the woman's brain.

"You didn't upset me, I did it to myself," Grace said. She took a grip on her emotions, centered herself mentally. She would deal later with the unsteadiness that had settled inside her. "I apologize for getting weepy." Grace sent Iris a determined smile. "I've got a great life, a wonderful husband. I don't have anything to sniffle about."

"I'm sure things will work out." Iris squeezed her wrist again. "And once you do have a baby, your life will be even better."

Chapter 5

Dressed in sharp-creased tan slacks, a black polo shirt and windbreaker, Mark let himself into the suite late that afternoon. He shrugged out of the windbreaker, grimacing when his sore muscles protested the effects of the eighteen holes of golf he'd played.

Anyone observing him earlier would have assumed that Mark Calhoun of Houston, Texas, had no connection with the threesome who'd invited him to join them on the links when he checked in with the golf pro. In reality, the trio of men consisted of FBI agents. They'd brought Mark up-to-date on Iris Davenport's activities since the Bureau had begun its surveillance.

One agent was charged with overseeing the tap, authorized by a federal judge, that had been placed on the phone in Davenport's hotel room. Another agent obtained and scanned daily copies of security tapes during the times Davenport spent shopping, gambling in the casino and eating in the various restaurants inside the Gold Palace. The other agent made sure the trash collected each day from Davenport's room got passed to him instead of dumped into a maid's cleaning cart.

So far Davenport had neither made nor received a single phone call. When she gambled, it was alone. Her meals were solitary affairs, usually spent with her nose in a po- lice-procedural paperback. To date, her trash had contained nothing remarkable.

Mark knew from experience that surface observations were necessary, even though they meant little. He had run across serial child killers whose looks and behavior were so benign they could get a job playing Santa at any mall in the country.

He laid his room key card on a table next to a vase that held enough fresh flowers to turn the air ripely funereal with their scent. Glancing around the suite's living room, he saw no sign that Grace had returned from the spa. He hoped her first encounter with Davenport had given her some instinctive sense of the type of person they were dealing with. As it was, they were currently in the familiar no-man's-land of suspicion without proof. Investigative hell. He and Grace both believed Davenport was involved in the murders and kidnappings, but without evidence, they couldn't be certain.

Mark rolled his shoulders, which seemed to be getting stiffer by the minute. Since his and Grace's cover was of husband and wife, their clothes shared space in the bed- room's chest of drawers and walk-in closet. He decided this would be a good time for him to grab a shower and change.

He strode down the short hallway, his footsteps muffled by the thick carpet the shade of pewter. Like the living room, the bedroom was spacious and refined. Long vertical blinds covered the glass doors to the balcony; a touch to a button on a remote would lever the blinds open to reveal the muted grays and blues of the soft desert evening that would soon settle in. Another button was programmed to raise a wall panel to reveal a wide screen TV, DVD player and hi-tech stereo system. A rich tapestry of flowers and ribbons covered the sofa and matching chairs that faced a marble fireplace. The bed was as big as an ocean, clad in cream-colored Irish linen.

Still gripping his windbreaker, Mark let his gaze sweep across the bed. He knew without question that tonight—*every night*—he would lie awake on the living room couch and picture Grace in this immense bed. In his mind's eye he carried the memory of how she looked while she slept—her black hair a gorgeous mess, her lips slightly parted, her dark lashes fanning her cheeks. Maybe after six years she *had* changed on the inside. He sure as hell had. But physically she was the same woman he had known and made love to. The same woman his body now ached for.

A noise filtered into his consciousness, a low moan that seemed to come from nowhere. Eyes narrowing, he tossed his windbreaker onto the foot of the bed. He did a visual scan of the adjoining dressing room as he strode past it, then paused at the bathroom's closed door.

"Grace?"

When he got no answer, he knocked. The light rap caused the door to push slightly open, bringing with it a cloud of steam and the sound of a muffled sob.

He took in everything at once: the long rose-toned counter over which hung a mirror ringed in lights. A separate shower constructed of wavy glass blocks. The lush green plants that lined the tiled shelf beside the oversize tub, its jets bubbling softly. And Grace, up to her neck in steamy water, her face buried in a snowy white towel.

She had her back to him, so he had a good view of her damp bare shoulders as they shook.

A cold fist tightened Mark's stomach. He moved to the tub and gripped her shoulders. "What's wrong?"

Her head snapped up. Her body jolted beneath his palms, sending a wave of water sluicing out of the tub and onto the gleaming marble floor. She crammed the towel against her breasts as she drilled him with a hostile look across her shoulder. "Get out."

Framed by her dark, wet hair, her face was pale as a sheet. Her dark lashes were spiked with damp from tears.

"Are you hurt?"

"Dammit, Santini, let go." She twisted to try to free herself of his hold. "Leave me alone."

"As soon as you tell me why you're crying."

He didn't catch her succinct reply, but he got the drift when she surged to her feet. His mind had time to register inviting curves and water-slicked flesh before she wrapped the towel around her, then rounded on him. "It's none of your business."

"It is if it has to do with your first meeting with our suspect."

A shadow flashed across her eyes then was gone. "It doesn't." Gripping the knot of the towel between her breasts, Grace stepped out of the tub, turned toward the counter, then lost her footing on the wet floor.

Mark grabbed her, gripping her upper arms to steady her. Beneath his hands, she felt as taut as a bowstring. "Careful," he cautioned. "Marble floors are like black ice when they get wet."

"Thanks for the tip." Lifting her chin, she sent him a look that could have caught a bush on fire. "Since you walked in without knocking, I assume you need to use the facilities. Back off, Santini, and I'll get out of your way."

"I did knock. You didn't hear me because you were crying." He tightened his fingers on her arms. "Why, Grace?"

"I just needed to." She eased out a breath that wasn't quite steady. "Leave it alone, okay? Some people need a good crying jag once in a while. I'm one of them," she added, then shifted her gaze from his.

He'd sat in prisons with killers cursing him, attended meetings in grim conference rooms with the grief-stricken parents of victims—and he'd maintained perfect control. Seeing Grace looking so fragile while secrets lurked behind her dark eyes shook that control.

The regret he'd shoved back earlier in the day welled up inside him. Old memories, too close to the surface to push away, tightened his chest until he could almost forget there had been no time between. He studied her profile, both angular and soft, while heat swarmed in his blood. His gaze skimmed down the long arch of her throat, still beaded with water.

He loosened his hold on one arm, grazed his fingertips upward to the hot, moist flesh of her shoulder. Her eyes fluttered shut. "Grace?"

When she still didn't look at him, he cupped her chin in his hand and nudged her head around, forcing her to meet his gaze.

"Do you remember that movie we saw?" he asked quietly. "The one where the dog died at the end? We had to sit in the theater for ten minutes after the lights went on because you were crying so hard."

"I remember." She sniffled. "It was sad. What about it?"

"You said the same thing then—that some people need a good crying jag every so often."

"It's true."

He closed his hand around her throat and felt her pulse jump under his fingers. "I didn't like seeing you sad then. I don't like it now." He rubbed his thumb against her soft flesh and dropped his gaze to her mouth. That smooth, lush mouth that he knew tasted of heaven. "What made you sad today?"

"Life. Life in general."

"That doesn't give me a lot of information."

"You don't *need* information." Her hands came up and pressed against his chest. But she didn't try to shove him away. "I'm not some suspect, Santini. You don't get to interrogate me." Her breathing was noticeably shallow, but her voice held steady. "Be sure and close the door on your way out."

"Interrogating you isn't what I'm thinking about doing right now."

"I know." Wariness, touched with heat, flickered in her eyes. "Mark, being here like this isn't good for either of us."

"Feels good to me." He speared his fingers up into her damp hair and angled her head back. "Damn good."

He dipped his head, settled his mouth on hers and felt sharp, edgy need spring up inside him. His lips moved against hers out of memory and longing, the fit he remembered. A perfect one.

When he felt her shudder, he wrapped his arm around her, banding her against him, trapping her hands that were still pressed to his chest. Angling his head, he kissed her quietly, slowly, deeply, his tongue sliding past her parted lips to perform a seductive dance with hers.

Her fingers clenched, gripping his shirt as if she were being tossed around by a storm. They may have said good-bye to each other, he thought hazily, but the heat igniting between them spoke of unfinished business.

He fed on her mouth while she softened against him and his arousal went rock hard. And then she moaned his name, a husky rasp in the back of her throat. He swallowed that moan like a man feeding after a lifelong fast. His kiss turned fierce. Mindless. He could no longer think past the hot, soapy scent of her, the press of her body against his, her succulent, ripe taste. Grace—*only Grace*—could make him forget the rest of the world, forget his responsibilities. Make him even forget the darkness.

Until this moment he had not realized how far he had descended into that black, hollow pit. Had not known how little of himself the ghosts of all the victims he'd been too late to save had left behind. And now he didn't want to let go—couldn't let go—not when he'd discovered the light and warmth that came with Grace's kiss.

The salvation.

He shoved one hand beneath the hem of the towel, his fingers splaying on the curve of her hip. Need barreled through him like a train out of control. He drew the room's moist air into his lungs and felt it turn to fire.

He wanted to take her right there. Drag her to the slick, wet marble floor and drive himself into her. Sate his gnawing, tearing hunger for her while she was moaning for him. While she was molten and damp and her mouth as urgent and impatient as his. Take her before she remembered she didn't want to give herself again to a man destined to walk away. To one who had no choice but to turn his back on the light and comfort she offered.

"Let me," he whispered against her mouth. "Let me have you, Grace. Now."

She couldn't breathe or think. All her cool, controlled logic had vanished. In its place were rioting sensations. The hard feel of Mark's muscled chest against her trapped hands. The urgent, desperate taste of his mouth. The spiraling heat, the thunder of his heartbeat, echoing that of her own hammering pulse.

Before, she'd had to divide her attention between focusing on breathing and making her legs support her. Now that his hand was beneath the towel and she felt the possessive press of his fingers against her hip, she'd lost all focus. All she knew now was need. Searing need and the thrill from his touch that snapped through her like a whip, with a quick, shocking burn.

The ache inside her was huge. She was close—*so close*—to surrender. To giving in to the madness where body ruled mind and blood roared over reason. A heartbeat away from giving herself up to the pulse that throbbed inside her as the heat of his mouth fanned the roaring fire between her legs.

So close to not caring how empty and hollow she would feel when he left her again.

But the part of her brain still functioning reminded her that she *did* care. That she'd been crying only moments before, grieving for people she had lost. One being the man who was currently kissing her as if he were starving for the taste of her.

She struggled to cling to the fine edge of reason, but discovered she no longer had the strength to resist him. Resist her own needs.

He slid one knee between her legs, forcing them apart so that he could press her closer. The hardness of his arousal against her belly filled her with a crazy sense of panic. The impatience, the heat, the hunger in his kiss all mixed together in a near brutal, thrilling assault. The urgency pumping from his body into hers nearly overpowered her. She wanted to race away to sanity. Wanted to stay in his arms and succumb to the reckless, maddening sensations.

Before she had to make the decision to stay or flee, the chime of the suite's doorbell spiked into her brain. Mark cursed against her mouth. Grace stood stock-still in his arms, her lungs heaving, her entire body trembling as the chime sounded again.

With his hand still fisted in her hair, Mark dragged her head back and gazed down at her with eyes so full of raw emotion they threatened to consume her. "Expecting anyone?" he asked, his voice a hoarse rasp.

"I don't... No." Her mind reeled. Dazed, she fought for some rag of sanity and forced her brain to start working again. "Housekeeping, maybe?"

"If no one answers, they'll let themselves in." He muttered another curse. "Don't want that."

"No," Grace agreed, and discovered that her lungs needed more oxygen than she could drag in.

He untangled his fingers from her hair. The hand molded against her bare hip slid down, his fingertips grazing her flesh so that she felt every second of his retreat from beneath the towel. "I'll be back."

She remained motionless, watching him stride out the door while her heart bumped madly against her rib cage and the echos of a million sensations rippled through her. She very much wished she had something specific to do, like see who was ringing the doorbell. Since Mark was handling that, all that was left for her was to think. Because she was afraid her legs wouldn't support her much longer, she plopped down on the edge of the tub.

She had gone temporarily, crazily insane. That was the only reason she had to explain her actions. She *had* meant what she'd told Mark earlier in the day—she couldn't pick up where they'd left off all those years ago, knowing it was only temporary. Knowing she might never see him again.

Grace stared at her reflection in the lighted mirror that spanned the length of the rose-toned counter. Her face was flushed, her dark hair a tangled mess from Mark's fingers, her lips red and swollen from his kiss. She looked like a woman who'd been on the brink of being ravaged. In this case, looks weren't deceiving. And if things had continued the way they'd been going, she was afraid—terribly afraid—it would have only been minutes before the towel still covering her would have been off, and Mark inside her.

So, *would* she have let things get that far? Or somehow found the strength to stop him? Stop herself?

"Damn," Grace breathed when she realized she didn't know the answer. The logical part of her *had* wanted to tell him no, she could at least give herself that. But with her body on fire and a savage need crawling through her like a swarm of ants, it was wholly possible she'd be on that wet marble floor, naked and wrapped around him at this very instant if the doorbell hadn't chimed.

Thank goodness, she thought, while slippery knots of panic tightened her stomach. Thank goodness someone from housekeeping had chosen that moment to ring the doorbell and rescue her from herself. She'd make sure to leave a big tip—

"Grace."

Her head jerked around at the sound of Mark's voice. Without waiting for him to step fully into the bathroom, she sprang off the tub, saying, "I can't do this. It was a mistake. I just can't."

He stepped swiftly inside and closed the door behind him with a soft click. "We have company."

The cool caution in his eyes and voice put her instincts on instant alert. "Who?"

"Your new friend from the spa. Iris Davenport."

"She's here?" Grace whispered.

"She said you got upset during your massage and wants to make sure you're okay. I invited her to join us for a drink. She accepted." He took a step closer, his voice low. "I covered by telling her I'd just gotten off the golf course and hadn't seen you yet. Didn't know what your emotional state was. Grace, what happened during your massage?"

"Nothing, really. *Really,*" she repeated when his eyes narrowed. "I just did a good job of acting. Showing her how upset I was over not having a baby." It was the truth, if a simplified version.

"You apparently did a good job."

"Looks like it." Grace thought for a moment. "Here's the short version," she began, keeping her voice low to negate any possibility of being overheard. "On the surface, Davenport comes off likable. Very friendly. She seemed empathetic, even concerned over my being upset because we can't seem to conceive a child. But an awareness settled in her eyes the instant I let on that we might have a fertility problem."

Grace swept her hand toward the counter where she'd taken off Mrs. Calhoun's diamond wedding ring. "I saw dollar signs in Davenport's eyes when she got a good look at that rock. And she made a point to ask what you do for a living. I could almost hear her mind working, doing the math on how much we might pay for a child. She's our girl, Santini."

"It's looking more and more like it," Mark agreed. "And it's reasonable to think she showed up here unannounced to see if we're who we say we are. Anyone murdering young girls and kidnapping their infants can't be too careful.''

''True.''

''Did she mention the possibility of adoption?''

''No, and I made sure not to bring it up,'' Grace added. When formulating their ops plan, she and Mark had agreed not to mention the prospect of the Calhouns adopting a child. Doing so might send up a flag of caution in Davenport's head. Plus, letting the suspect broach the subject on her own negated the possibility down the road of some defense attorney claiming his client had been the victim of entrapment.

Grace blew out a breath. She truly had lost her mind. She and Mark were working undercover, for heaven's sake. *Their suspect* was presently cooling her heels in the living room. Davenport's unexpected presence was a reminder that, when it came to working undercover, nothing was for sure. Anything could trip you up. A suspect, even an innocent passerby, could turn the tables at a moment's notice. Could transform what appeared to be a relatively benign assignment into a life-and-death situation. That she and Mark had let their personal relationship distract them was flat-out dereliction of duty. They *had* to pull back, act like professional cops instead of still-hot-for-each-other ex-lovers.

Grace shoved a hand through her still-damp hair. ''I should have already told you all about my encounter with Davenport. Mark, we should have been going over the case, not…each other.''

''You won't get an argument from me,'' he said evenly. ''Under the circumstances we'd be wise to postpone anything that doesn't have to do with the job.''

''Cancel it,'' Grace amended, well aware of the sensations still churning in her system. This man standing just inches away was everything she'd remembered and sought to forget. And she so desperately *wanted* to forget. Desperately wanted to let him walk away this time without losing another part of herself.

She stiffened both her spine and her resolve to close the door on further temptation. Both the personal and professional consequences were too great. "Cancel," she repeated.

Mark's dark eyes stayed cool and steady on hers. Then he gave a curt nod. "I'll go mix Davenport a drink. How much time until you join us?"

"Give me ten minutes," Grace said as she reached for the hair dryer.

Chapter 6

Cancel it.

Grace's words echoed in Mark's head while he strode through the suite's bedroom and headed down the short hallway.

Cancel all future kisses. Avoid potential brushes of flesh against flesh. Sidestep every reference to the past. Better yet, *forget* their past.

Sure thing, he thought with a cynical shake of his head. He might feel more optimistic about the prospect of success if he hadn't already *tried* to forget for six years running. In all that time he hadn't seen her, heard from her, yet Grace McCall-Fox had never been far from his deepest thoughts, even during the time she'd belonged to another man.

Even when *he* had been with other women. There had always been a voice in the dark recesses of his brain whispering to him that Grace was the one. She was his match.

Whatever hope he might have harbored that the passage

of time had at least taken an edge off the memories had been dispelled moments ago when his mouth settled on hers. The need, the longing had seemed much too fresh to have lain dormant for six years. The memories he carried of her were sharper than he had thought. Nothing was forgotten. *Nothing.*

Scrubbing a hand across his face, he paused at the end of the hallway. This was not the time to think about coiled lust, unbidden need, or the woman he'd recently made one hell of an attempt to swallow. He eased out a breath, then another, while the FBI agent in him ruthlessly diverted his thoughts to his quarry.

Iris Davenport, currently cooling her heels in the suite's living room, had possibly killed two young women and kidnapped their newborn infants. Chances were, she was deeply involved in a black market adoption ring that sold babies to the highest bidder. Experience had taught Mark never to underestimate a suspect, and he had no intention of starting with Davenport. Coincidence was not in his cop's vocabulary. In police work, things happened for reasons. Davenport had rung the doorbell of Mr. and Mrs. Mark Calhoun's suite for more purposes than to just check on the emotional well-being of a woman she'd met that day at a health spa.

He felt his muscles begin to tighten. Felt the adrenaline, the hunting hormone, slowly flow into his bloodstream. He'd always savored the feel of getting nearer to a suspect, the closing in. *One less monster left free to prey on innocents.*

He took a silent step around the corner and paused. Davenport was still seated on one end of the long, plush sofa where he'd left her, thumbing through a glossy magazine that presented an overview of high-end shopping locales in Las Vegas. While she was still unaware of his presence,

Mark glanced toward the console behind the desk in the alcove that served as a small office. He noted the green light glowing on the eavesdropping device he'd placed there that morning. Apparently, Davenport had not bugged the room during his absence.

He shifted his gaze back to her. She was tall and slender, with dark red hair that cascaded around her shoulders and down her back in a mass of curls. Her face was chiseled, with pronounced cheekbones, a strong jawline and a long, straight nose. She wore loose white pants made of some sort of drapey material, with a long slate-blue tunic top belted in black leather. Her hands were slender; her faux fingernails, long enough to be viewed as potential claws, were painted a rich cinnamon. Not quite the hands one pictured for a nurse, Mark mused. Of course, if she was guilty of murder and kidnapping, she wasn't like most nurses. Guilty or not, Mark had no trouble picturing the woman assuring a patient that a shot would feel like a small sting, when in truth it would raise a knot the size of a doorknob.

''Sorry to leave you alone,'' he said as he strode toward her.

Looking up, Davenport gave him a cordial smile and laid the magazine on the coffee table in front of her. ''That's okay.'' Her dark-eyed gaze slid past him toward the hallway. ''Is Grace coming?''

''As soon as she dries her hair and gets dressed.'' Frowning, he slipped his hands into the pockets of his tan slacks. ''I'm glad you dropped by. Grace knows it affects me to see her upset, and she's become adept at camouflaging her feelings. If you hadn't thought to check on her, I doubt I would have known how troubled she was earlier.''

Davenport leaned forward, as if to share a secret. "Is she okay now?" she asked in a whispery voice.

"She seems fine." Mark gave her what he knew looked like a forced smile. "If a little embarrassed that she made you uncomfortable during your workout session."

"But she didn't." Davenport raised a palm, let it drop. "It was the other way around. There we were having just met, and I started asking questions that were clearly too personal. That's something I routinely do on my job, and I just got carried away today."

"Your job?"

"I'm a registered nurse. One of my job duties is to take patient histories. Anyone who's ever visited a doctor's office knows there's all sort of personal questions involved in doing that."

"True," Mark agreed.

Davenport gave him a chagrined look. "So, I not only came by to check on Grace, but to apologize for being so nosy and making her feel uneasy."

"From the sound of things, you were just being friendly." Mark glanced across his shoulder toward the bedroom, then looked back at Davenport. "Frankly, I'm glad Grace has found another woman here to whom she feels she can talk about our attempts to start a family. She and I discuss things, of course, but it's emotional for both of us. Her having you to talk to eases my mind."

"I'm glad to lend an ear." Davenport raised a shoulder. "Ever ask yourself why it's sometimes a lot easier to unburden ourselves to a stranger than to someone who's close?"

"The thought has crossed my mind." Although Davenport's words seemed sincere, Mark glimpsed a flicker of the same awareness in her eyes that Grace had described. It was a look of cool stealth, as if the woman had spotted a target and was zeroing in. Mark looked forward to the day when he had Davenport in an interview room so he could do the same.

He stepped toward the wet bar, saying, "I've kept you waiting long enough for that drink I promised." Having brought up the subject of the Calhouns' failed attempts to have a child, he didn't want to dwell on it. "What can I fix you?"

"Vodka and soda would be good."

"Coming up." Davenport's choice of something alcoholic was to their favor, Mark thought as he poured her drink into a crystal tumbler. He could only hope she would stay a while and give the liquor time to take the edge off her defenses.

"Grace mentioned you live in Houston," she commented.

"That's right." As a concession to the perpetual burn in his stomach, Mark poured himself ginger ale, topped it with a lime wedge, then carried both tumblers across the living room. "Grace and I are both native Texans. How about you?"

"I'm from Oklahoma."

He raised a brow. "That makes us not only neighbors, but rivals during college football season."

"Friendly rivals," she amended when he passed her drink to her.

Mark felt her long fingernails brush his hand and instantly wondered if it was by accident or design. If Davenport *was* flirting, it could be a test to see if he would succumb to her advances. He had delved into the mind of enough criminals to know that a fair number of them possessed at least a modicum of conscience. If Davenport fell into that category, one way to justify her crimes would be to ensure the babies she handled went only to couples devoted to each other.

Instead of joining her on the couch, Mark settled into one of the wing chairs on the opposite side of the coffee table. "So, Ms. Davenport, do you work at a hospital?"

"Oh, call me Iris."

"I'm Mark."

"I work at a clinic in Oklahoma City right now." She sipped her drink, her eyes intense points of interest as she surveyed him over the rim of her glass. Although the clothes he'd worn to play golf in were casual, they were expensive. As were the solid-gold wedding band and designer watch he wore.

"Nursing must be a rewarding career," Mark commented. "To know you help so many people."

"It is. I think Grace said something about your being in the oil and gas business."

"That's right." Davenport's lack of interest in talking about herself underlined Mark's belief that she was there to learn if Mr. Calhoun's need to have a child went as deep as his wife's. If so, did the couple have adequate funds in the bank to meet those needs?

"Grace mentioned you're involved in some other energy concern," Davenport added. She slid her auburn eyebrows together, as if trying to retrieve a memory. "I can't remember what that was."

"Wind energy production," Mark said without missing a beat. "I own a controlling interest in a company that constructs wind farms."

Using an index finger, Davenport made a small circling motion. "You build windmills?"

"Actually, the correct term is wind turbines."

"Well, we certainly have a lot of wind in Oklahoma."

"Not as much as in California and Texas. Then there's

Iowa.'' Mark sipped his ginger ale. The woman's intense scrutiny made him feel like a lab specimen. ''However, we're in the first stages of expanding into your state.'' The FBI agent responsible for rifling through Davenport's trash had checked her room and noted she hadn't brought a laptop computer on this trip. Still, Mark would lay odds that she—or her unknown accomplice—would soon hit the Internet to research wind power and find out the amount of potential financial gain involved.

And if she directed her online research toward Mr. and Mrs. Calhoun, Davenport would find the photos the Bureau had downloaded of himself and Grace supposedly attending Houston art openings, political fund-raisers and charity auctions.

Behind him, Mark heard the tap of Grace's footsteps against the hardwood floor as she stepped into the living room. ''That didn't take long,'' he said, rising.

''Long enough to keep our company waiting.'' Grace patted her dark hair, pinned into a sleek, graceful twist. Her long-sleeved dress was a perfect curve of black knit that ended midthigh and snugged against her body in all the right places. Sheer smoky-black hose and spiked heels pulled Mark's gaze to her slim legs as she crossed the expanse of Oriental carpet. He allowed himself an instant to regret that those legs weren't currently wrapped around him. *Cancel it,* he told himself, then ruthlessly shifted his thoughts back to business.

''As always, you look gorgeous,'' he said when Grace slid a hand into the crook of his arm. Dipping his head, he pressed a kiss against her temple. ''Is that dress new?''

''Yes.'' She gave their guest a smile. ''Iris, I'm so glad you dropped by.''

''I told Mark I didn't mean to impose. I just wanted to apologize again for getting too nosy during our massage.''

"In that case, I'll say I'm sorry again for getting so emotional." Fluidly Grace moved to the couch and settled near her new friend. "Now that we have that out of the way, let's forget the entire episode and enjoy ourselves."

Mark stepped behind the bar and mixed a tonic water for Grace. "Iris, can I freshen your drink?"

"No, thanks." She glanced at her watch. "I can only stay a few more minutes."

"Are you sure?" Grace asked, accepting the tumbler Mark handed her. "We'd love to have you join us for dinner." Her mouth curved. "I twisted Mark's arm and talked him into hitting the casino with me afterward."

Iris glanced his way. "You're not a gambling man?"

"I prefer to think that I don't toss money away." He settled on the couch a few intimate inches from Grace. Her warm, soft scent instantly settled over him, into him. "When I make an investment, I want to know up front what the potential return will be." He skimmed a hand across Grace's shoulder. "But my wife enjoys playing blackjack, and I like to see her happy, so we'll spend time in the casinos while we're here." The smile he gave Davenport was full of polite invitation. "Are you sure you can't join us tonight?"

She glanced again at her watch, then set her tumbler on the coffee table. "I wish I could, but I've made other plans for the evening. If I don't leave now I'll be late."

"Our loss," Mark said as he and Grace rose together. He knew the agents trailing Davenport would advise them where she went after leaving the suite. "You'll give us a rain check?" he asked.

"Absolutely." Davenport threaded the chain of her small black evening bag over her shoulder, then looked at Grace. "Will I see you at the spa tomorrow?"

"Yes," Grace said as they moved toward the door.

"Keely—the sadistic attendant—talked me into booking the entire morning. Facial, shampoo and set, manicure. Pedicure."

Mark cocked his head. "None of that sounds too sadistic."

"Waxing of various sensitive areas," Grace added, shooting him a long-suffering look.

"Ouch," he murmured.

"I'll tough it out." Grace ran a hand down his sleeve. "Just think how great I'll look when you pick me up for lunch."

"You'll look more than great," Iris assured her. "I'm having a full-body paraffin dip and wrap in the morning. You can't imagine what that does for your skin."

Grace arched a brow. "Full body?"

"Actually…" Mark let his voice trail off and pursed his mouth, giving the impression he was a husband scrambling for a way out. In truth, while formulating their ops plan, he and Grace had come up with a variety of scenarios designed to keep Davenport in their sights after they made initial contact with her.

"Actually?" Grace asked.

"I'm afraid our lunch plans for tomorrow have hit a snag," he said. "Urgent business in the form of a conference call. It's slated to take several hours." He rubbed his thumb lightly against the frown line that had formed between Grace's brows. "I'm sorry, darling."

He sent Iris a look. "Ever see a man slide into the dog house so efficiently?"

Iris wrinkled her nose. "The way you did that was pretty good."

Nodding, he looked back at Grace. "I have an idea that might win me a reprieve."

"It had better be a good one, Calhoun."

"It is." He shifted his gaze between both women. "And it involves both of you, if Iris is free. How about I arrange for a limousine to pick you up when you're done at the spa?"

"Pick us up and take us where?" Grace asked.

"To the restaurant of your choice for lunch."

"Then?" Grace prodded.

Chuckling, he nudged a finger beneath her chin. Anyone watching them would buy it, Mark thought as he gazed down into her dark eyes. Willingly accept that he and Grace were devoted to each other, totally in lust. In love. "Shopping, darling. A full afternoon of shopping."

Grace slid Davenport a look. "What about your schedule, Iris? Can you fit me in?"

The woman sent them both a smooth smile. "I wouldn't miss it for the world."

"I'm buying," Iris said late the following afternoon when she and Grace settled at a table in one of the Gold Palace's lounges.

"Not necessary," Grace said. "But appreciated," she added while checking their surroundings. The lounge resembled a dark, masculine study with leather chairs grouped around tables that had some age and weight to them. Overhead were huge oak beams; across the room a fireplace on a raised hearth held a blazing fire. In one corner stood a massive Christmas tree decorated with white twinkle lights and ornate golden bulbs and bows. An ocean of white poinsettias sprouted beneath the tree.

Out of the corner of her eye, Grace noted a man in a gray suit slide onto a stool at the brass-railed bar. He was the FBI agent assigned to tail Iris when she left the lounge.

"I appreciated the limo ride and lunch your husband supplied," Iris said, smoothing the short, white wool jacket that matched her slacks. With her red hair swept into a loose chignon and her skin glowing, Iris looked like a model.

Grace slipped off her heels and sighed with relief. "My feet went numb about two hours ago."

Iris chuckled. "Mine, too. Why is it that something as enjoyable as shopping can render such pain?"

"You've got me," Grace said. She gave thought to the mountain of shopping bags the bell captain had unloaded from the limo for delivery to the suite. After the investigation closed, all the expensive clothing and accessories she'd charged to the gold card supplied by the FBI would be returned unused to the stores. Talk about pain.

When a waiter approached, Iris ordered champagne. "I hope that's okay with you," she said after the man left the table. "Since my time in Vegas is winding down, I want to make the most of it."

"Champagne's fine," Grace said, feeling a fist of apprehension tighten her stomach. Iris had mentioned several times that her vacation was nearing an end. Grace and Mark still had no hard evidence linking the nurse to the two murders and kidnappings of the missing infants. Iris hadn't brought up the Calhouns' inability to have a child during their shopping spree. If she didn't mention the subject soon, Grace would have to scramble to find an opening.

"In fact, I love champagne," Grace added, then tilted her head. "Do we have something to celebrate?"

"Maybe," Iris said, just as the waiter returned with their order. He made quick work of popping the bottle's cork and filling crystal flutes with a gush of bubbly champagne.

Iris retrieved her purse, saying, "I'll just take care of the bill."

"Yes, madam."

The waiter presented Iris with a small leather folder. She checked the amount, then pulled some items out of her purse in her search for her wallet. Grace kept her face expressionless when she identified one of those items as a thin, disposable cell phone. The background checks run on Iris had proved disappointing when no cell phone account was found, which shut the door on using that angle to track an accomplice. The disposable phones were new on the market—Grace had first seen one a few months ago when she'd taken it off a juvie first-degree burglar. The phones, sold in convenience stores, were a bane to law enforcement since users didn't have to establish an account and could remain anonymous. With no records maintained on the phones, there was no way to track calls made and received.

Iris dispensed with the waiter, slid her belongings back into her purse, then picked up her flute. "Grace, I want to ask you a question. I'll warn you ahead of time that it's personal." Iris eased out a breath. "To be honest, I've spent the entire day trying to muster my courage to bring up this subject. I just hope you'll keep in mind that I have your best interests at heart."

Grace infused a wary look into her eyes at the comment. She hoped to hell Iris was about to make her grand play. In case she was, Grace leaned forward minutely, ensuring that the transmitter sewn into the lapel of her tobacco-colored suede jacket picked up Iris's voice clearly. "All right," Grace said, lifting her glass. "I'll keep that in mind."

"I gather from everything you've said that the chances of you and Mark having your own biological child aren't good. Am I right?"

"After this last failure at in-vitro, the doctors don't hold out much hope." Grace lowered her glass. "Why do you ask?"

"I'm wondering if you and Mark have ever considered adoption?"

"Yes, of course. I've lost count of the number of agencies we've contacted. Mark and I are on so many waiting lists." She pulled her lower lip between her teeth. "The last agency we talked to said their normal waiting period is ten years. *Ten years.*"

"Hearing things like that must be dreadful for you," Iris said. "And I know personally about all the hoops and hurdles involved in working with adoption agencies." Reaching across the table, Iris patted Grace's hand. "You remember I said I work at a clinic?"

"Yes."

"It's operated by the state, so we see all age groups of people. Most of the girls who come in for prenatal care are single and in their teens. The majority are runaways who don't even give us their real name. Some of those girls have no idea how to care for themselves, much less their babies, so they give them up for adoption. Usually the babies go to agencies that have contracts with the state."

Dropping her gaze to her glass, Grace stared into the champagne's pale gold fizz. "Like I said, Mark and I have our names on so many lists."

"That's good because you want to keep every option open. But some of the young mothers who come to the clinic are more discriminating. They don't trust an agency mired in paperwork to place their baby in the best home possible. Those girls prefer to go through an attorney for what's called a private adoption."

And if they change their mind about doing so, you kill them, Grace thought, feeling adrenaline surge through her system. All of her instincts told her the investigation had finally shifted, the prime suspect had taken the bait.

Grace held up a hand, making sure it trembled slightly. "Mark and I tried going that route about a year ago." As if to steady herself, she took a sip of champagne that slid down her throat like liquid gold. "We even met a young pregnant girl about a month away from her delivery date who wanted to give up her baby. She told the attorney she thought Mark and I would be perfect parents for her child. We paid her medical and living expenses, and gave the attorney a substantial retainer. We were so thrilled. Excited. We even chose wallpaper and fabric for a nursery. Picked out names. And then the baby was born and the mother backed out." Grace shook her head. "Mark and I… Well, neither of us has the heart to go through that again."

"How awful for you."

"It was."

"I don't blame you for not wanting to open yourself up to the possibility of that happening again. It's just that through my job I deal with a lot of social workers. More than one has mentioned an attorney whose expertise is private adoptions. Grace, the social workers make this guy sound like the superhero of adoptions. His success rate of placing infants with couples unable to have their own child is one of the highest in the entire country. Something like ninety-eight percent."

"So high?" Grace asked, infusing a hopeful tone into her voice. "This attorney, is he in Oklahoma City?"

"I don't think so." Iris pursed her red-glossed lips. "Close by, maybe, but not in the city itself."

"Do you know his name?"

"I've been trying to recall it all day. It's on the tip of my tongue, but it just won't come. I could have called one of the social workers to get it, but I didn't want to make any inquiries until I talked to you." Iris paused, a hint of a frown marring her smooth forehead. ''I have no way of knowing, of course, but with a reputation like that, the attorney fees involved are probably substantial. Not to mention those for the biological mother.''

Big shock. ''The amount of money involved isn't really a...concern for us. Having a baby is.'' Grace placed a hand against her throat. ''A superhero,'' she repeated in a ragged whisper. ''It sounds so tempting, Iris. So hopeful. I just don't know if Mark or I can open ourselves up for another possible disappointment.''

''I understand.'' Iris gave Grace's hand a second pat, then eased back in her chair. ''I wouldn't have brought this up if I hadn't seen you and Mark together yesterday evening.''

''Really? Did we do something remarkable?''

''Just looked at each other like you were madly in love, is all.''

''Well, we are married,'' Grace said lightly. If she were working with any other cop, she would have taken Iris's comment merely as affirmation of the acting skills she'd honed during various undercover assignments. But Mark wasn't just any cop. He was foremost a man who had once been her lover. Had very nearly become her lover again yesterday. Grace was very afraid the emotional responses Iris had witnessed on Mrs. Calhoun's part had been more than just an act.

''These days, being married isn't necessarily an indication of how a couple really feels about each other.'' Iris retrieved the champagne bottle from the silver bucket near her chair and topped off their glasses. ''But where you and Mark are concerned, believe me, it's obvious you're crazy about each other.''

''We have our moments,'' Grace murmured, feeling a tiny catch in her heart. She and Mark did indeed have their moments in time. Every six years, or so. Even then, whatever emotion lingered between them was incidental. Mark had come back for a case, not because he needed her or missed her. And now that the investigation seemed close to shifting into high gear, he would no doubt be gone in a matter of days.

"Well, Grace, in my book you're a very lucky woman. If I could find your husband's twin, I'd grab him and never let go." Pausing, Iris tapped a red-slicked fingernail against her champagne flute. "The point is, it's clear you and Mark will make great parents. I'd like to help you if I can." She took a long, slow sip. "I won't bring the subject up again, you have my word. Just think about what I've said. Talk to Mark. If you decide you want to meet with this super attorney, let me know. I'll find out what arrangements need to be made."

"Thank you. I'll talk to Mark as soon as I get back to the suite." Grace gripped Iris's hand, aware she was holding herself back from squeezing hard enough to break a couple of bones. "I can't tell you how grateful I am that you'd offer to do this for us."

"It's nothing." Iris tapped the rim of her glass against Grace's, letting the crystal sing. "I just hope everything works out for the best."

"Yes," Grace agreed, picturing Iris in a bright orange prison jumpsuit. "You and me both."

Chapter 7

Two mornings later Iris Davenport stood in a hotel room registered to a pharmaceutical salesman from Orlando. Because the morning air carried a nip, she'd tugged the sheet off the bed and wrapped it around her, toga style.

The room was twenty-eight floors up; through the glass door off the balcony, Iris had a view of the azure dawn spreading across the desert landscape. Behind her, the closed bathroom door muffled the rhythm of the shower that mixed with the salesman's voice, currently booming out a slightly off-key rock tune.

Her mouth forming a smug curve, Iris glanced at the rumpled comforter and pillows spread across the mattress while she punched a series of numbers into her disposable cell phone. It sure as hell wasn't Troy Pacer's singing ability that had kept her in his bed all night.

She had caught sight of him the previous evening while they both gambled at the same roulette table in the Gold Palace's casino. He had beautiful dark, thick hair and wonderful shoulders, and his brown eyes were so expressive that when he looked up and met her gaze, she'd felt her legs go weak. The man had the most exquisitely masculine hands, big, competent looking, with clean, square nails. Even as he'd leaned over the table to make another roll of the dice, Iris had wagered those hands would be on her before the night was over.

She'd won that bet.

"Hello?"

She blinked when her partner answered her phone call on the second ring. "I told Grace Calhoun you were the superhero of adoptions," she said.

"Superhero, huh? Did she buy it?"

"Oh, yeah—you should have seen her face light up. She's so desperate to have a child, she grasps at any straw."

"Lucky thing for her we provide a lot more than straws. If the Calhouns are willing to pay enough money, they'll get a kid."

"They're willing. And the financial check we ran on them confirmed they've got money available to just toss away. I spent an afternoon with Grace while she did her best to max out her husband's gold card. Then, while she and I were in the lounge drinking champagne, Mark Calhoun strides in and slides this jeweler's box into her hands."

"What was inside?"

"A solid-gold bracelet encrusted with rubies."

A low whistle came across the phone line. "The shopping spree you were a part of and the bracelet are just additional confirmation that the guy's loaded."

The picture of Grace Calhoun that formed in Iris's mind had her frowning. With her dark, thick hair and sculpted, high-boned features, the woman was certainly a looker.

And the curve-hugging spandex she wore at the spa showed off a killer figure. But Grace's desperation to have a kid made her seem excessively vulnerable; pitifully clingy. Iris shrugged. The woman was just damn lucky she'd landed a man who found all that neediness attractive. One who looked at her as if she was the beginning and end of everything. A once-in-a-lifetime kind of guy who happened to be rich and gorgeous to boot, Iris thought. Even the perpetual weariness around Mark Calhoun's eyes seemed to add a fascinating depth to him.

"From all our checks on them and considering everything I've observed, I'm convinced the Calhouns are a sure thing," Iris said. "Since I'm the one who found them in the first place, I want a finder's fee."

The silence coming across the line pressed like fingers against Iris's eardrums.

"That isn't our deal," her partner said finally.

"Right. Our deal is that I supply the babies and *you* find the couples who'll pay to adopt them. In this instance, I've done both. You want to make your usual amount on the transaction, fine. Just tack it onto the Calhoun's tab."

"You don't think they'll try to negotiate for a lower price?"

"Maybe." Iris thought back to what Mark had said about gambling: he didn't toss his money away. When he made an investment, he knew beforehand what potential profits could be involved. "Probably," she amended. "You have to figure the husband didn't get rich by paying top dollar for things, so it's a good bet he'll try to get the price down. He'll give in, though, because he loves his wife and she's desperate to be a mother. He knows she won't be happy until she's changing diapers full-time. All you have to do is stand firm. Make noises you've got another couple in the wings willing to pay any price for the baby. Do that, and you'll get whatever amount you quote him."

"If you're sure about this."

"Positive." She pursed her mouth. "In fact, I may drop that little tidbit on Mark Calhoun. Start him thinking about what it will do to his wife if he allows someone else to outmaneuver him. When you mention that other couple later on, it'll add to the pressure he feels."

"Works for me. Have you checked on the biological mother?"

"I called yesterday. Everything's fine. She'll probably deliver toward the end of next week. I need to wrap up this vacation and get back to the clinic. Like I said, I'm taking care of *everything*."

A brief pause came on the line. "All right, Iris, I'll give you a finder's fee. This one time. The next adoption we do, we go back to the old way. Status quo. After all, except for the two unfortunate…events, we've operated without any glitches."

His comment reminded Iris of their last face-to-face meeting, during which he had referred to the events as *murders*. The nurse in her wouldn't allow her to think of them that way. Instead, she considered what she'd done more abstractly, as the solution to otherwise intractable problems. In both instances a certain issue had arisen, and she'd found a solution.

Granted, she'd been caught off guard the first time the *issue* had arisen. When DeeDee Wyman changed her mind about adopting out her baby while she was in the throes of labor, Iris had shoved back a sense of panic and reasoned it was just the teenager's hormones talking. If Wyman felt too sick and weak to take care of her child, then she would come to her senses and go ahead with the adoption.

That adoption *had* to go through! Iris had been counting on the money, she'd *needed* it to prevent the people she owed from making good on their promise to start breaking her bones, one by one.

The small amount of anticoagulant drug Iris had slid into Wyman's vein shouldn't have stopped the teenager's heart, but it did. No big loss, really. Wyman was homeless, she slept at various shelters on occasion, but mostly she lived on the street, turning tricks. Iris had seen plenty of other girls like her and knew Wyman would probably wind up trading the baby for drugs before it was three months old. The kid was now with a family that wanted it, loved it and had tons of money to give it whatever it wanted.

A'lynn Jackson had been a carbon copy of Wyman—a pregnant teen who'd already signed all the adoption papers, then balked about giving up her baby. Filling a syringe with the same anticoagulant and sliding the needle in the girl's IV had simply been a matter-of-fact decision on Iris's part. Just a solution to another intractable problem.

"I see no reason for us to change our basic agreement while the operation is running so smoothly," her partner added.

Iris narrowed her eyes. Things were running smoothly because *she* was the one who solved their problems. *She* took the damn risks.

Pointing that out to the bastard was on the tip of her tongue, but she held herself back. In truth, she needed him. Coming across the ripe-for-the-picking Calhouns had been a fluke. She didn't have the contacts—or the law degree— necessary to work the operation on her own. Without him, there would be no operation.

"I'm not trying to change things, darling," she said

through her teeth. "I'm pointing out the obvious—I've done double duty this time for which I should be compensated. Quite simply, I'm due a bonus, which I expect you to pay."

She thought about the untraceable cash she had stashed in a safe place. She viewed each bill now secreted there, each one she added, as a layer of protection. Insulation. Insurance that she would never have to go back to being the mousy redhead who'd carried around twenty-five pounds of extra weight. The boring woman who'd gotten her kicks gambling at Oklahoma's Native American–run casinos between working at a hospital and doing night shifts for a Hospice program.

How pitiful she must have been, caring more about the sense of anticipation gambling had instilled in her than even the winning and losing. Whether it had been the next card, the fall of the dice, what horse won or the number the little ball stopped on, it was those few seconds of waiting and hoping and wishing that had made her feel alive. The downside to that was the pit of debt she'd quickly dug for herself. When the opportunity came along that offered her a way out of the quagmire, she'd grabbed it and held on for dear life. Now, except for the occasional out-of-town trips she treated herself to, she no longer gambled. In short, she'd reinvented herself. She had no intention of going back to the hellish, pathetic existence that had once been her life.

As if needing visual confirmation of her transformation, Iris tucked the phone against her cheek and shoulder, then turned toward the mirror over the dresser. Loosening her grip on the sheet, she let it slither down to pool around her ankles. The image reflected back at her assured her there was nothing left of the woman she'd once been. Her body looked long, sleek and expensive, like a new Jaguar. She'd paid experts to teach her all the tricks about hair and makeup, so that even after a night spent in a man's bed she looked sexy and tousled, not *used*. Dammit, she was *entitled* to the new life she'd scraped and clawed out for herself. She'd earned it. And she wanted more. No one was going to get in her way.

"What about my bonus?" she asked into the phone.

"You've made your case," her partner said. "You'll get it. Let's move on."

Feeling a tug of triumph, she allowed herself a light laugh. "You sound like a lawyer, darling."

"I'm the superhero attorney, remember?"

From behind the bathroom door the rhythm of the shower continued. The salesman switched from rock to an achy-sounding country tune about lost love and strong whiskey. The thought of his hands—those hard masculine hands spreading soap over her flesh—fine-tuned every nerve in Iris's body.

She kicked the sheet aside. Strolling toward the bathroom, she said, "Actually, I have a date with a real superhero right now."

"Should I start calling you Wonder Woman?"

"I've got to go," Iris said, ignoring his attempt at humor. "I'll tell the Calhouns the birth mother has approved them and they'll have to meet with her attorney. You'll arrange for a suite for them? Say the day after tomorrow? Schedule an afternoon appointment for them at your office?"

"I'll take care of things on my end. If that baby arrives on schedule, you and I will have the Calhouns' payment to stuff in our Christmas stockings."

"Perfect timing," Iris said. Feeling the heat of desire

rising inside her, she clicked off the phone and tossed it into her purse.

Pushing open the bathroom door, she disappeared into a cloud of steam.

After dinner that evening, Grace headed for one of the blackjack tables in the Gold Palace's casino. Mark detoured to their suite to check for messages.

Clad in a slithery gown of midnight-blue sequins, Grace perched on a stool vacated seconds earlier by an overweight, balding man who'd left the table with a scowl on his jowly face. The air in the casino was filled with smoke, murmured conversation and the steady clatter of slot machines. Occasionally silver clattered into one of the slot's metal bowls. Overhead chandeliers glowed, spilling light onto players, tables and the dark copper art deco carpet.

Aware that she might be under surveillance, Grace opened her sequined evening bag. Using fingers that sported the fake, manicured nails she still wasn't used to, she pulled out a bill and laid it on the green baize.

"Changing a hundred," the lanky, bearded dealer said.

Grace gave the other four players a polite smile. The dealer, clad in a modified tux uniform, slipped the bill into a slot on the table, then counted out chips.

Twenty minutes later Grace's one-hundred-dollar stake was up to three hundred. She felt sure her fellow players mirrored her by sending up continuous silent prayers of hope for the elusive card combination of twenty-one. For some reason, luck had chosen to smile down on her tonight.

Sipping the tonic water a waitress had brought her, Grace peeked at her hole card while the croupier dealt her another. Satisfied with a nineteen, she made a wordless gesture with her hand, indicating she would pass on getting another card. One by one, the other players broke until the dealer was Grace's sole competition on the current hand. He dealt himself another card, and broke at twenty-three. Grace smiled, happily accepting the chips he deftly slid her way.

"New dealer," the croupier announced, indicating his shift at that table was finished.

A female dealer with spiky blond hair and electric-blue eyeshadow stepped up to take his place. Giving the players a businesslike nod, she said, "Good evening. New deck." She broke the seals on decks of cards and began shuffling them together.

Grace used the time to perform a slow survey of her surroundings. Sweeping her gaze over the sea of bodies, she searched for Iris Davenport. Although there were various women wearing sleek dinner dresses and sparkling sequins, none of them had the flame-red hair that made Iris easy to spot.

It had been a day and a half since Mark had phoned Iris to tell her he and Grace would take a chance on another private adoption. That chance, however, was contingent on the transaction being handled by the lawyer Iris had referred to as the "superhero." Davenport had dropped by their suite a few hours later, saying she had contacted a source she didn't name in order to put the wheels in motion. Supposedly, the source had told Iris the attorney would need certain background information from the Calhouns. Mark and Grace had supplied her with the fictional history the FBI had created on their undercover personas. Iris had left their suite, promising she'd be in touch.

Iris had not shown up at the spa that morning for their spin class. Grace knew that while she had been sweating on the exercise bike, Iris had been holed up in a hotel room registered to one Troy Pacer, a pharmaceutical salesman from Orlando.

The surveillance team that tracked Iris last night reported it had seemed the encounter between the two had been unplanned. A sudden meeting of gazes across a roulette table.

Grace shifted her attention to the nearby table where Iris had hooked up with Pacer. A crowd of people hovered nearby while the roulette wheel spun continuously. So far, the FBI had found nothing in the background check they'd run on Pacer that indicated the married father of twins had prior involvement with Iris and/or ties to a black market adoption ring.

Still, the man earned his livelihood traveling around parts of Florida, making calls at various doctor's offices, clinics and hospitals. Through those contacts Pacer might possibly get access to pregnant women willing to sell their babies to the highest bidder. And perhaps dispirited couples in the midst of seemingly futile fertility testing who would have no qualm forking over thousands of dollars in cash to buy a child.

"Darling, it looks like you got lucky," Mark said when he strode up beside her stool. Ever the indulgent husband, he placed a hand on her shoulder, his fingers squeezing lightly.

She felt the instant kick of her pulse as she shifted to face him. Tonight he wore a gray silk suit and a midnight blue shirt. A cream-and-blue tie was knotted at his throat. The lighting in the casino made his sinfully handsome face look narrow and raw-boned. The looks he garnered from several nearby women told Grace he was easily the best thing they'd seen all night.

She had to agree.

Since that day they'd exchanged those steamy kisses,

both she and Mark had adhered to their agreement to keep things between them strictly business while they were alone together. Doing so, however, wasn't an option when they were in public parading as a married couple. Nor did it seem to Grace that she had the option to prevent her body from instinctively reacting whenever Santini got near, whether in private or in public. The best she could do was hope the walls of resistance she'd erected around herself held steady until they closed their case and he winged away on his next assignment.

Looking up, she saw the intensity in his eyes and knew something had happened. Although her cop instincts went on alert, she stayed in character.

"Luck?" she repeated, sending him a flirty smile. "I prefer to think that I've tripled my money due to skill."

"You're too gorgeous to argue with." Mark leaned in, his mouth grazing her temple. "It appears the Calhouns got lucky, too," he murmured against her ear. "We had a message from Davenport, asking us to contact her as soon as we got back to the suite."

Grace felt her heart pick up rhythm. Telling herself it was solely due to Mark's words and not the closeness of his mouth to her flesh, she said, "And?"

"I called her. All she would tell me was that she has good news about the adoption. She's on her way down to meet us in the lounge."

"Bets?" the blond dealer asked.

"I'm done for the evening," Grace said. She eased off the stool while Mark collected her chips and handed them to her. She dropped them into her evening bag, knowing Grace Calhoun would be too eager to hear news about the adoption to take time to cash the chips in now.

Linking hands as they moved off, Grace gave Mark an expectant smile. "What about Iris's pill-pushing lover?"

She kept her voice low to negate any possibility of being overheard.

"Anything new come in to make us think he's some sort of baby merchant?"

"Nothing on the surface." Placing a hand at the small of her back, Mark matched her smile. "Not yet, anyway." He dipped his head, speaking as softly as a lover whispering endearments. "Agents in our Orlando office are digging into Pacer's background. The pharmaceutical conference he's attending here ends tomorrow. The hotel shows he's due to check out in the morning. He's booked on an early afternoon flight to Orlando. We'll have someone on the plane watching him and tailing him after he arrives in Florida."

In a matter of moments they reached the entrance to the dimly lit lounge where Iris and Grace had relaxed over flutes of champagne two days ago. Iris had already arrived and laid claim to one of the tables near the hearth where a fire blazed. Tonight, a pianist sat at the baby grand on the far side of the lounge, caressing a bluesy tune out of the keys.

"Mark said you were playing blackjack," Iris said while Grace and Mark settled into heavy leather chairs.

"That's right," Grace said.

"So, how'd you do?" Iris asked. She wore a short black silk dress, cut low front and back. Her long red hair was swept off her face with a single comb. Grace was sure the woman had not dolled herself up just to spend the evening alone. Earlier, she'd studied surveillance photos of the pharmaceutical salesman. She took a moment now to check the lounge for the man. As far as Grace could tell, Pacer was nowhere in sight.

"I won," Grace answered, then flipped her wrist. "Iris, I apologize for being abrupt, but I'm too on edge for chitchat. Mark said you have good news about the adoption for us?"

"I do," Iris confirmed just as a waiter stepped up to the table.

Mark made quick work of ordering drinks. "I take it the good news comes from the attorney?" he asked. As if offering support, he settled his hand on Grace's, linking his fingers with hers.

"Not just from the attorney," Iris answered. "But the birth mother, too." Her glossed lips curved. "They've both gone over the background information you gave me. At this time they agree you're the ideal parents for this baby."

"At this time?" Mark asked levelly. The small white lights on the massive Christmas tree in the corner nearest their table turned his chiseled features into a landscape of silver light and shadow.

"Well, you'll have to meet with the attorney in person, of course," Iris said. "That's when all the legal issues will be ironed out. The fees involved discussed. And, I imagine, he would like to get to know you a bit. From the sounds of things, it's just standard operating procedure."

The waiter arrived with their order. Grace waited until he left to ask the obvious question. "What about the birth mother? Will we meet her, too?"

"Right now it doesn't look like it." Iris reached for her vodka and soda, took a sip. "As I understand it, she's a student, going to college on a scholarship. She also has to work to make ends meet." Iris raised a bare shoulder. "Her boyfriend—the baby's father—was far from pleased with the news she was pregnant. He's totally out of the picture. There's just no way she can manage to do right by a child at this stage in her life. She's afraid if she meets you, a part of her will want to try to maintain some sort of contact. Bottom line is, she thinks a clean break will be best for all involved.''

''How awful for her,'' Grace said. ''She must feel so torn.''

''True,'' Iris agreed. ''But she's very fortunate that a couple like you is willing to give her child a good home. I asked the attorney to make sure she knows that.''

''Speaking of this attorney,'' Mark began. ''He's checked us out, but you have yet to give us his name. We learned from our first attempt at a private adoption that they can be…delicate. I want to do some checking on this guy before Grace and I meet with him.''

Grace knew Mark had used the word *delicate* due to the fact that, technically, private adoptions were legal. If the attorney involved collected only a reasonable fee for services in arranging the adoption and perhaps medical and living expenses for the birth mother, he or she was acting within the law. It was illegal, however, to buy or sell a baby—or any human being, for that matter. Not to mention killing young women in order to obtain their babies to sell to the highest bidder.

''It makes perfect sense you'd want to check out the attorney.'' All solicitude, Iris retrieved a folded piece of paper from her black silk evening bag and handed it to Mark. ''Here's his name and address.''

He unfolded it. ''Stuart Harmon, Sr., Esquire. Winding Rock, Oklahoma.''

Mark had read the name and town not just for her benefit, Grace knew. They both wore small transmitters; the FBI agents monitoring their conversation would now shift into high gear to check out the lawyer.

Mark glanced up. ''Where exactly is Winding Rock?''

''About an hour's drive west of Oklahoma City,'' Iris answered. ''By the name you'd think it was a small, quaint town, but it's not. It's more of a luxury community, built by families with old money. By luxury, I mean million-dollar homes, most built on the shores of this gorgeous lake. There's a resort with a wonderful golf course." Iris inclined her head toward the paper. "I've written the name of the resort at the bottom. Reservations have been made for you and Grace to stay there, beginning the day after tomorrow. You'll need to book a flight to Oklahoma City, then arrange for a car. I hope I'm giving you enough notice."

Mark dismissed it with a flick of the hand. "I'll deal with the arrangements when we get back to our suite."

"The day after tomorrow?" Grace repeated. She gave Iris a quick, hopeful look. "So soon?"

Iris nodded. "The baby is due within a week. If everything goes well, you'll be a mother before Christmas Day. I understand the baby is a girl."

"A girl." Grace let her hand tremble as she pressed it to her lips. "Oh, Mark, a daughter." She took a deep breath as she blinked out tears of gratitude. "I don't want to get my hopes up, but…"

"I know," he said, his voice a soothing murmur. Lifting her hand, he pressed her fingers to his lips. "I know, darling."

Iris studied them over the rim of her glass with eyes as sharp as a razor. "I wish I could give you a one-hundred-percent guarantee. From your previous bad experience, you know I can't. All I can do is tell you that I have a good feeling about this. That everyone will agree on all the terms and things will work out for you this time."

"Thank you," Grace breathed, anticipating the moment when she'd be able to slap a pair of cuffs around Iris's elegant wrists. "Will you be going there with us, Iris? To Winding Rock?"

"No, I'm leaving tomorrow. My vacation is over, and I'm due back to work at the clinic."

"I see." Grace's stomach tightened. She knew that upon Iris's return to work, Dr. Odgers would inform her that staffing vacancies had necessitated her temporary reassignment to the elder-care patients. Plus, the Bureau now had an undercover agent working inside the clinic to make sure Iris stayed clear of the young maternity patients. Still, Grace wouldn't rest easy until the baby-snatching killer was in custody.

Grace wiped at her tears. "Iris, when I think this is all happening just because fate put us on bikes next to each other in a spin class…" She tied up the lie with a quick, watery laugh. "How can Mark and I ever thank you?"

With soothing notes from the piano hanging in the air, Iris gestured her glass as if to make a toast. "How about you let me have one dance with your gorgeous husband? Then I'll leave the two of you alone to celebrate."

Chapter 8

Moments later Mark guided Iris around the polished wooden dance floor that formed a semicircle on one side of the baby grand. A handful of other couples also swayed to the classic Cole Porter tune.

Keeping his touch light and impersonal, Mark glanced at the table where he, Iris and Grace had been seated. Grace had made her excuses and scurried off to the ladies' room, claiming she needed a moment to dry the tears that had come with Iris's good news about the impending adoption. Grace had yet to return. Mark knew she would linger out of sight while using a receiver to monitor his conversation with their prime suspect. Mindful of the transmitter implanted in his gold designer watch, he angled its face toward Davenport.

"So, Iris," he began. "I get the impression you wanted to dance with me for reasons other than to celebrate that I may soon become a father."

"I guess this is why you're so successful in business,"

Iris responded, giving him an indulgent smile. "Not much gets past you."

The nurse was tall and her heels brought her flawless face level with Mark's so that he had a clear view of her kohl-rimmed eyes. Despite the lounge's dim lighting, he could almost see her mind working the angles.

"It's been my experience that business in particular and life in general runs smoother when I don't allow things to get past me," he commented. "What is it you can't say in front of my wife?"

"It's just something my source mentioned in passing. Grace seems so...vulnerable when it comes to the subject of having a child. I didn't want to give her anything to worry about."

"With all the disappointments we've had over the years, Grace has every right to feel vulnerable."

"Yes, of course. She's been through so much. You both have. I just didn't see any point in dampening her excitement, but I thought you should know." Iris raised a sleek shoulder. "It's best not to have something jump up and bite you at the last minute."

"I agree. In this case, what would that something be?"

"Fortunately, the inquiry I made to the attorney on your and Grace's behalf came in first, so you have priority. But I was told there's another couple interested in adopting the little girl."

Mark narrowed his eyes. No stranger to manipulation, Iris hadn't taken long to zero in on the heart of the matter. A bidding war would up the amount of money she and her associates raked in for a baby sold on the black market.

"How interested is this couple?" Mark asked evenly.

"Very. From what I could find out, it appears they've tried to have their own child even longer than you and Grace. Endured all the medical procedures. Added their names to waiting lists with numerous agencies. That's basically all I know about them, other than that they're very well off financially.''

Mark doubted that this specific desperate, childless couple existed, but he couldn't be sure. ''So, what you're saying is these people waiting in the wings will be more than willing to step in if Grace and I are found to be…lacking in any area.'' Considering the topic at hand, he kept his face tense, his eyes somber. ''In other words, this may all come down to money.''

''I really don't know.'' Iris sent him a frown that had a practiced edge to it. ''Something questionable could come up in the background of this other couple that would automatically eliminate them from the birth mother's consideration. That would clear the way for you and Grace. In these matters, I suppose anything is possible. But you're probably right. Money may be the deciding factor.''

He'd bet on it. ''If so, I assure you Grace and I will soon be parents. I intend to do everything in my power to prevent her from being hurt again. No matter the cost.''

Iris angled her chin. ''You know, Mark, just listening to you makes me want to sigh.''

He raised a brow. ''How so?''

''The way you talk about Grace. How protective you are toward her.'' Iris shook back her long red hair. ''I've seen you looking at Grace sometimes like you want to slurp her up in one big gulp. If I ever catch a man looking at me that way, I'll consider myself the luckiest woman in the world.''

Mark felt a line of heat shoot up the back of his neck. At least he'd done a far better job of concealing his profession from Iris than he had his true feelings for his undercover partner. He took a moment to wonder how

Grace—and the other agents monitoring the conversation—were reacting to Iris's comment.

"Slurp her up," he repeated lightly. "Iris, I had no idea you're such a romantic."

She laughed. "Guess my secret's out now."

"Apparently." Waiting a few beats for the moment to pass, Mark gave her a somber look. "You have my eternal gratitude for telling me about the other couple. If I can repay the favor, let me know."

"I'm going to hold you to that." She gave his shoulder a light squeeze. "Far be it for me to think it's a bad thing to have a handsome man in my debt."

Just then the music died away. Out of the corner of his eye, Mark saw Grace step around the corner.

"There's your gorgeous wife," Iris said, motioning Grace to join them.

"Darling, are you all right?" As he spoke, Mark slid his arm around Grace's waist, and felt tension in her as tight as a plucked string. He knew his conversation with Iris had filled Grace with the same deep-seated need he felt to haul their suspect away in cuffs.

"I'm fine." Grace smiled up at him. "More than fine," she added, then looked at Iris. "This is a wonderful night and we owe it all to you. I don't know how we'll ever be able to thank you."

"All I wanted was a dance with your gorgeous husband, and he obliged. I consider all debts paid."

Mark glanced at their table. "Shall we finish our drinks?"

"I can't." Iris placed a restraining hand on his arm. "I have an early flight in the morning so I need to get back to my room and finish packing."

"I can't believe you're leaving." Reaching out, Grace gripped Iris's hand. "Promise me you'll spend your next vacation in Houston with us. And the baby.'' Grace's voice bubbled with a kind of joyful hysteria. ''We'll have the baby then.''

''It's a date.'' Iris's lips curved in a suggestive arch. ''Since the two of you are already on the dance floor, stay where you are. I'm going to ask the pianist to play something in your honor.'' She gave Grace's hand a squeeze. ''Be happy,'' she added before moving off toward the piano, her ankle-wrecking stilettos clicking against the wooden floor.

''We'll be peachy,'' Grace murmured. ''The instant we take you down.''

Shifting, Mark curled a finger beneath her chin, tipped it up. ''Darling,'' he began quietly, ''I take it you listened to the conversation?''

''I heard it all, sweetheart.'' She smoothed the lapel of his suit coat. ''I wouldn't be surprised if the creeps involved in this operation hired an auctioneer to make sure they sell the baby to the highest bidder.''

''Greed.'' Dipping his head, Mark dropped a kiss on her hair. ''An eternal motive.''

''Murder, kidnapping, child selling.'' Grace slid a look toward the piano before giving him a bright smile. ''I'm so going to enjoy hauling that bitch's butt to jail.''

''Don't think I'm going to let you have all the fun.''

Just then the pianist swept his fingers across the keys, filling the air with a torchy love song.

Mark nodded to Iris as she gave a slight wave, then moved toward the door. He noted the sure set to her shoulders, the confident sway of her hips. Anyone watching would believe her to be a woman who had everything under control. He felt a surge of satisfaction that came with knowing it was only a matter of time before her world came crashing down around her.

As if to confirm that, the FBI agent nursing a beer at the bar slid off his stool. He tossed a couple of bills beside his glass, then strolled out the door after Iris.

Mark swept a casual, assessing glance around the lounge's dim interior. Every table and most of the long-legged stools at the bar were occupied. He turned back to Grace, knowing she was as aware as he that Iris might have left an associate behind to keep an eye on them.

"Looks like you're stuck dancing with your husband, Mrs. Calhoun," he said, offering her his hand.

"Just remember this is a public place, Mr. C." She arched a dark brow as she slid her fingers against his palm. "So try to refrain from slurping me up in one big gulp."

"I'll keep that in mind," he murmured. As he would the fact of just how perceptive Iris Davenport could be.

He clicked the stem on his watch to deactivate the transmitter. "Thanks for reminding my fellow agents of Davenport's remark," he said, then nudged Grace closer. "I imagine I'm in for some heavy razzing over it."

"You're most welcome."

"So, Mrs. C., has anyone ever mentioned that you've got great acting skills?"

"You think so?"

"Know so. That little hysterical laugh of happiness you laid on Davenport sounded like the real thing."

Grace gave him a demure smile. "An Oscar would look great on my fireplace mantel. Be sure to mention my name to the nominating committee."

"I'll take care of it," he said while the music swelled around them.

They had danced together many times, Mark thought as he tightened his arm around her waist. Years ago when they'd been lovers. When she had belonged to him in every way but one. Then, he wouldn't have hesitated to dip his head and kiss her while they moved to slow, alluring music. And while they swayed, the taste of her would shoot through his system, sharpening the clawing need he'd felt for her. Constantly felt. Then he would take her home to his bed and make love with her until they were both delirious, sated and spent. And always, always, the more he'd had her, the more he'd wanted.

But all that was history. They'd gone their separate ways. Years had passed. Plenty of time for the heat between them to cool.

The scorching kisses they'd shared just days ago proved nothing had cooled.

Mark looked down, saw that Grace was watching him, her eyes dark and intense. "Something on your mind?" he asked quietly.

"Mainly, I keep thinking about what Iris said about the other couple waiting in the wings for this baby. Logic tells me there probably isn't another couple."

"I agree."

He also agreed it was best that they keep their conversation focused on business. Centering his thoughts on the case, however, wasn't quite so easy. Not since he'd discovered their bodies still swayed together as if they were each half of an intricate puzzle created to move in perfect synchronization. Her hips shifted lightly against his. Their thighs brushed. He could feel her heart beating against his, quick now, and not too steady.

His own pulse was nowhere near steady.

The twinkling lights on the Christmas tree washed the piano in a sweep of light. The musician caressed the keys, coaxing out music to weep by. To make love to. To dream on.

"But suppose you and I really were the Calhouns," Grace continued.

"All right, let's suppose." He wondered if she realized her voice had taken on a breathy edge.

"And that there really was another couple wanting to adopt the baby as much or even more than we do," she said. "Just being told about them would make me feel a hundred times more desperate. Totally vulnerable. Much more willing to pay whatever amount they asked for the child."

"That's the game plan Iris and whoever she's working with have set up. They dangle the one thing you want most in the world within arm's reach. At the same time they let you know it's hanging there by a thread and might be snatched away in the blink of an eye. Gone forever, unless you come up with enough cash. It's easy to bleed their customers dry using that tactic."

"What leeches," Grace murmured. "At least our investigation is off high center now. We know the name of Iris's attorney pal so we can get the lowdown on him."

"And the agent we've got working undercover at the clinic will start combing files to see if they've got a maternity patient who matches what Iris told us about the baby's mother." As he spoke Mark splayed his palm at the small of Grace's back where midnight-blue sequins gave way to flesh. Beneath his fingers he felt her shudder.

"Hopefully—" Her voice faltered. The hand she'd rested on his shoulder flexed, then fisted. She cleared her throat. "Maybe we'll have a lead on the birth mother before you and I get to Winding Rock. With the baby due so soon, things will move fast."

"Yeah." Mark knew it was possible they might have things wrapped up before Christmas. He would then go wherever his boss sent him. He was the only agent in the Crimes Against Children Unit without a wife or a family, so he'd volunteered to work holidays. Most of them he spent in whatever small town or sprawling metropolis the latest vicious deviant had surfaced. While other people celebrated, he holed up with crime-scene photos and reams of reports, trying to figure out where the suspect might strike next. Doing his damnedest to find answers before another child suffered. Maybe died. All the while, he struggled to control his own thoughts, fought to separate one crime from another, to keep the cases he worked from running together like rivers of blood.

The prospect of what lay ahead in his future brought back the pounding exhaustion. Without conscious thought, he buried his face in Grace's hair and pulled in her soft, warm scent.

He felt like a sleepwalker, slipping between the past and present. The past, in which he'd had her but couldn't keep her. The present, in which she had transformed into a seemingly impersonal acquaintance. A co-worker, whom he'd agreed to keep his hands off. One whose soft, hot flesh shivered when the job required him to touch her.

Holding her close, he felt the heat of her body seep through the layers of his clothing. He didn't have to imagine what she looked like beneath the midnight-blue sequins. He pictured her and let the need rise inside him while he bit back a moan.

His fingers grazed up her spine, tangling with the ends of her hair. For as long as he could remember he had wanted no other woman except her. Only her. With his arms wrapped around her and the exotic, feminine scent of her perfume filling his lungs, it wasn't such a huge step to imagine she was his again.

Easing out an unsteady breath, she pulled back slightly and gazed up at him. The dim light darkened her eyes, shadowed her cheeks. "We may have the case wrapped before Christmas," she said, as if she'd read his thoughts.

"Probably." When they'd first met it had been right after the holidays, and his transfer to the CACU had come through eight months later. He and Grace had never spent a Christmas together. That hadn't stopped him from thinking about her every December twenty-fifth for the past six years. Wondering about her. Wishing he knew what she was doing. Speculating if her thoughts ever drifted to him, even during the years she'd been married to Ryan Fox.

Mark tightened his hand on hers as they continued to sway to the sensuous music. "Tell me about the McCalls' typical Christmas Day."

She gave him a puzzled look. "Why?"

"Just curious." He thought about the awesome meals he'd eaten at her parents' home. The rambunctious family that had gathered around the massive dining room table. And always after attending one of those meals, he'd been left to wonder about, to envy, to covet the love that was so evident. "Roma cooks on Christmas, right? She and your dad have everyone over?"

Grace nodded. "Mom takes care of what we call the spread. Gran helps, although arthritis has slowed her down some. All the kids show up in the morning with even more food and presents."

"Kids?" Mark grinned. "Isn't Bran in his midthirties?"

"Right." Grace shrugged. "Even when all six of us have gray hair and wrinkles, Mom'll still call us 'the kids.' Anyway, Christmas Day is basically a mad house. It'll probably be even more of one this year with Carrie and Morgan bringing their fiancés." A frown formed between Grace's brows. "Though Bran and Tory are still separated, so I doubt he'll be Mr. Holiday Cheer."

"Lucky for him he has you to help him get through it."

"Tell Bran that," Grace said with a smirk. "Whenever

PLAY THE
Lucky Key Game

and you can get

FREE BOOKS
and a FREE GIFT!

Do You Have the LUCKY KEY?

Scratch the gold areas with a coin. Then check below to see the books and gift you can get!

YES! I have scratched off the gold areas. Please send me the 2 FREE BOOKS and GIFT for which I qualify. I understand I am under no obligation to purchase any books, as explained on the back of this card.

345 SDL DVF4   245 SDL DVGK

FIRST NAME   LAST NAME

ADDRESS

APT.#   CITY

STATE/PROV.   ZIP/POSTAL CODE

2 free books plus a free gift   1 free book

2 free books   Try Again!

Visit us online at
www.eHarlequin.com

The Silhouette Reader Service™ — Here's how it works:

Accepting your 2 free books and gift places you under no obligation to buy anything. You may keep the books and gift and return the shipping statement marked "cancel." If you do not cancel, about a month later we'll send you 6 additional books and bill you just $3.99 each in the U.S., or $4.74 each in Canada, plus 25¢ shipping & handling per book and applicable taxes if any.* That's the complete price and — compared to cover prices of $4.75 each in the U.S. and $5.75 each in Canada — it's quite a bargain! You may cancel at any time, but if you choose to continue, every month we'll send you 6 more books, which you may either purchase at the discount price or return to us and cancel your subscription.

*Terms and prices subject to change without notice. Sales tax applicable in N.Y. Canadian residents will be charged applicable provincial taxes and GST.

If offer card is missing write to: Silhouette Reader Service, 3010 Walden Ave., P.O. Box 1867, Buffalo NY 14240-1867

BUSINESS REPLY MAIL
FIRST-CLASS MAIL   PERMIT NO. 717-003   BUFFALO, NY

POSTAGE WILL BE PAID BY ADDRESSEE

SILHOUETTE READER SERVICE
3010 WALDEN AVE
PO BOX 1867
BUFFALO NY 14240-9952

NO POSTAGE
NECESSARY
IF MAILED
IN THE
UNITED STATES

I ask if he's taking care of himself, I hear terms like pest and nag.''

"Isn't that the job of a big brother?" Mark asked. "To hammer his siblings occasionally?"

"True," Grace said, her eyes sharpening on his face. "So, I remember you telling me once that you're an only child."

"That's right," he answered. It was a fact he'd always been glad of. It had meant he'd only had himself to try to protect. Considering the beatings he'd taken, he hadn't done a very good job of it.

"Having only one kid around probably makes the typical Santini Christmas Day seem calm compared to a McCall one," Grace observed.

Growing up, Christmas had been like any other day spent with his mother—filled with the scent of stale cigarettes, the sickly sweet odor of yesterday's bottle and, always, *always,* the prospect of a beating.

Mark looked away, his gaze tracking the shadowy outline of the couples sharing the dance floor. Just thinking about the woman with the hard, callused hands and vicious addiction to alcohol dragged him back over the jagged distance to the past. No matter how he'd transformed himself, how successful he was in his field, it took only the mention of the cruel and hostile world he'd escaped from to jerk him back into that small, frightened boy who cowered in various hiding places, praying the monster wouldn't find him.

He was no longer a little boy hiding from monsters. He hunted them now, one by one. Locked them in a cage. Still, never talking about his own monster was on his shortlist of unbreakable rules. He saw no reason to tempt reopening the fleshed-over scars. No reason to have to deal with emotions that took too much from him when he already felt so hollow on the inside.

Grace's fingertips grazed his jaw, pulling his gaze back to her. "Christmas?" she prodded.

He studied her in an almost amused annoyance. Her tenaciousness was classic Grace. "Darling, is this an interrogation?"

"Think of it as quid pro quo. You asked me about the typical McCall Christmas. I told you. I'm just asking you the same question."

"So you are." Without thinking, he skimmed his knuckles down her cheek. "Your family is special, Grace. Priceless. I don't—have never—had that. For me, Christmas is just another day. I'm usually at a crime scene. Or trying to wrap up one case to get to another one."

She kept her gaze locked with his. "Okay, so what about the holidays when you don't have to work?"

There had always been limits to what he could and would give her. The biggest was his past. "I work every holiday. Can we just leave it at that?"

"Of course."

Despite the dim light, he saw the shadow pass over her eyes. He was holding her, yet he sensed her distancing herself a million miles from him.

Regret swelled in his chest. "Grace—"

Just then the music ended. Another couple bumped into them, then apologized.

"No problem," Grace assured them, then shifted smoothly out of his arms. "It's late, Mark." The scenario they were enacting had her mouth curving, a wife smiling up at her husband. Still, he saw the cool, focused look in her eyes when she stepped away, as though backing off from the edge of a cliff. "It's been a long day. Why don't we go upstairs?"

"All right."

As she turned and started moving away, Mark felt something twist in his gut. For the first time in his life, he realized how utterly alone he was.

Chapter 9

After briefly chatting on the phone with her brother, Grace slept—deeply for two hours, then fitfully as the dream closed around her: The night was clear and frigid; she walked out of the restaurant where she and Ryan had met for dinner and found her husband lying beside his patrol car. The bullet wound so close to his badge—*his heart*—pumped blood across the front of his uniform shirt.

"No!"

Frantic, she dropped to her knees, pressing her palms against his chest while a river of crimson oozed between her fingers. No matter how much pressure she applied, how fervently she prayed, she couldn't stop the flow. Couldn't slow the speed of the warm gush over her hands. Couldn't help her husband when he gasped her name, then took his last agonizing breath.

She woke with a start, fighting for air while nausea ground in her stomach. She pitched upright in the ocean-size bed at the same time consciousness slammed the door shut on the nightmare. There was a band around her chest; air heaved in and out of her lungs in hot, ragged gasps. Cold sweat plastered her T-shirt to her skin.

The blinds over the balcony door were levered partially open, allowing the glare of neon lights to leach in. Her gaze darted across the large bureau that loomed against the wall opposite the bed, then over the tapestry-covered sofa and chairs that faced the marble fireplace. The nausea began to fade when she saw she wasn't back in that frigid, harshly lit parking lot, fighting futilely to keep her husband alive. She was in a ritzy Las Vegas hotel suite. On assignment. Working undercover.

"God." She scrubbed her hands over her face, then plowed her fingers through her sweat-damp hair.

Why now? she asked, bringing her knees up close to her chest. Ryan had been dead for three years; it had been over a year since she'd last had the nightmare. Why all of a sudden had her subconscious zapped her back to the night that called up memories too terrible for words?

She had met Ryan on his dinner break because she'd been too excited to wait until he got home to tell him about the baby. That she was pregnant. Even now, after so long, she could still feel the press of his palm against her cheek. See his dazed wonder at the prospect of being a father. At that instant she had known their impending parenthood would finally close the emotional distance her past with Mark Santini had put between herself and her husband.

Moments later Ryan was dead.

She would forever question how that night would have ended if she hadn't taken a side trip to the restroom. If she had walked outside to the parking lot at the same time as Ryan. If there'd been two cops instead of one who'd surprised the gun-wielding auto burglar flying high on meth.

Maybe then, Ryan would be alive. Maybe her system

wouldn't have been so weakened weeks later when she caught the virulent case of flu and wound up in a hospital. Maybe then she wouldn't have lost the baby.

Grace closed her eyes. Though the passage of years had transformed the fierce pain of grief into a dull ache, there were still times the void in her life reached out and tore at her.

Like now.

And that was the cause of the nightmare, she reasoned. *Her baby.* She'd lost the child she'd wanted so desperately. The child she'd hoped would help restore the sense of closeness she and Ryan had once shared. Now she was working an assignment centered on babies. Innocents kidnapped from their murdered mothers. Lost, perhaps forever.

Where were those infants that DeeDee Wyman and Andrea Grayson had given birth to? Grace asked herself for the hundredth time. Would she and Mark find the babies? Or were they gone for eternity, like her own child?

Knowing she wouldn't find those answers tonight, Grace shoved back the comforter, then freed herself of the tangled sheet. She stood shakily, felt her legs wobble. When she was sure they would support her, she headed into the bathroom.

There she stared at her reflection in the mirror that spanned the rose-colored counter. Her face was pale as ice, her dark hair a disheveled mess, her eyes still clouded with memory. Shivering, she peeled off her clammy T-shirt and boxers, then shrugged into one of the hotel's thick terry robes.

She splashed water on her face, filled a glass and took a long, slow drink. Although the water eased her dry throat, it did nothing to steady her. Not when she could still picture Ryan so clearly, lying beneath her blood-soaked hands, the life gone from his eyes....

She shoved back the image into the dark recesses of her brain. Doing so, however, didn't rid her of the ice that seemed to course through her veins. She knew if she was ever going to get warm again, it would be with the help of something that came out of a bottle, not a tap. She took a moment to curse the fact that every drop of alcohol in the suite was in the minibar, a few feet from the couch where Mark slept. Knowing that, however, wasn't enough to dissuade her. Not when she felt so cold on the inside.

She pulled in a deep breath, then another. So, okay, she thought, squaring her shoulders. It apparently was a night for dealing with unsettling pieces of her past. And part of that past was the FBI agent asleep in the next room.

Her plan to quietly pad in undetected and pour a drink fell apart when she stepped into the living room. Mark was on the long sofa where she expected him to be, but he wasn't asleep. Far from it. He was working, studying the contents of a file folder that lay open on the expansive coffee table. Several lamps glowed, spreading a pool of warm, buttery light around him.

He'd stripped down to gray sweatpants and a black T-shirt. His dark hair was slightly rumpled, his face somber. She watched his eyes scan the page and saw his expression harden.

Despite the hurt she'd felt earlier over his refusal to talk to her about his personal life, she felt an unexpected jolt when she realized she was glad he was still awake. Glad he was there for her to talk to while she waited for her balance to return.

As if sensing her presence, Mark glanced up. Surprise flickered across his face, then his eyes narrowed. "Grace, is something wrong?"

"No." Remembering how wild her hair had looked in the mirror, she dragged her hands through it, wishing she'd taken the time to use her brush. "I didn't think you'd still be awake, is all."

"I can say the same about you."

"I was thinking about our case. The missing babies." She tucked her restless hands into the robe's deep pockets, then pulled them out. "I decided a drink might help me sleep."

His dark gaze focused on her with laser sharpness. "A drink probably wouldn't hurt," he said after a moment. Rising, he strode toward the bar. "I was planning to make myself some tea. How about I do the honors?"

"Only if you pour me something stronger than tea."

"Coming right up."

She glanced toward the alcove where the desk inlaid with intricate marquetry and matching console sat. "Have any faxes come in yet on Davenport's attorney cohort?"

"Not yet." Mark pulled a teabag out of a box. "I got a call on my cell a while ago from the agent who's doing the background investigation on Stuart Harmon. So far, Harmon looks to be Mr. Sterling Citizen. The agent has to wait until morning when the courthouse opens to find out how many adoptions Harmon has filed."

Not bothering to ask Mark if he wanted company, she crossed the wide sweep of carpet and settled on one end of the couch. Right now, she simply couldn't face going back to the bedroom. Couldn't shut herself in the dark while thoughts of all she'd lost still skimmed the surface of her consciousness.

"Is brandy okay?" he asked.

"Fine."

"So, what is it?" he asked.

"What's what?" She glanced across her shoulder toward the bar just as he began punching buttons on the microwave. Seeing him in the black T-shirt that didn't do a thing to hide the muscular contours of his chest and arms reminded her how deceiving the impeccably tailored suits he wore were. Though he didn't look soft in them, he looked elegant. There was nothing elegant about all those sculpted muscles.

"What's keeping you awake?" He retrieved a crystal snifter and brandy bottle from one of the glass shelves behind the marble counter.

"Hard to say. I talked to Bran earlier," she said, railroading the conversation onto another track. "He said to tell you hello."

"How's he doing?"

"Having a good time arresting bad guys. He hasn't seen or talked to Tory, so his personal life doesn't seem to be going as well. Since brother dear chooses to keep things to himself, that's just a theory on my part."

"It's probably on target."

"Why do you say that?"

"We law enforcement types are known to be proficient at theorizing."

"Good point." Grace flicked a look toward the hallway that led to the bedroom. Cops were also known for their bravery, but right now the last place she wanted to be was back in the big bed, risking a replay of the nightmare.

She shifted her gaze to the coffee table. A file folder with a red Confidential stamped diagonally across its front lay beside the report Mark had been studying. On one corner of the table sat the brown, nondescript mailing box that had been delivered to the suite while they'd been downstairs in the lounge with Iris Davenport.

"You mentioned earlier that the files you received tonight are on a case out of Buffalo, New York," she said.

"Right." The microwave dinged softly. Seconds later Mark rounded the bar, carrying the snifter and a mug with a teabag string fluttering in its wake.

"Is Buffalo a case you've been working or a new one?"

"It's ongoing." He handed her the brandy before settling onto the couch.

"Thanks." Now that he was only a few feet away, she noted the perpetual shadows of weariness under his eyes seemed to have deepened. "How many cases are you juggling right now?" Grace took her first sip of brandy. It slid down her throat like liquid silk and instantly began untying the knots in her belly.

"In addition to the one we're working?" he asked.

"In addition."

"Last time I counted, twenty-five." He swept a hand toward the files on the table. "I picked this one up in October when I was in Buffalo, speaking at a law enforcement seminar. A Buffalo PD homicide detective showed up when I got back to my hotel. He had two cases where the only similarity seemed to be that both victims were young girls. In his lieutenant's opinion, they had murders committed by different suspects. But the detective's instincts were telling him one guy did both. He asked me to consult on the cases. The detective called me last week when another girl about the same age as the first two was reported missing. They found her body yesterday. The Buffalo cop wants my opinion on whether the same guy murdered victim number three."

"So, what's the verdict? Do you think they have just one killer?"

"I'm ninety-nine percent sure of it."

She rolled her shoulders to help ease the tightness that had settled there. "Can you tell me the specifics of each case?"

"Why would you want me to?" Mark asked while dunking the teabag in his mug. "They don't exactly make for light conversation."

"Are you forgetting I'm a cop, Santini? One who worked a stint in homicide. Cops talk over their cases with each other." She cupped the snifter in her palm, swirling the liquid while reminding herself that the man sitting a few feet away wasn't just any guy with a badge. He was Mr. Close-mouthed Cop.

He gave her a pointed look. "I'm fully aware of your qualifications, Sergeant McCall." Easing back into the cushions, he sipped his tea. "Is our case the reason you can't sleep? Or did something come up while you were talking to Bran? I know you're worried about him."

She met Mark's gaze over the rim of his mug. He was watching her closely. Too closely. So close, she felt like a bug under a microscope.

The man wouldn't tell her about his past, she thought with a spurt of irritation. Why the hell did he think the reason she couldn't sleep was any of his business?

"Do me a favor, Mark, and stop trying to analyze me like I'm some do-wrong in one of your supersecret cases." She swirled the snifter, took another drink. She could feel the brandy's heat seep through her system, melting her muscles to putty consistency. "I suspect you have sleepless nights once in a while, even if you won't admit it," she added.

He raised a dark brow. "Why wouldn't I admit it?"

"Because, Special Agent Santini, you are a Fed. Acknowledging an occasional bout of sleeplessness might put you on the same level as a run-of-the-mill cop like me. Might even make you seem *human*."

His mouth twitched. "I'd forgotten about that nasty streak of yours, McCall. And it has apparently slipped your mind that you have this opportunity to lob insults at me because I requested your assistance on the Grayson case. I did that because you're such a good *run-of-the-mill* cop.''

"But not good enough to hear about your Buffalo case.'' She angled her chin. ''You know, Santini, cops talk over cases with each other not just so they can hear their own voices. Bringing in someone with a pair of fresh eyes can help spot angles no one else has clicked on to. Bring up a point that might lead to something. Maybe even help figure out who done it.''

"I do talk over my cases. With other agents in the CACU.''

"Well, ace, none of your pals are here right now.''

Shifting, Grace curled her legs under her and settled more snugly into the couch's pillowed corner. Thanks to the brandy, her nerves had steadied. ''Look, we can't do anything more on our case until we have the background information on Harmon. I can't sleep. You're working on another case that needs to be solved before there's a victim number four. Why don't you just talk it over with me as you go?''

"Fess up, McCall,'' Mark said, gazing at her with cool-eyed suspicion. ''You're using me as a momentary diversion, right? You couldn't sleep, so you decided the next best thing would be to come in here and harass me.''

She aimed an index finger at him. ''Don't let anyone tell you you're not perceptive.''

He gave a short laugh that took her by surprise when it curled around her heart. Before, when they'd been together, he had laughed easily and often. It had always been that way with them, so relaxed, so comfortable in the company of each other. How many Sundays had they spent huddled together on her couch? Reading the newspaper, listening to soft music, watching TV. Making love. Content just to be together.

And after he'd moved to Virginia, she had missed those Sundays desperately.

"McCall, has anyone ever mentioned you can be a pain in the butt?"

"You have, Santini," she said, her throat tightening around the words as she dealt with years-old memories that made her ache. "A couple of times."

"Yeah." The crinkles at the corners of his eyes deepened when he grinned. "The reasons why I called you that are all coming back now."

When her nerves scrambled, Grace tightened her fingers on the glass. She knew full well the heat in her veins had notched up to blast-furnace hot due to the man, not the brandy. She eased out a breath, forcing herself to relax, to push back passion. Her reaction simply proved the age-old theory that knowing something's not good for you doesn't stop you from wanting it.

"All right, Sergeant McCall, you win," Mark said, then set his mug on a coaster. "Let's see if you can help figure out 'who done it.'"

He scooped the reports up he'd been reading and shuffled them into order. When he looked down at the top page, his eyes sobered.

"Buffalo's first victim was murdered a month shy of her fifteenth birthday," he began quietly.

For the next hour Mark shifted through the reports and photos spread on the table in front of him. He used the information they contained and the theories he'd developed after his visits to the first two crime scenes to give Grace a chronological overview of the Buffalo homicides.

Surrounded by the suite's lavish elegance, he had the

sense that describing the murders was like talking about some parallel universe where three young girls took center stage in a hideous, violent play.

Propped in the corner of the couch, Grace listened, her eyes rarely leaving his face. Her questions were few, always germane.

Mainly she listened.

And Mark realized the longer he talked, the lighter the load he felt on his shoulders.

"That sums things up." He laid a handful of reports on the table, then eased back and met Grace's gaze. She was snuggled into the thickly padded corner of the couch, an oversize pillow propped behind her. Since the white terry robe reached only to her calves, she'd burrowed her bare feet beneath one of the cushions to keep them warm. Her eyes were dark and sleepy, her face relaxed. Clearly the brandy had taken effect.

"So, Sergeant McCall, what's your opinion?" he asked quietly.

"The Buffalo detective's boss thinks they've got different killers because the body disposal methods are so varied," she replied, sounding as tired as she looked.

"Right." Mark reached, took the almost-empty snifter from her hand and set it on the table.

"But you disagree. You think there's one killer who changes his MO between murders. He does that because he's growing more confident. Each time he kills, he gets better at it."

"Very good job at reading my mind, McCall. And since you're about to fall asleep on me, we can finish this discussion in the morning."

"What about you?" Her eyelids fluttered shut, opened.

"What about me?"

"You look as tired as I feel." She studied him for a moment. "More tired, maybe."

"Maybe."

Silently Mark conceded that *tired* wasn't the word for what he was. If he was lucky, he'd get a couple of hours of fitful sleep. Then the images of all the horror and death he witnessed on a daily basis would begin racing through his head and he'd jerk awake, sweating, his heart pounding. He knew from bitter experience that once awake the rest of the night would be shot.

So he would then dig out the files on one of the other cases he'd dragged here with him and go back to the unending cycle of reading reports and analyzing crime-scene photos. He wiped a hand over his face. Somehow his life had become a merry-go-round of death that never stopped spinning.

His life. Back in Virginia, he had a rented townhouse, a closetful of made-to-order suits and a vintage Mercedes sedan. He put the rest of his money away toward a retirement which he couldn't envision himself ever taking, since he had nothing but the job.

Grace's soft, steady breathing pulled his gaze back to the end of the couch. She was asleep now, her dark lashes shadowing her cheeks, her lips slightly parted, her raven hair rumpled and glossy on the pillow behind her.

Watching her, he noted the natural color, bleached out of her face when she'd first stepped into the living room, had returned. He furrowed his brow, wondering again what it was that had kept her from falling asleep. What had prompted her to come in search of a drink strong enough to settle the nerves he'd seen in her eyes? What had compelled her to spend time with him when she'd been so annoyed earlier after he'd refused to talk about his past?

Right now he could be selfish for himself and admit he

didn't much care what had brought her out of that bedroom. He was just glad it had.

Rising, he switched off the lights. In the dark he stood at one of the floor-to-ceiling windows, looking out at Vegas's eternal neon light show. Beyond the glare, the desert was an ocean of inky black.

Behind him Grace shifted; he heard the delicate change in her breathing as she slid deeper into sleep. Mark closed his eyes as fatigue shuddered down through him, giving his stomach a kick as it went.

Her mere presence was like a seductive song, calling to his battered senses. Unable to resist, he moved to the couch, eased down beside her. She stirred, then cuddled against him.

He smiled to himself. Grace was a cuddler. Always had been.

Over the raw yearning inside him, Mark felt an even more potent satisfaction. For this one night she was his again. At least until the dreams came back, jarring him out of whatever fitful sleep he could manage.

He slid his arms around her, closed his eyes and dropped into sleep.

Mark woke wrapped in woman.

He blinked against the shafts of morning light that streamed in the long windows, tossing diamond patterns against the living room's polished woods, brasses and marble. He wasn't sure what surprised him most—to wake with Grace McCall draped against him, or that he'd slept through the night. He hadn't accomplished the latter feat in at least a year—close to two. What was it about this woman—this one woman—that had the power to hold back the demons inside him?

They lay on their sides, pressed close together, almost

nose to nose. A shapely yard of leg was tossed over his sweatpants-clad thigh; one of her palms was pressed against his chest, as if she'd decided to check his heart rate during the night.

Not wanting to break the spell, Mark remained unmoving, one arm trapped beneath her waist, while an enveloping silence hovered around them. His gaze traced the curve of her cheek, her lush, unglossed mouth. The closure of her terry robe was slightly parted, giving him a view of one supple swell of breast. While her soft, distinctive scent filled his lungs, the struggle built inside him rapidly, almost painfully, to prevent his hands from pulling aside the robe to find her.

Even as lust slapped at him, he acknowledged that his need for her wasn't just physical. It was emotional. She was bringing something back to him, to his life, he hadn't known he'd missed. Something he wasn't quite ready to pin a label on. Still, whatever it was, he was no longer certain he could do without it.

But did he really have a choice?

With a conscious effort of will, he tried to put himself into the same mind-set he used when he analyzed a case. It had always felt to him, then, as a kind of separation. As if he were in some other dimension, devoid of emotion. Lying there, he tried to get to that place but failed. Where once he had found it easy to separate himself from his feelings, he found doing so was no longer possible.

Not when it came to Grace. She was the only person who made him wonder what his life would be like if he'd made other choices. The years he had gone without seeing her, touching her, crowded in on him. Just the thought of walking away from her again tightened his chest and made his throat go dry.

With only a whisper of space separating them, she slept on.

Mark grazed his fingertips down the length of her dark hair. Where would life have taken them if their backgrounds had not been so diverse? If he'd learned something growing up other than how effective violence could be? If some adult in the town where he'd lived hadn't looked the other way and had helped the small, terrorized boy he'd been?

Feelings he had suppressed for years bubbled to the surface, clawing at him. He had grown up a victim. Now he felt like one all over again. An unwilling victim of his past. Unable to reach out and take what he wanted because he was too busy chasing the same type of demon who'd made his childhood a terrorizing hell. How many children would suffer if *he* looked the other way?

From the small alcove came the faint ring of the fax machine that sat on the credenza. He figured the information coming in was the background data on Stuart Harmon, Sr.

He closed his eyes. He and Grace would spend the biggest part of the day going over the information now pouring out of the fax. In the morning they were scheduled to fly to Oklahoma City, then drive to Winding Rock to meet with Harmon. By then they would have formulated a plan on the best way to deal with Davenport's lawyer pal.

Asleep, Grace sighed and moved against him. For an instant blood ruled. She was as warm and lovely as any fantasy, yet she was real. More than anything, he wanted her. With reason slipping against the need ripping at his insides, Mark held himself back.

Logically, he agreed that keeping their relationship on the level of colleagues was the smart thing to do. Problem was, his body didn't give a damn about smart. Not while her scent seeped through his system like a quiet promise, lulling him into believing he could have her again. He ached to touch her. To strip off that robe, fill his hands with her breasts. Feed on her warm, scented flesh while her body melted against his.

Gritting his teeth, he reminded himself he and Grace had no future. Less than a week from now he'd probably be God-knew-where, working some other case. She would be back home, getting on with the life she'd made for herself. A life that in no way was in synch with his.

As desire rippled along his skin and regret filled the air like invisible smoke, Mark forced his thoughts to business. Easing away, he rose and left her.

Chapter 10

Grace and Mark flew from Las Vegas to Oklahoma City the following morning. After an hour's drive west through a cold December rain, they arrived in Winding Rock. Even through the downpour Grace could see that Iris Davenport had been right—the town boasting cobblestone sidewalks and wrought-iron street signs had a refined elegance that spoke of money.

As did the Mirador Resort.

Seconds after Mark pulled their rental car beneath the hunter-green awning, a uniformed valet swung open Grace's door and offered her a white-gloved hand. The instant she slid out of the car, an icy awareness rose inside her like a floodtide, lapping at the back of her throat. Instinct told her the sensation wasn't due to the cold, wind-driven rain. She'd been a cop long enough to know she was under surveillance.

Her sense of being watched heightened when she and Mark walked through the revolving door into the lobby's gilded silence. They paused at the marble-topped counter where he dealt with checking in to the suite that had been reserved for the Calhouns. While she waited, Grace slipped out of her wool coat and smoothed the lapels of the black silk blazer she wore over gray wool slacks. She swept her gaze around the lobby, its floor, walls and soaring ceiling all done in soft pink granite.

Several men had settled in a grouping of bloodred leather chairs near a copper-faced fireplace that held a blazing fire. From the coffee carafes, cups and file folders littering the low table in front of them, it appeared they had chosen the spot for a business meeting. A woman clad in a white blouse and red blazer affixed with a gold name tag rearranged several intricately tied bows adorning a massive Christmas tree. A man wearing an identical blazer sat at the concierge's desk. Holding a phone tucked between one cheek and shoulder, he jotted notes on a pad. Across the lobby, a couple whose very attire bespoke wealth and status paused to admire one of the large oil paintings that lined the walls at precise intervals.

Grace couldn't peg anyone who seemed to have even a vague interest in Mr. and Mrs. Mark Calhoun. Yet, she *felt* the surveillance.

Which in no way surprised her. The stakes had risen when Iris Davenport revealed the identity of the attorney who allegedly handled illegal adoptions. Putting the Calhouns of Houston under close surveillance simply provided another layer of security for those involved in the operation.

Grace stepped to the counter and laid a hand on Mark's arm. "Almost done, sweetheart?" she murmured.

He handed a signed credit card slip to the clerk behind the counter. "Just about," he said, then shrugged off his black wool overcoat. "I feel the same as you." The pointed look he gave Grace sent the message that he, too, sensed eyes on them. "Anxious to get to our suite and relax."

The clerk gave Grace a polite smile while handing her a small folder. "When your reservation was made, spa time was also booked for you, Mrs. Calhoun. Your exercise class schedule is inside."

"Thank you." Keeping her smile in place, Grace glanced at the schedule. When this operation ended, she was never again climbing on another damn spin bike.

The clerk checked his computer's screen, then looked back at Mark. "A dinner reservation has been arranged for you at seven this evening in the Sabroso Room."

"Fine," Mark said.

The clerk motioned to the bellman waiting beside a brass cart that held their luggage. "Charles will show you to your suite. If there's anything you need to make your stay at the Mirador more enjoyable, let us know."

They rode in a glass elevator that smelled of lilacs and zipped busily up to the top floor. Charles keyed open a nearby towering wooden door and stepped aside to allow Grace to lead the way.

Her heels tapped against a gleaming hardwood hallway, its walls covered with oil paintings. Light sparkled from a small cut-glass chandelier. The short hall led into a sitting room with a rolled-arm sofa covered in ivory damask fabric, two raspberry leather chairs, polished tables and floor-to-ceiling windows.

Moving to one of the windows, Grace edged back the sheer drapes. The lake Iris had mentioned was visible a hundred yards below. The water looked as gray as old quarters through the sheeting rain.

Charles rolled the cart through a set of doors into the bedroom. Leaving her purse and coat on the couch, Grace peered in after him. From where she stood she could see a four-poster bed with a red satin duvet flanked by dark wooden end tables holding leaded glass lamps.

When the bellman reemerged with his empty cart, Mark handed him a folded bill. ''Any idea how long the rain is supposed to last?''

''For several more hours at least, sir.''

Mark glanced at Grace while he laid his briefcase on the coffee table in front of the couch. ''We may have to swim to Harmon's office.''

''Doesn't matter,'' Grace replied. She knew the bellman could be on the attorney's payroll, monitoring her and Mark's every word and move. Just another layer of safety to ensure the Calhouns were what they seemed: a couple excited by the prospect of an adoption. ''We'll get there in a rowboat if we have to.''

Mark gave her an understanding smile. ''Don't worry, darling. Nothing's going to stand in our way this time.''

He waited until the door bumped shut behind the bellman to pull out the two small surveillance devices that resembled cell-phone chargers. Without comment, he handed one to Grace. When she switched the unit on, a red light flashed. She felt her throat tighten. The red light meant an eavesdropping device was nearby, emitting electronic radio waves.

''This suite is lovely,'' she said, angling the unit in Mark's direction. ''So cozy.''

''Smaller than the one in Vegas,'' he commented. ''But you're right. It has a certain atmosphere.''

Carrying the second unit, Mark strode into the bedroom. A moment later he reappeared in the doorway. ''Darling, our early wake-up call and flight are catching up with me. I'm going to squeeze in a shower and nap before our meeting with Harmon. Interested in joining me? Or are you headed for the gym?''

''The gym can wait,'' she said, lowering her voice to a silky murmur. ''I prefer the kind of exercise you have in mind.''

Arching a dark brow, Mark gave her a slow smile. ''I'll certainly try to make the next three hours worth your while.''

His voice was as soft and warm as the press of velvet, his dark eyes unnervingly watchful as Grace walked toward him.

Noting the surge in her pulse rate, she reminded herself they were merely actors in a play. Putting on a necessary performance for whomever was eavesdropping on their conversation.

She stepped past Mark into the bedroom, its air laced with the scent of warm vanilla. He shut the door behind her, then tipped the surveillance device in her direction to show her the green light.

''They only bugged the sitting room,'' he commented. ''This room and the bath are clear. Which makes sense. If we were cops posing as a married couple, we wouldn't spend time together in the bedroom. We'd use the sitting room to write reports, talk over the case and make phone calls.''

Grace agreed with this logic. Still, she kept her voice whisper-soft. ''Are you sure we can't be overheard through the door? The walls?''

''Positive.'' He bounced the surveillance device in his palm. ''The frequency is too high for us to hear, but this unit emits electronic noise that prevents our voices from being picked up outside this room.''

Turning, he positioned the device on the nearby bureau. The piece of furniture was dark and heavy, and looked identical to some Grace had seen in high-dollar antique shops.

"We need to keep in mind that whenever we talk to each other outside of this room, we're the Calhouns," Mark added.

"Got it."

Grace felt her stomach jitter when she slid a look at the big, firm four-poster, piled with pillows. In no way did she want to bring up the subject of sleeping arrangements. But with the surveillance device planted in the sitting room, the matter had to be discussed. Too much was at stake for her and Mark to make what might be a crucial mistake.

"We need to discuss where I'll sleep," he said, his thoughts mirroring hers.

She looked back at him. "Yes."

"My bedding-down on the couch worked in Vegas because we weren't under surveillance, at least not inside the suite. I can't do that here, Grace. Not with a listening device planted out there."

"I know." She snicked open the locks and raised the lid on the suitcase the bellman had left on the bed. "The Calhouns are happily married," she reasoned. "Crazy in love. Ecstatic that their dream to have a child is about to become reality. It's a moment they've been awaiting a very long time and there's no way they'd sleep in different rooms." She scooped several pairs of shoes out of the suitcase. "One of us can sleep on a pallet on the floor."

"That would be me." Mark pulled off his navy suit coat, laid it on the end of the bed. "I realize this is more than you bargained for when you agreed to join this operation."

She flicked him a look before turning toward the closet. "You gave me the opportunity to get out of working the assignment. I chose to stay in. Which means I deal with whatever comes my way, like it or not. So do you.''

''True.'' Settling beside his suit coat, Mark pursed his mouth. ''Good thing the problem of sleeping arrangements didn't come up during my last undercover gig.''

''Why's that?''

''I was partnered with a two-hundred-plus-pound DEA agent. After college he played tackle for one season for the Green Bay Packers. I doubt sleeping in close proximity with him would have been the same as with you.''

''You always did know how to give a girl a compliment, Santini,'' Grace murmured while tucking a handful of sweaters into a drawer on the bureau. ''We're adults. Professionals. We've agreed to keep our minds on the job,'' she said, not totally sure if she brought up the point more for his benefit or hers. ''We shouldn't have a problem.''

''We shouldn't,'' Mark agreed softly, his eyes fixed on hers.

A whisper of awareness stirred Grace's senses. The room that had seemed so spacious when she'd first stepped inside now felt smaller. Intimate.

''So, speaking of the job,'' Mark began. ''In three hours we've got an appointment with an attorney who we suspect sells kidnapped babies to childless couples who pay him immense fees. However, on paper the guy appears to be Mr. Upstanding Citizen.''

''Mr. *Loaded* Upstanding Citizen,'' Grace amended. ''Thanks to the trust fund he inherited from his great-grandfather.''

Grace thought about the background information on Stuart Harmon, she and Mark had spent the previous day studying. ''Harmon donates thousands of dollars annually to various charities,'' she said. ''Mentors in a literacy program. Volunteers time to his church, which he attends regularly. Does a man who is falling-down rich and goes around doing good deeds have the time or inclination to sell babies kidnapped from their murdered mothers?''

''If there's one thing I've learned from this job it's that there is an appetite, and therefore a market, for anything and everything. And sometimes the appetite belongs to the last person you'd suspect.'' While he spoke, Mark loosened his perfectly knotted crimson tie.

''Yes, you're right.'' Grace forced the words past the sudden constriction in her throat while she watched his long, strong fingers unhook the button on the collar of his shirt.

The familiar movement shot her back six years, to when they'd been lovers. Assigned to the same task force, they invariably ended the day reviewing their case, winding down while they changed into comfortable clothes. How many times had Mark sat on the end of her bed, tossing out theories while he loosened his tie, opened his shirt? And unfailingly, they'd wind up in that bed, mindlessly tearing off the remainder of their clothing, half-crazed to get at each other.

The memory seemed so real, so sharp, so hotly erotic that Grace could hardly breathe against the desire that wrapped around her like a thick, glossy spider's web. Dragging her gaze from him, she grabbed a handful of lingerie and moved to the bureau.

With her back to Mark, she closed her eyes. The longing, the need clawing inside her was so quick, so strong that for a moment she didn't want to resist it. Wanted only to act on it.

''During the past five years, Harmon has represented couples in more than seventy adoptions,'' Mark said, unaware that her libido had kicked into overdrive.

Grace knew the heat blazing inside her, the depth and

suddenness of it, held its own special danger. Knew, too, she needed to control it. *Had* to control it.

Because she in no way wanted to analyze why her emotions had gone on this sudden roller coaster ride, she forced her thoughts to follow Mark's.

"More than seventy adoptions," she repeated, vaguely amazed that her voice sounded even. Level. "In all of those, legitimate adoption agencies were involved in the process. Everything was approved by the courts. The documents properly filed."

"Then along comes Iris Davenport. She forged paperwork to make it look like a social worker picked up the babies and turned them over to adoption agencies. Instead, those babies disappear into thin air. And Davenport drops Harmon's name in our lap."

"Mr. Upstanding Citizen." Grace slid the last of her clothing into the drawer, slid it shut. "If Harmon is in on this with Iris, it's hard to imagine he's doing it for money."

"Some people never have enough."

"Good point." Grace frowned. "The man's an enigma. It's like we're looking at a good-twin, bad-twin scenario. Maybe after we meet him we'll have a better sense of who he is. What drives him."

"Maybe."

Grace rubbed at the tension that had settled at the back of her neck. "I keep thinking about the young girl who's giving up her baby to the Calhouns. The FBI agent undercover at the clinic where Iris works hasn't yet pegged who that girl is."

"She may not be a patient there. Davenport never specifically said she was."

"She didn't," Grace agreed. "We can't even be sure what Iris told us about the girl's background is true. What is true is that she's due to deliver any day. What if she changes her mind? Decides she doesn't want to give up her baby?''

''If Davenport is in the vicinity, the girl is in danger of getting shot full of anticoagulant.''

''Mark, we can't just leave her on her own with no protection. We need to try to convince Harmon to let us meet the mother. If that doesn't work, maybe we can get him to tell us something more about her background. Some details that will point us in her direction.''

''I agree.''

Thoughtful, Grace lowered the lid of the suitcase, set the locks. ''When I work a case, I equate it to picking up a piece of knitting.''

Mark angled his chin. ''Knitting?''

''Threads,'' she explained. ''Pull at the right one and the entire garment comes unraveled. We need to find the loose thread in our case.''

''The sooner the better,'' Mark agreed. ''Right now all we've got are two murders and kidnappings, and a circumstantial case against Davenport, at best. We need solid proof to take her down. Not to mention evidence of where those two babies wound up.''

''If Senator Grayson knew how little progress we've made in finding his granddaughter, he'd probably have a stroke,'' Grace said.

''That would happen only *after* he reduced the Bureau's budget by half,'' Mark drawled. He rubbed his right temple, as if an ache had settled there. ''When you're dealing with murder, it only takes a tiny mistake to leave a hole for someone to peer through and learn the truth. Senator Grayson was Davenport's mistake.''

''How so?'' Grace settled on the bed, leaving a safe distance between them.

"All Davenport knew about the two young women she killed was that they were drifters. Homeless. They lived on the street or at a shelter. Neither put the name of a contact in her file at the clinic. Davenport assumed they had no one who cared about them or their babies. Andrea Grayson's father cares."

"And the senator has a very loud voice," Grace observed.

"If it wasn't for him, Davenport would have committed two murders and no one would have known. Just goes to show how fate has played a hand in this case."

A big one, Grace thought, studying Mark's hard, chiseled profile. If not for that same twist of fate, she might have lived the remainder of her life without ever again seeing Special Agent Santini.

Without having to watch him walk away for a second time.

Fate, she already knew, wasn't always kind.

Mark and Grace, as the Calhouns, were shown into Stuart Harmon's office at three o'clock that afternoon. Mark had the sensation of stepping into an English study that boasted polished expanses of mahogany furnishings, gleaming brasses and expensive rugs. Shelves filled with law books lined the walls; leather armchairs formed a half circle in front of a small stone fireplace filled with flaming wood.

It struck Mark that the office itself instilled confidence. Trust. A good place to start a family.

"Mr. and Mrs. Calhoun, a pleasure to meet you."

"We're glad to be here," Mark said, returning Harmon's brisk handshake.

The attorney was in his early seventies, dapper, tweedy, with a sedate tie tucked beneath his vest. He was tall with thick silver hair and carried himself with an old-fashioned ramrod-straight posture.

Grandfatherly was the term Mark applied to him. Still, it was obvious from the way he enfolded Grace's hand in his that age hadn't dampened Harmon's appreciation for a beautiful woman.

The outfit Grace had chosen for the meeting was perfectly tailored—the slate-blue blazer and pleated slacks, the white shirt with the slim, diamond bar pin at the collar. Mark had worn a pin-striped charcoal suit, white tab shirt and red and ivory tie. Together the Calhouns presented the picture of the perfect couple whose clothes and jewelry were a study in understated good taste. And, most important, wealth.

"You've been out in that nasty rain," Harmon said. "Let's sit by the fire and take off the chill."

"That sounds wonderful," Grace murmured.

Before settling into the chair beside Grace's, Mark swept his gaze across the massive desk on the far side of the room. There were no files in sight, no stacks of legal documents awaiting Harmon's review. Not exactly standard for an attorney's office.

Harmon took a seat across from them, their chairs separated by a small coffee table. "Shall I have my secretary bring in coffee?" he asked. "Tea, perhaps?"

"Nothing for me," Mark said. "Darling?"

"No." Grace sent Harmon a jittery smile. "I'm such a bundle of nerves, I'd probably spill coffee all over me."

Harmon inclined his head. "This is an emotional time for you."

"Yes." Grace fingered the diamond pin at her throat. "Mr. Harmon, my husband and I are so pleased to have found you. *Thankful,* is a better word. We've wanted a baby for so long. I can't tell you what this means to us."

The nerves in Grace's voice and the shaky breath she pulled in had Mark admiring her acting skills all over again.

Harmon smiled. "My wife and I have three children of our own, Mrs. Calhoun. Had we not been blessed, I can only imagine how empty our life together would have seemed. So, in some small way I understand how you and your husband feel. I'm glad I can be a part of this happy event."

Mark leaned forward. "From having read the background information Grace and I supplied, you know we've attempted a private adoption before."

"You said the birth mother changed her mind at the last minute." A glimmer of sympathy settled in Harmon's eyes. "Unfortunate. That would have been very disappointing for you."

"*Deeply* disappointing." Mark reached, took Grace's hand. "We hadn't been allowed to meet the birth mother. Later, we wondered if our doing so would have made a difference in the outcome."

"How so?"

"She could have gotten to know us," Grace explained. "Seen for herself how much Mark and I love each other. How much love we had to give her baby." Grace's voice wavered. "Mr. Harmon, we have so much love to give a child."

"I can see that."

"Can you also see our reasons for wanting to meet the biological mother this time around?" Mark asked.

"Of course," Harmon said. "I fear, however, that isn't possible."

"We're asking you to make it possible," Mark persisted. Not wanting to push too hard, he kept his tone light, even. Still, they were talking about a young woman whose life might be in danger if she changed her mind about giving up her child. He and Grace *had* to find out her identity.

"I've had several conversations with the young woman," Harmon explained, his tone all patience. "The fact that the child's father is no longer in her life played a large role in her decision to seek an adoption for the infant." Harmon propped his elbows on the arms of his chair and steepled his fingers beneath his chin. "She's insistent about not wanting to meet the adoptive parents. Prefers not to see her child after its birth. Basically she intends to get on with her life as if the child never existed."

"That's not possible." Even as Grace blurted the words, Mark felt her hand shudder against his. "She's carrying her daughter next to her heart. How is it possible for her to forget her child ever existed? How can she *deny* that small, precious life?"

"Darling." Mark spoke softly as his stomach knotted. Grace's voice had dropped to a trembling whisper. Tears welled in her dark eyes; her skin was as pale as paper. He had no idea what was behind her emotional reaction. All he knew was that she was no longer acting.

He tightened his hand on hers. Any alteration to their cover story could put the entire undercover op in danger. Still, it wasn't thoughts of their case that had every protective instinct in him shifting into overdrive. Grace was a determined, tough cop; yet, sitting beside him was a woman who looked fragile and defenseless.

"Let me take you back to the Mirador." He lifted their joined hands, pressed his lips against her icy fingers. "You can lie down for a while. I'm sure Mr. Harmon understands the stress you're under. That we're both under."

"Of course," Harmon said. "We can certainly reschedule—"

"No, I'm fine." Grace pressed her free hand to her stomach. "I'm sorry, I'm just…" She gave Mark a weak smile. "I'm fine."

"Giving up a child is an emotional issue for everyone involved," Harmon put in.

"Yes." Her hand tightened against his, and Mark could almost feel her struggling to regain control. "Mr. Harmon, you've handled so many adoptions," she continued. "I'm sure you understand my reaction. Mark and I have waited so long for a child. *So long.*"

"You must also try to understand the birth mother's feelings, Mrs. Calhoun. She's giving up her child. Though voluntary on her part, it's a type of loss many people equate with death. One that changes lives. I can't fault the young woman for trying to make the situation as easy on herself as possible."

"There's nothing easy about this." Mark ran a soothing hand down the dark fall of Grace's hair. Color had returned to her face, her eyes were dry and she seemed steadier. He bit down on a gnawing curiosity over what had caused her reaction. He would find out soon enough.

He shifted his gaze back to Harmon. "Because there's nothing easy," he repeated, "Grace and I are concerned the biological mother might change her mind before the child is born. Perhaps even after. That's why we'd like to meet her. To try to prevent that from happening down the line."

"The contract you sign will protect against her doing that, Mr. Calhoun."

"No contract is ironclad," Mark countered. Since it was clear they weren't going to get Harmon's help in learning the mother's identity, Mark shifted the conversation in another direction. "Speaking of the contract, I'd like to see it. I want my lawyer to review it, too."

"The document hasn't been prepared."

Mark narrowed his eyes. "I was under the impression we would deal with the paperwork and other details today."

"To be candid, the birth mother asked me to meet with you in person. Do my own evaluation of you and Mrs. Calhoun as prospective parents. Conduct one final test, if you will. If you failed, there would be no need for a contract."

"A test." Grace lifted her chin. "Did we pass or fail, Mr. Harmon?"

"You passed, most splendidly," Harmon said, compassion sounding in his voice. "It's obvious you will cherish the child. Love her as if she were your own." He rose, indicating their meeting had ended. "I'll have my associate draw up the contract."

"Thank you," Grace said quietly. "Thank you."

"When do we see the contract?" Mark asked, keeping a firm hold on her hand as they both stood. It was hard for him to believe Harmon would let them walk out the door without first asking for a healthy retainer.

"Come back tomorrow afternoon, the same time as today. I believe we can finalize all the issues then." A twinkle settled in Harmon's eyes. "Well, all issues, except for the birth. The timing of that is up to a higher power."

He stepped toward them, his smile deepening. "If all goes as planned, you'll have your daughter by Christmas Day."

Chapter 11

For Grace, the drive through the pelting rain from Harmon's office back to the Mirador Resort seemed unending. It wasn't only her over-the-edge reaction in the attorney's office that hung in her mind like a shadow. The small detector Mark carried in the pocket of his suit coat had alerted them to the presence of a bug that had been planted in the rental car while they'd been with Harmon. Out of necessity they'd kept their conversation on the drive back in line with that of the Calhouns.

By the time they walked into their suite, an ache had settled in the center of Grace's forehead. In the bedroom she glanced at the bureau, saw the green light still glowed on the surveillance device. For good measure Mark used his small detector to recheck the bathroom for bugs.

Rubbing at her forehead, Grace clicked on the lamp on the nearest nightstand.

"It's clear," Mark said when he strode out of the bathroom.

"Iris and her pals mean business." Grace slipped off her coat and hung it in the closet. Her slate-blue blazer followed.

"They do."

She hadn't realized Mark had come up behind her. She turned, saw that he, too, had shrugged out of his suit coat. When he reached for a hanger, the space between them narrowed. The rich, musky scent of his cologne slid around her, filling her lungs. He was too close, but then, even at opposite ends of the room, Mark Santini would have been too close for her peace of mind.

"I've complimented you before on your acting skills." His dark gaze locked with hers, his eyes revealing none of his thoughts. "Your reaction in Harmon's office was no act. What's going on, Grace?"

Because he was so close—*too close*—she stepped around him and moved to the heavy, antique bureau. She had opened her entire life to him, while he'd given her nothing of his. That she and Ryan were going to have a child was one of the few things she hadn't shared with the man whose presence had hung like a dark cloud over the last year of her marriage. She didn't want to share that with him now.

You have to, the cop in her countered. Her reaction in Harmon's office was proof that her losing her child had an impact on her ability to effectively pull off Grace Calhoun's role. She and Mark were undercover; their very lives might depend on knowing in advance how each other would react in the presence of the bad guys.

For that reason, she owed Mark an explanation.

"I didn't tell you before because I had no idea I would react that way." She unhooked the diamond bar pin from the collar of her blouse and placed it in a drawer. "It…just hit me."

"What hit you?"

Outside the temperature had dropped; the wind-driven rain was now mixed with sleet that pecked against the windows. Feeling as though she would never again get warm, Grace wrapped her arms around her waist, then turned and met Mark's gaze.

"Ryan and I decided to start a family," she said quietly. She felt no need to tell Mark that she'd hoped a baby would close the emotional distance that her past with him had put between herself and Ryan. "We'd always planned on having a huge house filled with kids."

She trailed a hand through her hair. "I felt sick a couple of mornings in a row and suspected I was pregnant. I didn't tell Ryan, because I wanted to be sure. Didn't want him to be disappointed. I took two home-pregnancy tests. They were both positive. But I still didn't tell Ryan because I wanted the doctor to confirm it.

"His nurse called me late one afternoon with the results. I was so excited. Jumping up and down like a kid on Christmas morning. I wanted to share my news with Carrie or Morgan, both of them, but Ryan first. He was working the swing shift. I called and asked him to meet me at a certain restaurant on his dinner break." Grace pressed her fingertips to her mouth. "I was so anxious, I got there nearly an hour early."

She paused to collect her thoughts. Mark stood across the room, watching her. Silent. Waiting.

"When I told Ryan, he was as excited as I was. Maybe more." She smiled, remembering. "I'd had this sense all along that the baby was a girl, so right then we started picking out names. Ryan and I couldn't wait to tell our families. We sat in the booth, ignoring our food while we made calls on our cell phones.

"After dinner Ryan paid the bill and I went to the rest

room. When I came out, the cashier said he'd gone out to the parking lot. I turned toward the door and heard the shot." The pain swept through her, thickening her voice. "I knew. Somehow I knew that Ryan... I yelled for the cashier to call 911, grabbed my gun out of my purse and raced outside. I spotted the guy. He still had the gun in his hand and he was running away. He had a strange gait, a limp.

"Ryan was still alive when I got to him." Tears formed in Grace's eyes, clogged her throat. "He...said my name...and then he was gone."

His face grim, Mark moved to where she stood, placed a hand on her arm. "Grace—"

"No." She shifted from his touch. "Let me finish." She drew in a choppy breath. "What happened affects our job, so I need to finish."

"All right."

"After that, things were a blur," she continued softly, her voice barely loud enough to be heard over the sleet pinging against the windows. "I don't remember doing it, but I gave the patrol cops the suspect's description. One of them pegged the guy because of the limp. They arrested him that night, still with the gun."

"Bran told me he's on death row now."

Grace nodded. "My family, Ryan's—they were all there for me. I couldn't have gotten through... No one blamed me for what happened."

Mark narrowed his eyes. "Why would they?"

"I kept thinking if only I'd waited until Ryan got home that night to tell him about the baby. If I hadn't called him, chosen *that* restaurant for us to meet at, then he'd probably still be alive."

"You can't know that." Reaching out, Mark grazed his

fingertips down her cheek. "You can't let yourself think that."

An echo of age-old grief washed over her. "I'd wake up every morning, feeling sick. I didn't mind, because my first thoughts even before I opened my eyes were about the baby. Then it would hit me that Ryan wasn't there. Wouldn't be there to see his child grow up.

"I woke up one night feeling awful. At first I thought my internal clock had gone haywire and morning sickness had hit me. But I started shivering and burning up all at the same time. I called Mom and Dad. I had a raging fever by the time they got me to the hospital." She raised a hand, then let it drop. "I'd picked up a nasty case of the flu. Nasty enough for the doctor to admit me to the hospital. I remember lying in bed, so weak I couldn't even raise my head, thinking that my being sick couldn't be good for the baby. That I needed to get better for my little girl."

Grace felt a fist clamp around her heart as the memories closed in. "I lost her, Mark." Every word she spoke hurt her throat. "Two days after I went into the hospital, I lost her."

Compassion, deep and depthless, settled in Mark's dark eyes. "Grace, I'm sorry. I'm so sorry."

"I was only a few months along, but that didn't matter. It made no difference that I had never seen her, would never see her. She was my child. Ryan's child. I could never *forget* her."

"And today, when Harmon said the baby's mother intends to give birth and then forget about her daughter, it hit you."

"Yes." Pain lanced into the soft, vulnerable part of her that still throbbed and bled. "I learned to get on with my life, but I'll never forget. How could any woman forget a child she's given life to?''

"A lot of women aren't like you, Grace. They don't view their children as something to cherish. They hurt them. Abuse them.''

The splinter of contempt in Mark's voice had Grace searching his face. "Is that what happened to you? Is that what you meant when you told me your childhood was wretched? Did your mother abuse you?''

"What happened to me while I was growing up doesn't matter.''

"Mark—''

"It doesn't matter.''

His refusal to share his thoughts and his feelings behind them after she had just poured out her soul touched a nerve. What had been pain and grief flashed to simmering temper.

"Well, Santini, let me tell you what matters *to me*,'' she said, jabbing a finger against the center of his chest. "The minute we fell into bed, I opened my life to you. Told you about my past. What I wanted for the future.'' She took another stab at his chest. "I shared my family with you. And they shared themselves with *you*. How many dinners did you eat at my parents' table? How many McCall birthday parties did you attend?''

He wrapped his fingers around her wrist, stilling her hand. "A lot.''

"And what part of your life did you share?''

"The present. I gave you what I was then. Trust me when I tell you there's nothing in my past you would have wanted me to parcel out to you.''

"Wrong. Like it or not, your past helped mold you into who you are.''

His eyes glinted. "You think I'm cruel and vicious?''

His fingers tightened on her wrist. "You think I go around slapping children just because they get within hitting distance? Cursing them, solely because they exist?"

"Mark, no." How could she hold herself aloof from that? Grace thought. Good Lord, what had he endured? "Of course I don't think—"

"I didn't just walk away from my past, Grace. I *escaped* it. It's dead to me."

"Maybe you wish it was." She eased her wrist from his hold. "What I see in your face, hear in your voice tells me it isn't."

He looked away, the muscles in his jaw clenching.

"Why do you think you have to be different from other people?" she asked quietly. "Everyone drags around baggage from their past. I'm one of those people. Which is why I just told you what it was like to watch my husband die. To lose my baby. Do you think those things are easy for me to talk about?"

"No." He looked back at her, his expression somber. "I know it took a lot out of you. It's good that you told me."

"Of course it is," she agreed, unable to block the sense of resignation that coursed through her. "It's always been *good* that I open my life to you." She set her jaw. Since it seemed to be a time for talking about the past, she decided she might as well go all the way.

"We were lovers for nearly a year, yet you never let me in," she began. "Just once, Mark. Just once I wanted to be invited into your world. I wanted to know about your terrible childhood. I wanted to know how you felt about me. About us. Know if you cared."

She saw surprise flicker across his face a second before his hands settled on her shoulders. "You *know* I cared.

Why else would I have asked you to move to Virginia with me?''

''You asked me to move with you. You never once mentioned sharing your *life* with me.'' Her fingers clenched. ''Of course, there wouldn't have been much sharing, would there? I would have been the one to give up my home, my job, seeing my family only on rare occasions. I'd have been in a strange town, left on my own while you traveled from crime scene to crime scene. We would have seen each other whenever you could fit me in. What kind of life would that have been?''

''The only one I had to offer.''

''Willing to offer,'' she tossed back, her eyes staying level on his. ''Did you ever once consider staying with me in Oklahoma City? Working out of the Bureau's office there?''

''I can't stop doing what I do. I can't turn my back on what I do best.''

''You are the best,'' she agreed. ''Because you put the job first. Always first.'' She hadn't known until she'd said the words how much the truth behind them still hurt. ''You shovel up facts, dig into people's lives all in the name of catching monsters. But if anyone starts looking too closely at *your* life, at the man you are, the walls shoot up.''

''Dammit, I can't change who I am.'' His fingers tightened on her shoulders. ''What do you want from me, Grace?''

''Nothing.'' She closed her eyes for an instant. ''We've been down that road. It's a dead end for both of us.''

All the emotion that had swirled inside her since the moment her control slipped in Harmon's office died like an extinguished fire. Now she felt spent. Hollow. All she wanted was to soak in the tub. Immerse herself in warm, frothy water and use the next hour or so to regroup. Before she could do that, however, she had to deal with the man who towered over her, his dark eyes turbulent, his fingers like shafts of steel against her shoulders.

"I don't regret what we had," she said quietly. "But I do regret that you had so little of yourself to give me. It was nothing personal—I understand that. It's simply how you are. The man you are. You don't allow yourself to get involved emotionally. Don't give of yourself to anyone. It wasn't just me."

When she would have stepped away, he jerked her against his chest, lowered his head. "You're wrong, Grace, it *was* you. Always you. *Is* you."

The simmering storm in his eyes had every nerve in her body vibrating like the strings of a plucked harp. "Mark—"

He dipped his head, his mouth hovering above hers. "Dammit, I can't get you out of my system," he said, his voice a hot sweep against her cheek. "I've tried to wipe you from my mind for six long years. Even when I knew you belonged to another man I couldn't forget you." His mouth inched closer to hers. "How's that for baggage from the past?"

With her breasts pressed against his chest she could feel his heart pound. She remembered all the times, long ago, when their hearts thundered while they made wild, reckless love. Long ago when she'd thought what they had might last forever.

Even as need swept through her, she pressed her palms against his chest and looked away. Seeking the last crumbling remnants of control, she reminded herself he had come back for the job, not her. That he would leave again. Walk away. She was determined it not be with another piece of her heart.

How unfair that she felt so good with him, she thought.

That looking at her life from the vantage point of his arms revealed all the missing pieces. All the need she had locked away deep inside her.

It was that need—aching and fathomless—that burned away the last of her resolve to hold strong. Fisting her hands against his chest, she turned her face up so that his lips could find hers.

His mouth was firm and possessive, and hers opened to his on a moan of pleasure. He kissed her long, slow, a languid meeting of lips that lingered until she was floating on a warm sea of sensuality.

"I am involved, Grace," he murmured against her ear as one of his arms wrapped around her waist. Locked against him, she could feel the iron evidence of his desire for her. "I've been involved since the moment I laid eyes on you. I wanted you then. I want you now."

Her legs were trembling, her pulse hammering in a hundred places. The air was too thick to breathe, and each gulp of it made her head reel. "That…was a long time ago," she managed weakly. "A lifetime."

"A lifetime I've spent wanting you. Only you." His hand streaked up, his fingers fisting in her hair. "I feel like I've wanted you my entire life." Dragging her head back, he latched his mouth on to her throat.

Blood raced through her veins. Flames licked at her. Raw hunger sprang free inside her, and she could almost hear the last tenuous wire of her control break.

Desperate for more, she tugged his mouth back to hers. She wanted to taste the heat, the need. *Him.*

Her fingers fumbled at the knot of his necktie, jerked it loose. While she grappled with the buttons on his starched shirt, he yanked her blouse free from her slacks, popping buttons with ruthless disregard. The room's cool air settled against her heated flesh as he peeled the fabric back from her shoulders, shoved it down to her elbows. With the cuffs still buttoned, she was bound by silk, wildly aroused, helpless as he toppled her back onto the bed.

He went down with her, settling between her legs as if he belonged there. His hands were instantly on her, flicking open her bra, shoving aside lace as he loomed over her. He gazed down at her, fierce emotion churning in his eyes.

A thrill shot up her spine when she saw the dark, reckless side of him that he kept so tightly controlled.

"You're as beautiful as I remember." His voice was thick, his fingertips as soft as a wish as they traced the curve of her breast. "More beautiful."

The persistent ping of sleet against the windows was drowned out by the thundering of her own heart. He tore off his shirt, tossed it aside, then lowered his mouth. His teeth scraped over one budded nipple, then the other. The heat of his mouth was wild, burning with wet fire as he fed on her. Light from the small lamp glowing on the nightstand fractured into star bursts before her eyes.

She writhed against the small, exquisite pain. Her flesh ached and hummed with an urgency that spread downward from her breasts to the pulse throbbing between her legs.

Her blood heated, flash-firing beneath her skin, roaring in her head. Jerking her arms, she freed one wrist from the silk binding, then the other. A hum of pleasure surged up her throat while her hands skimmed across his shoulders, his back, savoring the power of sinew and muscle.

He raised his head. The flash of passion, the hot desire that darkened his eyes as he lowered the zipper on her slacks had her stomach quivering. His hands stroked over her hips, slipping beneath the loosened waistband as he peeled off her slacks. His mouth lowered, nuzzled her through the thin silk of her panties.

Grace trembled at the first touch of his tongue, the

tender, stroking flicks, until she thought she would shatter into a million pieces. She wanted to push him away, but at the same time she pressed him against her.

Her breath snagged in her lungs as she arched back, her fingers digging into his shoulders. Time and place became nothing against a hard, driving desire for him. Only him.

Minutes, or hours later, his impatient hands peeled away the silk.

She tore at his remaining clothes, all sense of denial and self-preservation a memory. Sweat beaded her flesh. His kiss shifted, hardened, something reckless shimmering at its edge.

She could hear his breath come ragged and strained as he fanned his fingers low over her belly. Their eyes locked as he grazed his thumb over the hardened nub of flesh between her legs. His other hand moved low at her back; he lifted her hips and plunged into her.

A gasp of pleasure strangled in her throat. Memories swirled in her head, the past fusing with the present. Day and night, ice and fire. They all came together in a wild torrent of desire that lay somewhere between pain and pleasure.

Her blood was a river now, rushing hot and fast. Greedy, she wrapped her legs around his waist and drew him in deeper.

Reality focused to the point of a pin. This man—this one man—touched something in her that she'd tried to keep safe and untouched. He made her feel when no one had made her feel anything in a very long time.

And she had no way to keep him in her life.

She wanted to protect her heart. Wanted to resist, to push him back before he dragged her over a line she'd sworn to never cross again. But then his mouth grew more urgent on hers, his hands more impatient, stoking the terrible, glorious heat just beneath her flesh. Thoughts of caution blurred. Faded. Her hips moved like lightning, meeting him thrust for thrust. There was no resisting the driving desire that clawed inside her, frantic to break free.

She felt his body go rigid, his muscles bunch. Her low moan of release echoed his as he drove her with him over that crumbling edge.

And then they lay still, clinging to each other, their flesh flushed, hot and slick, their breathing unsteady while they absorbed the aftershocks of sensation.

Accepting fate, Grace pressed her lips to his still-raging heart. She let them linger there, knowing he'd stolen hers all over again.

Chapter 12

The bedroom was dimly lit, the warm air filled with the dark, sensual scent of lovemaking. The silence was broken only by the mix of rain and sleet beyond the windows.

And Grace's soft breathing.

Mark savored the moment, feeling simultaneous surges of contentment and desire. Beneath the soft sheet, he and Grace lay on their sides, spooned together, her back and bottom pressed against him, his arms wrapped around her. Her scent was gentle and sensual, drifting over him like a stroke of velvet.

With her dark hair fanned back, he had a view of the slender arch of her nape. He had to hold himself back from sinking his teeth into that exposed, vulnerable flesh and ravaging her.

He wanted to stay here with her, without tension, without puzzles to solve, without responsibilities.

He wanted to stay with her for the rest of his life.

If only, he thought.

During the years they'd spent apart there'd been times he would catch himself wondering whether his plaguing, unrelenting need for her would end if only he could have her one more time. Just once more.

The frantic, urgent passion they had just shared confirmed what he'd already known. There had never been a woman who made him want so badly. Would never be another. Grace McCall was the one. The only one. He could have her a million times and his desire for her, *need* for her, would forever remain desperate and greedy.

She was his again, for a few more days. Priceless days.

If only, he thought again. If *only.*

He couldn't give her the type of life she needed. She'd made it abundantly clear earlier she wouldn't settle for the bits and pieces of time he had to offer. He didn't blame her. It wasn't much of a life.

Just for a heartbeat he considered altering that life. Turning his back on the job, walking away. In the next instant, thoughts of the cases he was currently working closed in on him. The little girl murdered in California, the preteen boys missing in New Orleans. The young female victims in the small town in Alaska. The serial killer in Buffalo. The missing infants he and Grace now searched for. The thought of all the children helpless to save themselves hung in the air like smoke.

Who would help them if he walked away?

Always before, thoughts of all the defenseless victims had been enough impetus for him to shovel his emotions and feelings into a pit and just go on. He could no longer do that. Not now when he knew how deeply his holding everything back had hurt Grace. He might not be able to give her a life, but he could damn well give her something of himself.

Unable to resist, he pressed a soft kiss against the slender, seductive curve of her throat.

"I'm glad one of us has still enough strength to move," she murmured. "If this place catches fire, promise you'll toss me over your shoulder and carry me out."

He fingered the small gold hoop piercing her earlobe. "I'll try to remember to take you along."

"Thanks, Santini. You're one heck of a nice guy."

"Yeah." He placed his palm against the soft hollow of her stomach. He pictured her as she'd been earlier in Harmon's office, looking fragile and defenseless, her hand pressed against her stomach where she had carried her child.

She had lost so much, he thought. Her husband. Her baby. *He* had taken so much from her and never given back.

Now he would.

"Grace, I need to tell you something."

She rolled to face him, giving him a seductive, under-the-lashes look as she ran a fingertip down his chest. "Why don't you show me instead?"

He brushed his mouth over hers. "I plan to. Later." Ignoring the heat washing into his belly, he sat up, pulling her with him. "Right now I want to tell you how it was for me growing up."

Surprise flickered in her eyes. "Why?" Easing back a few inches, she studied him, her dark hair a glossy tangle around her shoulders. "Why, Mark? Why now?"

"You made me see how much I hurt you by not telling you." He settled into the banked pillows, the sheet bunched over his waist. "I never intended to hurt you, Grace."

"I never thought you did."

"Happened all the same." He watched her pluck his

shirt off the end of the bed, slide it on. "Hurting you is something I'll always regret," he added.

She pulled her legs up under her. "Tell me about growing up," she said quietly.

He shoved a hand through his hair. He had never discussed his past with anyone and he wasn't sure where to start. So he just plunged in.

"My mother drank." Instantly he let out a low, humorless laugh. "That sounds so benign, and that's the last thing she was. What she did was guzzle cheap booze. Swilled the stuff like it was some sort of magic potion. In our house, we didn't mark the passage of time with a calendar. We used liquor bottles. Had to have a new one every twenty-four hours, or there'd be hell to pay."

"What about your father?"

"I never knew him. At least I don't think I did. She brought home lots of men, but none stayed around very long. The one time I asked who my father was, she told me it was none of my damn business. Then she cracked me across the face with the back of her hand. I never asked again."

"Oh, Mark."

"It wasn't the first time she hit me," he said levelly. "Or the last."

"Could she work at all, drinking that much?"

"She didn't need to work. We lived in a small town outside of Chicago in a house that belonged to her older brother." Even now, Mark could smell the airless rooms that forever stank of cheap booze and acrid cigarette smoke. "My uncle was the local drug kingpin. A small-time operator, but his was the only game in town so he called the shots when it came to the local do-wrongs. In addition to drugs, he ran prostitutes and fenced stolen goods. I'm sure there was a lot more going on behind the scenes. Suffice it to say if it was illegal, Uncle Max was in it up to his eyeballs.''

"So, he supported you and your mother?''

''One of his thugs delivered a check the first day of each month, like clockwork. Every morning my mother would give me cash from what she called Max's monthly allotment. I'd go to the alley behind the liquor store and knock on the door. The owner would take the money, then hand me a bottle of booze in a brown bag. I'd stuff it in my backpack and cart it home.''

Grace shook her head, her eyes grave. "How old were you when you started doing that?''

''About five, I guess. Which explains why I had to use the alley to make my purchases.'' He scrubbed a hand over his face. ''The bad days were when my mother would drink an entire bottle while I was at school and by the time I got home, she'd forget I'd bought that day's bottle. She'd get mad, thinking I still had her money, that I was holding out on her. She was an angry drunk anyway, but on those days she'd turn mean. Vicious.''

"She'd hit you?''

''Yeah.'' Mark shifted his gaze toward the window, listened to the steady drum of rain and sleet. His past wasn't as hard to talk about as he had imagined. Not to Grace.

''She beat the crap out of me, when she could find me. Of course I knew every hiding place in the house. There was even a secret compartment in the dining room credenza where I used to hide. Over time she found all my cubbyholes. And knowing I hid from her made her even more vicious when she found me. I finally came up with a place she never thought to look.''

''Where?''

''The clothes dryer. Sometimes I would have just finished running a load of clothes through when I'd hear her yelling for me. I'd jerk out the clothes, stuff them into a laundry basket and climb into the dryer. Those times, it'd still be hot inside the drum and burn like hell. And the dry heat would nearly sear my lungs. But all that was preferable to a one-on-one with dear old Mom."

"You said you went to school. Surely you had bruises. Didn't your teacher see them? The principal? A school nurse, maybe? Did you ever ask for help?"

"I lied about the bruises in school. Made up stories about how I got them."

"Why? Someone could have helped you."

"Uncle Max had this thing about how blood kin had to stick together. He told me more than once that if I ever got taken away from her, he'd petition to get me. He meant it. I knew what it was like to live with a drunken mother. The unknown was what I'd face living with a drug dealer who ran whores and had thugs on his payroll. I was smart enough to know I didn't want any part of that life."

"The cops, a social worker, someone could have blocked him from getting you. If they'd known what was going on."

"People knew." The bitterness, lodged deep for years, swirled into Mark's throat. "It wasn't until I was older that I realized everyone in town had to have known what was going on. I mean, you've got a kid who shows up with fresh bruises on a weekly basis. It isn't hard to figure out someone's using him for a punching bag. People kept their mouths shut because they were afraid if they said anything they'd get a visit from one of Uncle Max's goons. And the sheriff was a good old boy who took payoffs to look the other way when it came to Max's business endeavors. That's what everyone did when it came to me. They looked the other way."

"And you suffered."

"Yeah."

"How long did you stay there? With your mother?"

"The morning of my thirteenth birthday I said something she didn't like so she busted my lip. Instead of going to school, I took off. From that instant my luck changed. I caught a ride with a trucker on his way home to Chicago. I told him my Dad lived there and I was on my way to see him. The trucker took one look at my lip and knew I was lying, but he didn't say anything. I fell asleep. When I woke up, we were in Chicago, parked in front of a church shelter for homeless kids. The trucker told me he had two sons who played softball on the church's league and that the minister was an okay guy. He was. He fed me, gave me a bed and didn't ask questions. He got me into school, interested in sports. I stayed there until I graduated and joined the service."

"Is your mother still alive?"

"She was murdered in the alley behind that liquor store. Someone shot her in the face, then stole her purse and the bottle she'd just bought."

"And your uncle?"

"After I joined the Bureau, I turned a DEA agent pal of mine on to Max's operation. He's now a guest of the Illinois department of corrections."

"Justice," Grace said.

"Yeah." Mark ran his knuckles along the curve of her jaw. "The other night while we were dancing, you asked me what Christmas was like at the Santini household. My mother drank up our Christmases. Every last one of them."

"I'm sorry," Grace said, her voice whisper soft. "I'm sorry there was no one to help you." Leaning in, she cupped a hand against his cheek. "Thank you for telling me."

"I'm glad I did," Mark said, meaning it. He felt a kind

of euphoric high, flooded by the relief of having told her. Of having opened the door he'd locked so long ago and letting out some of the bitterness and hate.

He settled his hand over the one she still held to his cheek. "You were right when you said the past makes us who we are. I knew what it was like to be alone and abused. A scared kid who had no one to turn to. After I got out of there, I vowed to do something with my life where I could help kids like me. The victims. Vowed I'd never look the other way."

Linking his fingers with hers, he pressed his mouth against her knuckles. "That's why I do what I do. Why I can't give up. Why I can't look the other way, Grace. Why I can't stay in Oklahoma with you."

She closed her eyes. "I understand."

He tugged her closer. "I don't regret what we had, either. What I do regret is that I can't give you the kind of life you need. One that will make you happy. If I could, I would. I hope you believe that."

"I do." She rested her forehead against his. "This has been an emotional day for both of us."

"That sums it up."

She angled back, her gaze meeting his. "For so long, I thought what we had was over. That it was finished. Then I walked into my lieutenant's office and saw you there."

"It was the same for me, Grace. The minute I saw you, I knew it wasn't over. Not for me, anyway."

"After all the time that has passed, how can what we feel still be so intense? How can all the heat still be there?"

"I have no idea." He feathered back her hair, nuzzled her throat. "I just know it is."

When the phone rang, Mark bit back a curse, then grabbed up the receiver. While he listened to the voice on the other end, he cupped a hand possessively over one of Grace's breasts. His thumb brushed across the nipple that budded hard and tight against the shirt he planned to strip her of very soon.

"Who was that?" she asked when he hung up. Already she was breathing deeply, heat rising from her invisibly, the warm scent of her perfume inundating his senses.

"The concierge." Within the space of seconds, Mark had her naked and stretched out on her back. He nibbled at one bare shoulder. "He called to remind the Calhouns about their dinner reservations." His mouth journeyed slowly up the length of her throat. "In the Sabroso Room."

"Sabroso," Grace breathed. "If my high school Spanish hasn't failed me, *sabroso* means tasty."

"Tasty." He slid his hand between her legs, cupped her, and watched her eyes turn smoky. "Great word," he murmured.

"Do you…think the Calhouns could pass on that reservation?" Her hand slicked down his belly, her fingers wrapping around him. "Call room service instead and have dinner in bed?"

Mark clenched his teeth against a jolt of pure animal lust. "Mrs. Calhoun, you can have anything you damn well want at the moment."

"You," she said, guiding him inside her. "I want you."

"You've got me, Grace. All of me."

"Your appointment today is with Stuart Harmon, Jr., not Sr.," a silver-haired receptionist dressed in sedate gray politely informed Grace and Mark the following afternoon.

Grace slid Mark a look as they stood before the law firm's waist-high mahogany reception counter that rose from thick coral-colored carpet. She knew the Bureau had done an intensive background check on the firm. Three attorneys practiced there, in addition to the firm's owner, Stuart Harmon, Sr. Junior wasn't listed as an attorney—or even as an employee—on the roster she and Mark had studied.

Somber and all business in his dark pin-striped suit, Mark gave the receptionist a level look. "My wife and I were not informed there was a 'Junior.' Or that we had an appointment with him."

Apparently not surprised at the news, the woman flicked a wrist. "Harmon, Sr. sometimes forgets to mention Junior when he meets with clients." She wrinkled her nose. "He's the boss, so we just have to work around that."

Leaning in, Grace gave the woman a fluttery, anxious look. "Will Junior have our contract ready? We're supposed to see our contract today." She clenched her hands. "We're adopting a baby, you see."

The woman's expression softened. "And you're concerned about everything getting done."

"Yes." Grace put a hand to her throat. "We've waited so long. And the baby is due to be born any day. We're hoping to have her home before Christmas. I hate to think there will be a holdup of any sort."

"Don't worry, dear." The woman's sympathetic smile had Grace thinking about her own grandmother. "The Harmons have worked as a team for several years on our adoptions. Senior always meets first with the prospective parents, and then Junior takes over the business details. He explains the terms of each contract, sees that it's executed properly. Both the Harmons are very good at what they do."

"I'm sure they are." Grace eased out a breath. "Thank you."

The woman glanced at the phone near her elbow. "Junior is on a conference call that got started late and is apparently running overtime. I'll show you to our lounge so you can have a cup of coffee or tea while you're waiting. It's just down the hallway a bit.''

Mark glanced at his watch, then nodded. "Fine."

They were still waiting fifteen minutes later. Figuring the room might be bugged like the sitting room of their suite and their rental car, they doled out their conversation with care.

''At least the sun came out today,'' Grace commented as she stood before the wall of windows that looked down on the parking lot. ''And it's warmer.''

Settled in a nearby leather chair, Mark glanced up from the financial magazine he pretended interest in. ''Still too cold to play golf, though.'' He sent her a slow, intimate smile that had her throat clicking shut. ''Fortunately we have other interests to keep us occupied.''

''We are blessed.'' Grace knew if someone were surveilling her they would see a woman gazing at her lover. At the man she'd given her heart to. The man who would walk away with it in a matter of days.

Her chest tight, she turned and looked back out the window. Last night, while lying sated and snug in Mark's arms, she had resolved not to think about the future. Special Agent Mark Santini had ridden into the sunset before and she had survived. She would do so again. He was a warm, caring man who'd grown up knowing nothing but hate, and her heart was lost to him. For now, she intended to make the most of the time they had together.

Looking down three stories onto the building's parking lot, Grace idly studied the vehicles that filled the slots. When her gaze snagged on a day-glo-yellow van, her eyes narrowed. As a juvie detective, she had constant contact with the various shelters in Oklahoma City. One being

Usher House, the shelter where Andrea Grayson had stayed for a short time before the birth of her baby. Grace knew Usher House had several vans painted the same eye-popping yellow so street kids needing a place to stay could easily identify the shelter's vehicles.

Unhurriedly she moved to a window closer to the lounge's center. A monster SUV prevented her from getting a look at the van's door to see if it displayed a logo.

What were the odds a van painted that off-the-chart color belonged to anyone else but Usher House?

Grace knew from having scanned the directory downstairs in the main lobby that Harmon's law firm was the only business operating in the building. So it stood to reason that whoever parked the van in the lot had business with the Harmons.

Was that person possibly a young, pregnant girl who'd decided to give up her baby for a private adoption? If so, was she a patient at the same clinic where Andrea Grayson and DeeDee Wyman died after being dosed by Iris Davenport with an anticoagulant drug? Was she the soon-to-be mother intending to give up her baby to the Calhouns?

Those possibilities had Grace's heartbeat picking up speed. The first thing on her list was to get a better look at the van to find out if it belonged to Usher House. If so, she and Mark had to find out who had reason to drive the vehicle an hour west of Oklahoma City for an apparent meeting at the Harmon law firm.

Grace drifted to Mark's chair. Since it was almost a sure thing they were being observed, maybe even listened to, she couldn't risk explaining her interest in the van. "Sweetheart, I left the list in the car," she improvised.

He closed the magazine, sat it on the coffee table in front of him. "The list?" he asked casually. Although his expression remained relaxed, Grace sensed his cop instinct going on alert.

"The one we made last night with the questions we want to ask Mr. Harmon." They had indeed come up with questions, but had committed them to memory instead of writing them down.

"Ah, *that* list."

She held out a hand. "I need the keys so I can run down and get it."

Mark stood, slid back one flap of his suit coat and retrieved the keys from the pocket of his slacks. "The sun may be shining, but it's still frosty. Why don't I go instead?"

"That's okay. Standing around waiting makes me as nervous as a caged cat." Plucking the keys from his palm, she raised on tiptoe and pressed a kiss against his cheek. "Watch the yellow van in the lot," she murmured. If the driver exited the building and drove off before she could get downstairs, Mark might at least get the person's description.

"Want me to get your coat from the receptionist?" he offered.

"Don't bother." She dropped the keys into the pocket of her plum-colored wool blazer. "This jacket's warm as toast and I'll only be outside a minute or two."

"All right." He picked up a different magazine and began leafing through its pages as he wandered toward the windows.

Since Grace Calhoun would predictably be in a hurry to get back for the meeting with Harmon, Jr., Grace bypassed the elevator and took the stairs down to the main lobby. Five minutes later she reentered the building, shivering from the sharp wind that made the afternoon seem colder than it was.

She had been right—the driver's door of the day-glo-yellow van bore the logo of Usher House. High priority on Grace's list was to call Millie Usher, the shelter's director. Grace and Millie had a good working relationship, and Grace knew the woman would tell her which of her shelter live-ins had reason to come to Winding Rock. The call would have to wait, though, until she and Mark could get to a secure phone.

Grace was almost to the staircase when she heard the elevator's faint hydraulic hum. Five feet away, the doors opened with a soft sighing hiss. Out of the corner of her eye she glimpsed a young woman step off the elevator, followed closely by Stuart Harmon, Sr. Grace moved smoothly out of sight behind a pillar.

"Sorry I didn't call first, Mr. H., but this is really starting to bug me."

The girl had a petite, slender build. Her short, spiked hair was black at the roots with bright purple tips. A diamond stud had been drilled into one side of her nose. Her face was bare of makeup, her eyes red from crying. Grace calculated she was in her late teens.

And pregnant. Close to her due date, considering the girth of the sweater-covered belly that jutted between the flaps of her unbuttoned wool coat. Instead of fitted maternity jeans, she wore regular ones that swallowed her legs and had frayed hems that hung over scuffed boots.

Looking as sedate and grandfatherly as he had the previous day, Harmon patted her shoulder. "It's all right to drop by anytime. The decision you've made is very serious. Once the papers are signed, it would be an almost impossible task to regain custody of your child. If you're going to change your mind, now is the time to let me know."

Grace held her breath. If this girl was the young mother

whose baby the Calhouns were slated to purchase, her changing her mind could get her killed.

"Yeah, I figured that." When the girl rested a hand on her protruding belly, Grace spotted the small lightning bolt tattooed on her little finger. "There's no way I can manage with a kid, especially since Slash did his disappearing act." She sniffed, then swiped the back of her hand beneath her nose. "Creep. I figured he'd walk when I told him about the baby and I was right. That was months ago. Don't know why I'm even thinking about him. I woke up this morning all emotional or somethin'."

"That's understandable." Harmon gave her a long, assessing look. "Are you sure you don't want to meet the couple who plan to adopt your baby? As I said in my office, they're anxious for a meeting if you're willing. I'm convinced they'll make excellent parents. Love your daughter as if she were their own. Meeting them might make you feel better about the decision you've made."

"Nah, I'd probably just blubber all over 'em."

"I don't believe they would mind if you did, but the decision is yours. Are you sure you'll be all right driving back to the shelter?"

"I'm cool." She forced a smile. "I'd better get started. I sort of borrowed the van without remembering to ask nobody's permission. Just had to get out of there for a while, you know? Sometimes the walls start closing in."

"I know the feeling," Harmon said as they moved toward the door. "I'll be happy to call and tell them we had a meeting, if you'd like. Smooth over the rough spots."

"That'd be good. Might get me out of a night or two of the kitchen duty I'll get for takin' the van." She stuck

The Cradle Will Fall

out her hand. ''Thanks for the talk, Mr. H. You remind me of my grandpa. Nice.''

''Where is your grandfather now, Lori?''

''Dead.'' She shrugged. ''Everybody went and died on me.''

Chapter 13

With time creeping by as slow as a glacier, Mark aimed an occasional glance out the lounge's third-floor windows. Pretending interest in the latest magazine he'd picked up off the coffee table, he flipped a page every so often while his gaze returned intermittently to the parking lot.

What had Grace seen? Why was the bright-yellow van significant to their case?

Below, a young girl with short dark hair moved into his range of view, apparently having just exited the building. Her tan coat was unbuttoned; at one point the wind picked up, blowing back the coat's flaps as she lumbered across the parking lot.

Pregnant, he realized. *Very.*

Just then Grace appeared through one of the lounge's doors. The smile she sent Mark held an edge of nervousness. "I just knew I wouldn't get back before Mr. Harmon got done with his conference call." She finger combed her windblown hair. "I was afraid you'd start the meeting without me."

Mark tossed the magazine onto the coffee table and went to her. He took her hand in his, found her fingers to be ice cold.

"Harmon and I would have waited for you." Eager to find out what she knew about the van, Mark attempted to read something in her dark eyes, but saw nothing revealed. "Did you find the list in the car?"

"No." She rolled her eyes. "I must have left it in the suite. I've just been so scatterbrained lately."

"Mr. and Mrs. Calhoun?"

They turned in unison toward the door on the lounge's opposite side.

A short, heavy woman whose suit was the same drab brown color as her hair gave them a polite smile. "Mr. Harmon, Jr. will see you now."

The office they entered three doors down from the lounge was the same size as the one they'd met in the previous day. It, too, boasted a fireplace in which flames currently blazed, along with dark wood and masculine leather furniture. That was where the similarity ended, Mark decided. Unlike the senior Harmon's neat-as-a-pin surroundings, his son's work area resembled an avalanche of papers, file folders and bulging brown accordion files tied with string.

And there was no sense of cultivated politeness about the man who rose from behind the desk inches deep in clutter. Stuart Harmon, Jr. had inherited height from his father, but not leanness. The black cashmere jacket he wore over a gray cashmere T-shirt and black slacks did nothing to camouflage his muscled, powerful build. *Burly* was the word Mark decided on to catalog the man whose age was probably edging toward thirty.

"Stu Harmon." Stepping around the desk, Junior offered his hand. He had a narrow face and wore small wire-rim glasses. His coal-black hair lapped over the collar of his jacket; his eyes were deep-set, guarded by heavy brows. Up close, Mark noted his eyes were red-rimmed and shadowed with fatigue.

"Mark Calhoun," he introduced himself, returning the handshake. "My wife, Grace."

Out of the corner of his eye, Mark watched Grace offer the attorney her hand. Her expression reflected just the amount of nerves and apprehension expected of a woman hoping everything would go right with yet another attempt to adopt a child. If she noticed the surreptitious examination Junior gave her breasts, Grace didn't acknowledge it.

With ancient instincts surging to the fore, Mark had to hold himself back from baring his teeth.

"Good to meet you," Harmon said, keeping Grace's hand encased in his. "I hope your suite at the Mirador meets with your approval."

"It's lovely," Grace said. "From what I've paid attention to. I'm afraid I'm so nervous about the adoption that you could have stuck us in a closet and I wouldn't have noticed." She eased her hand from his. "My nerves just aren't going to settle until Mark and I have our baby."

Nodding, Harmon, Jr. gestured toward the visitor chairs in front of his desk. "Once we take care of business details and have the contract signed, things should go fast."

Mark settled into the chair next to Grace's, then leaned in. "Your father said you would have our contract ready today."

"I do." Harmon shoved aside one stack of papers, then began shuffling through another. "As you can see, handling adoptions keeps me busy."

Mark didn't doubt the man's resolve—he was in some

capacity working with a nurse who murdered young women and kidnapped their newborns. Mark knew he and Grace were about to hear for the first time the price tag the Harmons and Iris Davenport put on each baby.

Harmon unearthed a file folder, pulled out paperwork and handed it across the desk to Mark. "Here's your contract. The language is standard for all adoptions, but feel free to have your attorney check it." He paused, then added, "I feel it's my duty to point out that doing so will no doubt hold up the adoption process."

"How?" Grace's gaze whipped up from the contract. "How will having our attorney review the contract hold up the adoption?"

Giving her a self-deprecating smile, Harmon leaned back in his chair. "Not to criticize the law profession, but do you know any attorney who does things fast? Even if we get a document that's perfect, there's always the urge to demand a change to the language, just because we can. Same thing could happen in your case, so be prepared." He rubbed his hands over his face, his fingers sliding under his glasses to press against his eyes. "Sorry," he mumbled. "Didn't get a lot of sleep last night."

"I hope you're not getting sick," Grace said.

He raised a shoulder. "Like I was saying, there could be a delay. That's not good, considering the baby you're adopting is due any minute. You won't get to even see her until the paperwork is signed by the parties, and all other business is completed. That's our policy. It's carved in stone. We don't make exceptions."

That was one hell of a good squeeze tactic to put on desperate parents-to-be, Mark thought while he continued to study the contract.

As expected, Grace clamped her hand on his. "Mark,

you deal with contracts daily in your business. Surely you can tell if this one is okay.''

''I deal with a lot of legal documents,'' he agreed. ''That doesn't qualify me as an expert on interpreting legalese.''

''Mr. Harmon just said the language in his contract is standard,'' Grace persisted. ''If that's the case, I can't see why we really need our attorney to look at it. What if we fax it to him and he doesn't check it right away?'' When she fisted her free hand against her thigh, her diamond wedding ring glinted beneath the lights. ''It just hit me that our attorney always takes a vacation before Christmas, so he's probably already gone.'' The reedy panic building in Grace's voice with each sentence now glimmered in her eyes. ''I don't want to wait until after the holidays to see our baby, Mark. *I can't wait.*''

''Darling, take a deep breath.'' As if weighing options, he lifted her hand, pressed a kiss against her knuckles and gazed at her for a cluster of seconds. ''All right, Grace, we won't wait,'' he said finally. Mark wanted Harmon to believe the husband was as desperate as the wife to take a shortcut in order to obtain the child they wanted.

''The contract's okay?'' Grace asked, her voice filled with hope.

''As far as I can tell.'' Mark shifted his gaze to Harmon. ''Grace and I will sign all the necessary paperwork before we leave today.''

''Good.'' For the first time, Harmon's fatigue-shadowed eyes took on an intensity, as if he'd just received verification that the Calhouns were easy prey. ''The way the contract's written, it virtually guarantees there's nothing that can come back and bite you later.''

''I'll hold you to that, Mr. Harmon.'' Mark raised a brow. ''I'm sure you're aware the document doesn't state the specific amount we're required to pay for…" He let his voice drift off as he thumbed through the pages until he found the clause he wanted. "'…fees incurred by all parties for legal representation,'" he read. "'In addition to medical, living and other miscellaneous expenses for the infant and its biological mother. Said fees to be paid in advance in full by the prospective adoptive parents prior to their acquiring the child.'"

"We don't put dollar amounts in the contract because the fees vary from adoption to adoption," Harmon explained. "That's because the expenses paid to each birth mother are different."

And because there's one less piece of evidence if you don't put the amount in writing, Mark added silently.

Harmon slipped a small calculator out of his desk's lap drawer. "In your case, I figured all fees and expenses last night. Here's the total." He punched the amount into the calculator, then handed it across the desk to Mark.

He studied the green digital numbers that glowed back at him. "Seventy thousand."

Harmon spread his hands. "That amount ensures you're first in line for the infant."

"First?" Grace asked. "There's another couple interested in our baby?"

"Two couples, actually."

Mark handed the calculator back to Harmon. He would have preferred to snap the man's neck while he was at it. "Money is not a problem for us," he said levelly. "How and when do you want to be paid?"

"A wire transfer. I'll give you an account number before you leave. To keep yourselves at the top of the list, the money has to be deposited in the account by this time tomorrow. If not, the deal's off."

"The deal won't be off, Mr. Harmon." Mark checked his watch. "You'll have the money in the morning."

"Good." Harmon plucked a pen from the clutter on his desk. "Let's get that contract signed."

By the time the Calhouns left his office, Stu Harmon's head was throbbing like a toothache, making his brain feel too big for his skull.

Shoving back from his desk, he made a beeline in the direction of the fireplace. He pushed back a panel on the wall, revealing a small wet bar. Snatching up a crystal decanter filled with vodka, he removed the stopper and took a long, greedy chug.

He was coming down hard.

He had been flying on cocaine for two days, getting everything done. *Everything.* He glanced across his shoulder at his desk, swamped with file folders and papers. His old man drove him like a slave. Used him as a glorified clerk, forcing him to take care of the mundane, eye-crossing work inherent with practicing law.

Only *he* wasn't practicing law. The thought clogged Stu's throat with bitterness, compelling him to swill more vodka. He had taken—and failed—the bar exam three times. Until he passed the damn thing, his father refused to pay him more than pauper's wages. As a way of openly showing his displeasure, the old man wouldn't even make him an official employee of the firm.

Bastard.

Fine. Daddy dear could keep his money because Stu had stumbled onto his own gold mine in the guise of a sexy redheaded nurse. Stu considered it a bonus that Iris Davenport was damn good in the sack. All he'd had to do when they'd met was steer her in the right direction. He'd gotten her a job at the clinic. After that, the money had started rolling in.

Not to the firm. *To him,* Stu thought smugly. Some to Iris.

His eyes narrowed at the thought of how Iris had turned greedy when it came to the Calhouns. Since she'd met them, brought them into the process, she wanted a finder's fee. He'd agreed, mainly just to keep her in line. He had a payment past due to his supplier, and he needed the Calhouns' money. *Yesterday.*

Knowing the damage his supplier's thugs would do to him if he didn't make good on what he owed had fear manifesting as a sharp pain in the center of Stu's forehead. He considered taking another snort of cocaine just to calm himself, then decided against it. After a two-day high, the only thing that would prevent him from going into a full crash-and-burn landing was vodka to smooth out his nerves and about twelve hours of sleep.

If Lori Logan still hadn't given birth after he'd gotten his shuteye, he would do something to speed the process.

Just as he was about to take another hit from the decanter, Stu heard the door open behind him. He reached for a glass, poured himself a shot of vodka, then turned.

"Dad."

"Stuart."

"Care to join me?"

"I don't drink. You know that."

"Yeah." Stu turned, leaned a negligent shoulder against the bar. "I know."

"And neither should you."

"So you continually tell me."

As always, his father's spine was stiff beneath his tidy three-piece suit. Closing the door behind him, Mr. Stiff-As-a-Board moved to the center of the office, a glint of disdain settling into his eyes as his gaze swept across the cluttered desk.

"Was your meeting with Mr. and Mrs. Calhoun successful?"

Although he wanted to chug the vodka in one gulp, Stu sipped at it. "They signed the paperwork. I'll have their certified check tomorrow." And a lot more of their money in an offshore account you'll never find, Stu added silently. *This* was his revenge. Justice for the way his father had treated him since his mother's death. "All that's left is for the baby to arrive so the Calhouns can start changing diapers."

Harmon, Sr. raised a silver eyebrow. "That's why I'm here, Stuart. To inform you there might be a problem with the adoption."

Stu paused, the glass partway to his mouth. "What the hell do you mean by 'problem'?"

"The Logan girl was here this afternoon."

"You didn't tell me she had another appointment."

"She didn't. She commandeered one of those big yellow vans that belongs to Usher House and drove herself here." Concern settled over his father's face. "I wish she hadn't done that. There's another storm moving in and the roads could turn bad."

"Why?" Stu asked, flicking away his father's comment with a snap of his wrist. "Why did Logan come here if she didn't have an appointment?"

"She needed someone to talk to, and she chose me." His father's mouth lifted at the edges. "I apparently remind the girl of her late grandfather. I asked Miss Logan if she still intends to give up her baby. She assured me she does. However, I sensed she's dealing with a great amount of turmoil over her decision. I'm not sure we can depend on what she'll do between now and the birth of her child.''

"Did she say that?" Stu set his glass on the bar with a snap, then took a quick step toward his father. "Did she actually *say* she wants to keep the kid?" He could feel the panic rising inside him, burning the base of his throat. He had to have the Calhouns' money tomorrow. If not, he was a dead man.

"No, to the contrary." Harmon, Sr. picked a piece of lint off his shirt's starched cuff. "She said she isn't able to support her daughter. Still, Miss Logan is having second thoughts, so I want you to put the Calhouns on hold. Don't accept any money from them until the child is born and we know for sure what Miss Logan is going to do."

"Fine. Sure thing." Stu's mind was racing. Whirling. He weighed his options. Found he had only one. "When did she leave?"

"Excuse me?"

"Logan. What time did she leave here?"

"A half hour ago. Why?"

Half an hour—it would take her thirty more minutes to drive to Oklahoma City. Stu had seen the shelter's yellow vans during previous visits from other birth mother clients. The vehicles were big and lumbering and even in favorable weather he doubted they made good time on the highway. Unlike his Porsche, which ate up the pavement.

"Just curious," Stu answered. "I was wondering if Logan ran into the Calhouns when they left a few minutes ago. She was adamant about not meeting them, after all."

"She still is. She arrived before they got here and I walked her downstairs when she left. Thankfully, Miss Logan and the Calhouns didn't cross paths."

Stu checked his watch. "Gotta go. I just remembered I

have a date.'' He grabbed his coat and walked fast out the door, leaving his father behind.

Five minutes after she and Mark returned to their suite at the Mirador Resort, Grace had the director of Usher House shelter on the phone.

''I was in a meeting all afternoon,'' Millie Usher explained. ''So I didn't know Lori Logan took the van until Mr. Harmon called. He wanted to let me know she'd needed someone to talk to and had come to his office. He asked me not to be too hard on her for taking the van without permission.''

Because the woman's voice sounded tinny, Grace rose off the bed and moved to stand at the windows, hoping to improve the reception on the secure cell phone the FBI had provided. Her gaze settled across the room on the small writing desk where Mark sat, his own cell phone clamped between one cheek and shoulder while he jotted notes on a pad.

''Is Lori back yet?'' Grace asked while thunder rumbled in the distance.

''I'm upstairs in my office, looking out the window at our parking lot. All three of our vans are there. So, yes, she must be back from Winding Rock.'' Millie sighed. ''Sergeant McCall, that young girl just breaks my heart. She's barely fifteen years old and has no family. No one. When her baby's father dumped her, she cried for days. I'm working to get her into a foster home after the baby's born, but there's no guarantee a child her age will make a good fit.'' Millie paused. ''I don't have to tell *you* that. You're a juvenile detective—you know how rarely we find a perfect fit for a lot of kids.''

''I know.'' In her mind's eye, Grace saw Lori Logan with her spiky, purple-tipped hair, diamond nose stud and

oversize clothes. Saw, too, the way she had held her tattooed hand against her belly, as if protecting the child she
carried. Lori didn't know it, but Grace was determined to
keep her and her child safe.

"Millie, what clinic does Lori go to for prenatal care?"

"The one on Sixth Street, run by Dr. Tom Odgers."

The clinic where Iris Davenport worked, Grace thought
with a shudder. Odgers was cooperating with the investigation and had reassigned Iris, so she no longer worked in
the delivery room. Further, the Bureau had an agent working undercover at the clinic. Still, those safeguards weren't
enough for Grace. Not when a young woman's life might
be on the line.

"Millie, I can't tell you right now why I'm asking about
the Logan girl. I'll explain everything later. I just need you
to make sure she doesn't go back to that clinic."

"Her records are there, Sergeant. She's due to give birth
any day."

"I know. Trust me on this, Millie. Lori Logan can't go
back to that clinic. And I need you to keep an eye on her,
just to make sure she stays okay. I want you to call me
the minute she goes into labor," Grace added, then rattled
off the number of her cell phone.

"All right, Sergeant. You can depend on me."

"Thanks, Millie," Grace said, then clicked off the
phone.

While Mark's call continued, she pulled off her plum-
colored wool blazer and hung it in the closet. She toed off
her heels. Another rumble of thunder, closer now, had her
padding back to the window. It wasn't even five o'clock,
yet dusk was already settling, like thick soot drifting down
through gray water. Behind her Mark's voice was a quiet
murmur.

She closed her eyes. If someone had told her two weeks

ago she'd be sharing a series of hotel suites with Mark Santini, she would have called them crazy. Told them there was no way in hell that would happen. But it had. And here she was, not only sharing a suite with Mark but a bed.

They were lovers again, for a few more days.

She swallowed past the knot in her throat. She could handle this, she assured herself for the nth time. Could handle having only days—instead of a lifetime—to spend in Mark's arms. She had resolved not to dwell on the past. Promised herself she wasn't going to obsess about the emptiness she knew lay in the future. She wouldn't let herself think about anything but now. Refused to contemplate what her life would be like when he was gone.

"I've got some background on Harmon, Jr.," Mark said.

Blinking, Grace turned away from the window, saw he'd ended his call. "What have you got?"

"What we *haven't* got is a licensed attorney." Grabbing up his pad, Mark rose and carried it across the room to where she stood. "Junior has taken the bar exam on these dates."

Grace raised a brow as she gazed at the pad. "Three times and he has yet to pass?"

"Crashed and burned each time. Bet that made Dad proud. And here's an interesting tidbit—Junior got popped for possession of cocaine a little over three years ago. The charge was dismissed. We're trying to find out why now, but I'll wager Harmon, Sr. used his influence to get his kid out of hot water."

Grace settled on the edge of the bed. "When you and I talked last night, we agreed Senior doesn't seem the type to black-market babies. Junior, on the other hand, does."

"He fits the mold," Mark agreed, taking a seat beside

her. He had his shirt collar unbuttoned, sleeves rolled up, and the knot of his tie loosened. "A person could afford to buy lots of coke if he were selling babies for seventy grand each."

"I can picture Iris Davenport teaming with Junior," Grace said after a moment. "Killer nurse supplies kidnapped babies to coke-head wannabe lawyer. He operates out of a prestigious law firm with a rock-solid reputation, so prospective parents have no reason to question if everything's on the up-and-up."

"Junior doesn't have a license to practice law, so his name doesn't appear on any of the adoption papers. Senior's name goes on all the legal documents." Mark paused. "Last year, Senior handled more than seventy adoptions. Duly decreed through the court. The receptionist told us standard operating procedure is that Senior meets with the adoptive parents, then Junior takes over and deals with the paperwork. And the money."

"The money," Grace repeated. "If the Calhouns are like all the other adoptive parents the Harmons deal with, they get a contract to sign that has no dollar amount shown. And Junior wants payment in cash, wired to an account that it's possible only he knows about."

"Yeah," Mark agreed. "So, hypothetically, it's possible Dad believes Junior charges a lot less money per adoption. If Junior is still putting coke up his nose, he might be funding his habit by squeezing a lot more money out of each desperate couple than Pop knows about."

"And we have to wonder if all the adoptions are legal," Grace pointed out. "FBI agents are taking a look at those seventy adoptions. So far, everything appears to be aboveboard."

"Since the babies born to Andrea Grayson and DeeDee Wyman have yet to surface, we can probably go with the theory that there was no real adoption where they're concerned. No legal proceeding through any court. All Junior had to do in these cases was draw up fraudulent papers and get the adoptive parents' signature. Junior never filed the papers in any court, he just forged signatures and seals so the new parents wouldn't get suspicious.''

Grace's hands balled into fists of frustration. ''This case is the worse piece of knitting I've seen. All we've got are loose ends. We still have no solid proof that Iris Davenport committed the two murders and kidnapped two infants. Then there's Troy Pacer, the pharmaceutical salesman she spent at least one night with while in Vegas. So far Pacer looks clean, but he's got a lot of connections to the Florida medical community. He could use them to acquire newborns for the black-market ring.''

''Both Harmons,'' Mark added, ''Junior for sure is involved, because after meeting with him today we know he's the money man. As soon as he accepts the Calhouns' money, we can make a case against him for the fees he's charging. It's a felony to overcharge for an adoption. There are federal statutes as well as state.'' Mark narrowed his eyes. ''At this point Senior's involvement is unknown.''

Mark tossed his pad aside. ''Damn it to hell.''

Grace stiffened at the snap of anger in his words. ''What?'' She shifted to face him, saw the frustration in his dark eyes.

''If all we can collar Harmon on is a lame adoption charge, we'll never find those two babies. Never know if they're dead or alive. And if they are alive, they're at the mercy of whoever this coke-snorting scum sold them to.''

At the mercy of a monster, Grace thought. Now that she knew about Mark's childhood it wasn't hard for her to read his thoughts. To know he would naturally wonder what fate had befallen the two helpless infants whose mothers had been murdered. Just two more children who Mark felt he needed to protect.

She laid a hand on his clenched fist. "I need to brief you on my call to Millie Usher."

"Right." Mark blew out a breath. "I take it she gave you the last name of the pregnant girl who was driving the Usher House van?"

"Lori Logan," Grace said, then ran down the rest of the conversation to Mark. She ended with, "Millie promised to keep her eye on Lori. And to call me the minute she goes into labor. I wish we could take her into protective custody now. Hide her away to keep her and her baby safe."

"If we do that, word might get back to the Harmons. We know they hedge their bets—that's why they've bugged the living area of this suite and our rental car. It's more than possible they're paying someone at Usher House to keep an eye on things. Let them know if any cops show up, asking questions. If that's the case and Lori Logan all of a sudden disappears, the Harmons might call off the Calhouns' adoption. That happens, this investigation folds with no real proof against any of the parties involved."

Grace nodded. "Iris would remain free to kill again on a whim. And we'd lose all hope of finding the two kidnapped babies."

"Yeah." Mark wrapped his hand around hers. "The Calhouns' money is scheduled for transfer by ten o'clock in the morning. The minute it hits Junior's account, we move in on him. After we get him into interrogation, we start talking about charging him with accessory to two murders and kidnappings. I guarantee he'll roll on Davenport. Then we'll have cause to pick her up."

"In the meantime, the Calhouns wait."

"We wait," Mark agreed. His thumb glided across her knuckles. "Any suggestions on how the Calhouns should pass the time?" he asked softly.

Grace slid him a sideways look. "They could go downstairs. Eat dinner in the Sabroso Room."

"I am hungry for something tasty," he murmured. Feathering her hair back, he pressed a whisper-soft kiss against her throat. "But not for food."

Instant heat, delicious and amazing slid through Grace's veins, pooled beneath her flesh. *Now,* she reminded herself as she closed her eyes on a soft moan.

The past could wait until tomorrow. Now was all that mattered.

Chapter 14

By the time Stu parked his Porsche in Iris Davenport's driveway, his system was jumping for a hit. He would take one, he promised himself as he dashed up the porch steps two at a time. Right after he had Iris where he needed her.

"Where have you been?" she demanded when she swung open her front door. Her green sweater was as skin-tight as her jeans, and she'd piled her red hair up on top of her head. "I've left messages for you since I got back from Vegas. Something's happened."

"You're telling me," he shot back as he stalked past her. He glanced to his right, his gaze taking in the small living room. When he'd met Iris, she'd been a hospice nurse, working two jobs. Her rental house had been furnished with Salvation Army castoffs. Now new furniture filled the room. A TV with a thin screen the size of a helicopter pad took up the entire wall opposite the couch. Although the sound was muted, the pictures of several infamous murderers, currently displayed on the wide screen, had Stu theorizing that Iris had been watching a documentary on serial killers. Appropriate, he thought, looking back at her. She'd killed twice. Committing one more murder shouldn't make a difference to her.

"I need you to pack a bag," he said.

She slammed the front door shut then advanced on him, her eyes boring into him like a pair of cold lasers. "I'm not doing squat until you tell me why you've dodged my calls for two days."

"I was taking care of things." *Everything.* "Adoption papers. Monitoring the Calhouns' conversation." Getting stoned, Stu added silently. He vaguely remembered the messages Iris had left on his voice mail. He'd intended to return them. Then his coke high had become unsustainable and everything had started bleeding out of his brain. "I don't have time to stand here while you throw a fit. Something's come up."

"You're damn right it has. When I got home from Vegas and went back to work, I found out I'd been transferred. I'm no longer assigned to work with maternity patients."

Stu narrowed his eyes. "Why? Why were you transferred?"

"I don't know. Dr. Odgers said several staff members needed cross-training so we could fill in for each other."

"So, you're not the only one who got transferred?"

"Five of us did." Her glossed mouth tightened. "Do you realize what that means? I no longer have easy access to the homeless mothers. The ones who want to give up their babies."

He held up his hands. "We'll deal with that later. In the meantime, pack a bag with enough clothes for a couple of days. There's no heat, so bring heavy stuff. And blankets." Stu shoved a hand through his hair, forcing his overloaded

The Cradle Will Fall

brain to function. "If you've got any medical supplies for delivering a baby, bring them."

"Delivering a baby?" The total disbelief in Iris's face sounded in her voice. "What the hell are you talking about?"

"I'll tell you on the way there." He gave her shoulder a light prod. "Start packing."

She knocked his arm aside. "I can tell by the way you look that you've been on another binge. Snorting. Drinking. You show up here, talking nonsense at a hundred miles a minute and expect me to pack a bag and go with you, no questions asked. Forget it—"

"Shut up!" He clamped a hand on her elbow and pulled her a few feet down the hallway. "You don't go with me, we're out the money from the Calhouns. I don't know about you, but I *need* that money. *I have to have that money.* So shut your damn mouth and do what I say!"

"Why would we be out the Calhouns' money?" Iris attempted to jerk her elbow free, but adrenaline and strength made his grip iron tight. "They were a sure thing."

"They still are. The mother's waffling."

Iris stopped struggling. "Lori Logan? She changed her mind about giving up her baby?"

"Let's just say she's *thinking* about changing her mind. I'm not giving her a chance to do that. I snatched her up a couple of hours ago. Stashed her in a place where there aren't any bleeding hearts telling her it's okay if she decides to keep her brat. *It's not okay.* I need you to deliver the kid."

"What about Logan?"

"You deal with her, the same way you did with the other two who waffled. 'Out of forced necessity,' you called it."

"Oh, my God. *Ohmygod!*"

Stu froze at the sudden panic in Iris's voice. She had stopped looking at him and was staring past him into the living room. Her eyes were huge; she'd gone so pale her skin looked nearly translucent.

Loosening his grip on her elbow, he pivoted toward the living room. He stared at the image on the TV, searching, searching.

The show on serial killers was still on, the setting having switched to a press conference, taped at some previous date. A silver-haired man stood at a podium with several men clustered behind him. Lights from media minicams glared as the speaker answered questions fired by reporters. The information line at the bottom of the screen identified the man as an FBI Special Agent.

"He's a damn cop!"

Stu gave her a baffled look. "You know the FBI guy with the silver hair?"

"Not him, idiot!" Iris jerked from his grip and rushed into the living room. She grabbed the TV remote off the coffee table and turned up the volume.

"…from those facts, the group of agents standing to my right from the Bureau's Crimes Against Children Unit surmised that the Lolita Killer had previously spent time in jail."

"There!" Iris stabbed a finger at one of the men standing in the cluster behind the speaker.

When Stu focused on the face, his body instantly went rigid. The man had sat in Stu's office only a few hours ago. Mark Calhoun.

"Christ." Bands of tension wrapped around Stu's chest, tightening as he moved into the living room.

"If he's a cop, she is, too!" Iris was trembling now, her

lungs heaving, her breath rasping. "Mark and Grace," she spat. "They're onto us. *They know!*"

Iris dropped the remote, then whirled. "I can't stay here. They'll come and get me. Put me in a cell. I've got to get out of here." She snatched a ring of keys off the coffee table. "Now."

"Wait!" Stu snagged her arm as she turned. He felt the same panic that clearly held Iris in its grip, but he wasn't so far gone that he was going to run out into the night and just take off. He didn't have a license to practice law, but he had no problem thinking like a lawyer. "You can't just leave. We need a plan."

She yanked against his hold, her body twisting. "Let go!"

He clamped his free hand on her other arm and gave her a shake. "We have to think."

"*You* think. I'm leaving." She struggled to get free. "I can't live in a cell. *I can't stay alive in a cell.*"

Her eyes were wild now, her voice shrill enough to shatter glass. Stu knew if the cops got her while in a panicked state she'd give them everything. Including him.

He dug his fingers into her arms. "Calm down, dammit. Get a grip."

She smashed the ring of keys against his right cheek. The pain from the keys' jagged metal edges was like an explosion, as clear as a star on a cold night.

"Bitch!" He pressed a hand to his cheek, felt blood seep against his fingers. In a sudden rush of black fury, he swung his arm, hitting her with an open-handed blow to the side of her head.

The impact sent her reeling backward like a drunken dancer, momentum pitching her down. Stu heard the crack when her head hit the edge of the coffee table.

"Get up." He had ice picks stabbing into his cheek, and

his breath escaped in a grunting rush. "You're going to take care of these cuts. We'll figure out our next step after that."

When she didn't move, he spat a crude oath. "I said get up." He squatted, gripped her shoulder then rolled her onto her back.

The eyes that stared up into his were open, glazed and lifeless.

Grace was sprawled across the bed, her body slick with sweat, her heart thundering in unison with the storm roiling outside when Mark's cell phone rang.

"Damn." With his mouth pressed against the curve of her left breast, she felt the warm wash of his breath when he muttered the word. He lifted his head, his eyes lazy and sated. "Duty calls."

"Us civil-servant types live to serve," she murmured, drumming up the strength to smile. Her smile became dreamy when she watched him walk to the small desk and snag his cell phone. Santini had one hell of a body. And that magnificent body had one heck of an effect on her own.

"The latest victim was how old? Seven?"

Hearing Mark's questions, Grace's smile evaporated. She sat up against the bank of pillows, watching as he reached into his briefcase and retrieved a file folder. It was evident from the conversation that another CACU agent was calling about one of the cases Mark was working. Grim-faced, he continued to ask for details while jotting notes.

"Dammit, Zabel, I know I could be more help getting a handle on this bastard if I was there." Mark's voice was as hard and unyielding as his profile. "The case I'm on should wrap in a day or two. I'll catch a flight to Anchorage the minute I get free.''

Grace closed her eyes. She could hear her heartbeat pounding in counterpoint to the rain that beat against the windows. Now, however, her pulse wasn't hammering due to lust. Realization had just hit her with the strength of a sledgehammer.

He was leaving.

She dragged in a breath. Then another. Mark had told her he would leave. She had made up her mind that thinking about the past could wait. That she would have hours, days, years to *think* after he was gone.

Despite the assurances she'd given herself, regardless of how she had thought she'd prepared herself, hearing Mark talk about leaving sent cold reality swooping down in the form of searing pain.

She had talked herself into believing she could handle being Mark's lover again on a temporary basis. *Fooled* herself into thinking that was more like it. Had she ever truly believed she could deal with being right back where she was six years ago, totally wrapped up in a man already planning to walk out the door?

In love with a man she might never see again.

Oh, God, she loved him.

She knew it was possible that in his own way Mark loved her. But whatever his feelings, they weren't deep enough for him to stick around.

He ended the call, stuffed the file back into his briefcase, then pressed the heels of his palms against his eyes. ''That was Zabel. He's filling in for me on the Alaska murder investigation until I can get back there.''

''So I heard.''

When Mark dropped his hands and turned to look at her, Grace realized the pain shimmering through her had sounded in her voice. "I have to go, Grace," he said quietly. "We both know that."

"Yes." Sitting there naked, she suddenly felt totally vulnerable. Rising, she went to the bureau, opened a drawer and snatched up the first sweater she came to. It was white and soft and hit her midthigh. "Knowing you have to leave is one thing." She pulled the sweater over her head, then turned to face him. "Sleeping with you one minute, then listening to you make plans to walk out the door when you've barely crawled out of bed with me is another."

Jaw set, Mark reached into the closet, snagged a pair of jeans off a hanger and hitched them on. "I have a job to do. I thought you understood that."

"I do."

"Then understand something else." He took a step toward her. "I don't intend to say goodbye to you when I leave. I don't want this to be like six years ago. We can work something out. Figure out how we can spend time together."

"Between your cases."

"Yes." Muscles flexed in his jaw as he jabbed his hands in his hair. "Dammit, that's my life."

"I know." Grace felt tears welling in her eyes. His life had been the same six years ago. There hadn't been a lot of room in it for her then, and she'd been smart enough to know what little he had to offer wouldn't be enough for her.

It still wasn't.

She fisted her hands against her thighs, unfisted them. Last night, he had opened up to her, stripped away all his defenses, and told her about his past. He had given her that part of himself so she could understand why he was the man he was. Why he couldn't turn his back on his job.

She figured she owed him the same.

"We have to make a clean break," she said quietly. "Because last time we didn't, and people I loved got hurt."

His brows slid together. "We *did* make a clean break. When you told me you wouldn't move to Virginia with me, you asked me not to call. Not to write. No e-mails. I respected that. You said you were sure it was what you wanted."

"Turns out I wasn't so sure."

He took a step toward her. "What are you talking about?"

"When I met Ryan, there was something between us instantly. A spark. I thought there could be more. But not while I still had feelings for you. Feelings I'd tried my damnedest to shake. Because I couldn't shake them, I had this gnawing sensation in the back of my mind that maybe I'd screwed up royally by not going to Virginia with you."

Turning back to the bureau, she opened another drawer, pulled out a pair of jeans and tugged them on.

"You were still inside me," she continued after a moment. "My head, my heart. I wanted to be fair to Ryan. I couldn't give myself to him until I figured out what to do about you. So, I decided to go for broke. I arranged to take a leave of absence from the job. I called your office. You weren't in town but were due back the next day. I caught a flight back east. My plan was to show up at your condo, announce my intentions to live with you, then jump your bones."

"You didn't…" Mark stared at her in dawning dismay. "Are you talking about that one time you showed up at my condo?"

"Yes."

"You said you were in D.C. to attend a conference. Law enforcement training."

"I lied."

"Why?" He closed the distance between them, his brows set in a thunderous line. "Why the hell didn't you tell me the truth?"

"Two reasons. One being the long-stemmed blonde who was perched on your couch when you answered your front door. The second was because you were packing to take off for yet another crime scene."

"The blonde didn't mean anything."

"Her name was Brenda."

"I don't give a damn about her name! She was just someone I dated."

"I know. I could tell by the way you looked at her. There you were, with this gorgeous blonde snuggled on your couch, and what were you doing? Packing to leave town."

"I had a job to do."

"Exactly." Grace lifted a hand palm up, let it drop. "I had known all along that the job came first with you. Until last night, when you told me about your childhood, I didn't understand why. I just knew you'd never let anything or anyone take precedence over your work. I *knew* that, but it didn't sink in until the day I showed up in Virginia. I saw then that no matter what woman was sharing your life, she didn't stand a chance—not pitted against your job. So, I came home."

"You should have stayed," Mark retorted. "You should have given what we had a chance."

"What we had didn't stand a chance," she countered quietly. "Turns out my showing up at your place and see-ing what I did was the best thing that could have happened to me. I shut the door on my past with you and I fell in love with Ryan. I did love him. Totally.''

Mark closed his eyes. "I know that."

Her emotions roiling, Grace paced to the windows, glanced out into the rainy black night. "What you don't know is that about a year before he died, Ryan overheard Carrie, Morgan and myself talking about my trip to see you." Grace turned and braced her back against the wall. "It was just girl talk. Idle stuff about guys from the past."

Mark angled his chin. "Let me guess. Ryan's reaction was anything but 'idle.'"

For a moment, no more than a blink of the eye, Grace was right back there, facing the pain and hurt that had roiled in her husband's eyes. Her throat aching with regret, she wrapped her arms around her waist.

"When Ryan confronted me about what he'd overheard, I told him the truth. All of it. He said he believed me. But I could tell there was still doubt. Uncertainty that maybe I'd settled for him because I couldn't have you." Grace dragged a hand through her hair. "From that day on you stood between us."

"Christ."

"You were a ghost, Mark. One I couldn't exorcise. Always there, hanging over my marriage."

"I feel like I should apologize." He scrubbed a hand over his face. "Tell you I'm sorry."

"Not your fault," she said quietly. "No one's, really. But it's the reason I can't do this again. I can't let you hang over the rest of my life like smoke that I can't quite get clear of. If we keep this up, keep falling into bed together, that's exactly what will happen. For me, anyway."

"Dammit, Grace, I don't want to lose you. We can work something out—"

"No. I can't sit home for months on end, hoping you'll

find a big enough hole in your schedule so you can drop by to see me. Then while we're together, spend my time wondering how long it will be before you leave again.''

For want of something better to do, she moved to the bed, began smoothing the blankets and sheets they'd rumpled while making love. When it came down to it, she thought, the only time she'd ever felt Mark Santini was hers—totally hers—was during bouts of mind-blowing sex. Out of bed, the job took priority. Always the job.

She plumped the pillows banked against the headboard. ''I thought last night when we wound up in this bed that we were starting something.'' She grabbed a pillow off the floor, propped it with the others. ''I realize now we were finishing what we had in the past. For good this time.''

''Like hell.'' He stalked across the bedroom and clamped his hands on her shoulders. ''Do you think making love with you was just a casual roll in the hay for me? Think again, McCall. We're not over.'' He leaned in, his dark eyes as turbulent as the storm outside. ''I asked you to move to Virginia with me because I cared about you. If you had told me why you'd shown up on my doorstep, what we had wouldn't have ended. We wouldn't have spent six years apart.''

She lifted her chin, studied his face. ''If I had told you the truth that day, would you have still packed your bags and left town?''

''You know the answer to that.'' His fingers dug into her shoulders. ''I couldn't change the fact a kid had gotten butchered. That my job was to find the bastard who'd done it before another kid died. I *had* to leave.''

''So did I.''

''Grace—''

''I know what it's like to have a normal life with a man who's always there. That's what I had with Ryan, and it was really special. If it weren't for him, if we hadn't had what we did, maybe I could settle for what you can give me.'' She shook her head. ''I don't want to settle, Mark. Someday I'll have the kind of life I need with another man. What I don't want is the specter of what you and I once had—or might have had—hanging over that relationship, too.''

The ringing of the phone on the nightstand had Mark swearing viciously.

Grace eased out of his hold. ''Better answer that, Mr. Calhoun.''

''We're not done with this, Grace. Not by a long shot.'' The undertone of steel in his voice backed up his words.

He stalked to the night stand, snatched up the receiver. ''Calhoun.'' He listened, then said, ''You're not interrupting anything, Mr. Harmon.''

While he listened, Grace watched Mark's expression transform from fiery emotion to a cop's sharp intensity.

''Of course we still want to meet the mother of the child we're going to adopt.'' Meeting Grace's gaze, Mark mouthed the word *Junior* so she would know which Harmon he was talking to.

''The location isn't a problem,'' Mark said, checking his watch. ''But like you said, it's an hour's drive from here. It will take us a while to get there. If you're sure she wants to meet us tonight, Grace and I will leave right away.''

She was doing both of them a favor, Mark decided as he steered the rental car off the interstate. After forty-five minutes of driving through the rainy night, he had finally figured out how Grace had worked things in her mind. By breaking off their relationship before they got in too deep, she thought she would do them both a favor and save them some pain.

Good try, he thought, but it wouldn't work. Not for him, at least.

What she didn't understand was that he had spent the past six years with her crowding his thoughts. Day after day. Month after month. Year after year. Maybe it was a fluke that an investigation had brought them back together. One huge coincidence. Karma, brought on by a shifting of planets. He didn't care why their lives had intersected again. The point was, they had, and he damn well wasn't going to let her go this time. They would deal with their different lifestyles. Figure out some way to see each other more often than every six years.

Somehow. Some way. They would make things work.

Mark tightened his hands on the steering wheel as rain continued to pelt the windshield. He had grown up bereft of love. Spent his adult life budgeting his emotions meticulously. As a result, he had no way to compare his feelings for Grace with anything he'd experienced before. He might possibly be in love with her. Love, after all, meant giving and sharing deep intimacies. They had definitely done a lot of emotional and physical sharing over the past two days.

He slicked a look toward the passenger seat. Lights from the dash illuminated Grace's face in a pale glow. If there hadn't been a bug planted in the car, he wasn't sure what he would have said to her during their almost silent drive. And even if he'd known what needed to be said, he had no idea *how* to say it. Not yet, anyway. He would figure out something before he left Oklahoma City.

"I wonder what changed for her," Grace said. "Why she suddenly decided to meet us."

"We'll find out soon enough, darling," Mark said. He

shifted his attention back out the windshield. The car's headlights stabbed through the darkness and sheeting rain to illuminate the curved road that had narrowed to two lanes.

The directions Stuart Harmon had given over the phone were to a small café on the outskirts of Oklahoma City. Believing he and Grace were the Calhouns from Houston, Harmon had no way of knowing they were both familiar with the area that sported poorly maintained roads, farmhouses and an occasional mom-and-pop convenience store. Their final destination was just beyond the upcoming wooden bridge, and Mark surmised that business wouldn't be booming at the café on the rain-soaked night.

Just then, glaring headlights snapped on behind them. Narrowing his eyes against the bright beams, Mark realized a car had turned in behind them at some point after they'd left the interstate. With the rain coming down in sheets, he'd had no clue it was there.

And because of its bright lights, he could barely make out the vehicle's shape. The headlights were positioned higher and wider than those on the rental car. Some sort of SUV, he theorized.

He sensed Grace tensing beside him. "Mark—"

His name was all she got out before the SUV rammed them.

Years of training prevented Mark from slamming on the brakes. Doing so on the wet pavement would have sent the car into a spin. Instead, he pumped the brake pedal, attempting to reduce the car's speed before they reached the narrow bridge.

The bridge that spanned deep banks and a rushing creek.

"Your seat belt fastened?" he shouted.

"Yes. Yours?"

"Yes."

The SUV rammed them a second time. Mark gripped the wheel while the car fishtailed. The headlights did a wild dance, glinting off the railing that stood between the narrow edge of road and the creek below. He had the sudden image of the car smashing through the railing and plunging into the dark abyss.

Not going to happen, he told himself, using the next half second to think, to anticipate, to plan. He couldn't let the SUV come up beside them. It was massive, higher off the ground than the car and could easily shove the lighter vehicle's rear wheels into a sideways skid. Doing that would force the car into the bridge's not-so-stable-looking railing.

When the SUV surged into the lane beside them, Mark yanked the wheel to block its path.

The sound of metal on metal screeched above the thunder of the engines as the side of the SUV smashed against the bridge's railing. Obviously fighting for control, its driver slammed on the brakes. The SUV crashed against Mark's side of the rental car with teeth-loosening intensity, then careened back against the bridge, ripping off pieces of railing.

Pumping the brake, bearing down on the wheel, Mark battled against momentum that tossed the car sideways. Skidding wildly, the car smashed into the bridge.

Over the roar of blood in his head, over the squeal of tires, Mark heard the thud when Grace's head hit the passenger window.

Chapter 15

When Grace opened her eyes, everything swam in and out of focus. The right side of her face throbbed. She closed her eyes again.

"Baby, open your eyes. Grace, look at me."

Mark's voice, and his unrelenting tapping on her left cheek with his fingertips made it impossible to sink back into the darkness.

"I'm okay." Blinking and disoriented, she shoved his hand aside. "I'm okay." When she started to sit up, her stomach took a dip and she hissed out a breath.

"Easy." Mark gripped her shoulder. "Keep your eyes open, but stay down for a minute longer."

"Good idea." She touched a finger to her cheek, instantly clenching her teeth against a jolt of pain. Her brain felt fuzzy and disjointed. Which was exactly how Mark's face looked, hovering above hers. "What…happened?"

His hand, warm and gentle, curled around hers. "You

used the side of your head as a battering ram against the car's passenger window."

"Oh." It all came rushing back now. The glare of lights, the jarring impacts when the vehicle rammed their car from behind. The sickening screech of metal. Her head slamming against the window. The way her vision doubled, then tripled before she blacked out.

Taking a deep breath, she eased herself up. Only then did she realize she was on a gurney in the back of an ambulance. A female EMT with blond hair scraped back into a ponytail hovered at Mark's side. Grace recognized the woman whose fingers were currently wrapped around the pulse in her wrist from the years she'd worked in Patrol.

"Hi, Stella. How you doing?"

"Better than you right now, Sergeant McCall." Stella looked at Mark's hand wrapped around Grace's. "In some areas. How many fingers am I holding up?"

"Two."

"What's the date?"

"December twenty-third."

"Who's the governor?"

"Of which state?" Grace asked. "Do I pass?"

Stella nodded. "With flying colors."

Grace looked back at Mark. "I'm still fuzzy on some details. I remember Junior called the suite and told us Lori Logan wanted to meet the Calhouns at that café."

"A ruse," Mark said. "I sent a cop to check the café. Lori hasn't been there. Junior called because he wanted to get us out in the open. The way things look, our cover got blown somehow, and he decided to kill us. Our car running off a narrow road on a rainy night and crashing into a creek would have probably looked like an accident."

Grace closed her eyes, opened them. "I take it Junior was driving the car that rammed us?"

"Yes. Actually, it was a minivan," Mark said. "Registered to Iris Davenport. She wasn't in the van, though. An agent from the Bureau's Oklahoma City office and an OCPD black-and-white are on their way to pay Iris a visit."

"What about Junior? Did you get him?"

"Nabbing him was a piece of cake since he was passed out in the van." His expression concerned and intense, Mark ran his knuckles down Grace's uninjured cheek. "Junior wasn't wearing his seat belt. When the van slammed into the bridge, his head hit the steering wheel. He came to while being transported to Baptist Hospital. Which is where you're going."

"Not in the back of an ambulance."

"Grace—"

"I'm fine."

"You hit your head. You've been unconscious. You need to get checked by a doctor."

"I will. We have to go to Baptist to see about Junior, so I'll ride with you. I can have an E.R. doc take a look at me."

"Our rental car is out of commission. I've got an OCPD patrol car waiting to take me to Baptist." Mark glanced across his shoulder. "Your call, Stella. Is Sergeant McCall cleared to ride to the E.R. in a black-and-white, or does she go in this ambulance?"

"Her pulse is steady, memory good, vision and speech are clear. She can ride with you as long as she sees a doc at the hospital."

"I'll make sure of that," Mark said, looking back at Grace. She glimpsed something in his dark eyes, some emotion she couldn't read.

The EMT shifted her gaze from Mark to Grace, then back to Mark. "I get the feeling that while Sergeant McCall hangs with you, she's in very good hands."

The E.R. was the usual bevy of nurses, ambulance personnel and patients.

While a distant radio broadcasted nonstop Christmas music, a still-wet-behind-the-ears intern pronounced Grace fit to return to duty the following day. Ignoring the "following day" part of his prognosis, she turned down his offer of a prescription painkiller. Instead she swallowed aspirin for the headache that snarled in her right temple.

Less than a minute after the doctor disappeared through the privacy curtain circling the exam table, Mark stepped in. His expression was set, his eyes grim.

"What's happened?" Grace asked, still perched on the edge of the table.

"Iris." He handed Grace her purse, which he'd retrieved from the wrecked rental car. "When the FBI agent and patrol cop showed up at her house, they found her dead."

"Dead?" Grace's eyes widened. "How?"

"The M.E. says it looks like she fell and hit her head on the edge of a heavy wooden coffee table. Whether she had help falling is something we don't know at this point." Mark reached into the pocket of his trench coat, pulled out photos and handed them to Grace. "The agent snapped these at Iris's house. He brought them by, knowing we'd want a look at the scene."

Grace studied the photos. Iris, dressed in a green sweater and jeans, lay on her back, her eyes open and glassy. The last two photos had been taken in the garage. A silver, mud-spattered Porsche was parked on one side. "Does the Porsche belong to Iris?"

"No. It's registered to Stuart Harmon, Jr. The lab guys

found cocaine in the glove box. They've towed the Porsche to their evidence garage and are already going over it.''

"Interesting," Grace murmured. "Any idea why Junior was driving Iris's minivan tonight?"

"My guess is he decided a Porsche was too easy to identify while running cops off the road. We can ask Junior his reason whenever you're ready. His forehead is stitched and he's in a room down the hall with a cop guarding the door." Mark paused. "I talked to the doc who treated him. He's also got several scratches on one cheek. The doc isn't sure, but he doesn't think Harmon got them when the van crashed."

Grace remembered the fake nails Iris had worn in Vegas. They could do major damage to a face. "You think they're from fingernails? That he and Iris struggled and she scratched him?"

"Maybe. But the doc said they don't look like fingernail scratches. The lab people will check under Iris's nails for traces of skin and blood."

"What about his father?" Grace asked while using a fingertip to gingerly explore her throbbing cheek. "We don't know where he fits in. How deeply he's involved in illegal adoptions, if at all. We need to interview him tonight, too."

"We will. One of our agents picked him up in Winding Rock, told him Junior was under arrest and injured. They should be here soon. I've got another agent working on getting a search warrant for the Harmons' office and residence. Since Junior lives in the same house as Senior, that means we can look for evidence of involvement on both their parts at the same time."

Angling her chin, Grace conducted a slow study of the man standing a few feet away. His black trench coat hung open; she could see his pressed jeans and gray turtleneck sweater beneath. The exam room's harsh fluorescent lights seemed to emphasize the dark, somber handsomeness of his features. Loving him, wanting him, Grace knew the way Mark looked at this one moment in time would haunt her secret dreams for the rest of her life.

She swallowed around the lump that settled in her throat. "You've had a lot on your plate tonight, Santini. Taking care of business while your partner was unconscious, then getting poked by a doctor. I haven't exactly held up my end of the workload."

Mark stepped to the edge of the table, placed a hand on her thigh. "Seeing you hurt. Unconscious..." His eyes stayed steady on hers while a muscle in his jaw tightened. "There are things I want to tell you, Grace. *Need* to tell you."

Whatever he intended to say was lost when a uniformed cop stuck his head through the curtains.

"Sergeant McCall? Dispatch got a call from a woman trying to locate you. Her name's Millie Usher. You need her number?"

"I've got it." As the cop stepped out of view, Grace looked at Mark. "She might be calling to tell me Lori Logan has gone into labor."

"You can use my cell," Mark offered.

"Here's mine," Grace said, pulling her phone out of her purse. She checked the display. "Millie's tried to call me twice. Must have been while I was unconscious." Grace stabbed the recall button. Less than a minute later she had the director of Usher House on the line.

"Thank goodness I've found you, Sergeant McCall." The reedy panic in the woman's voice stiffened Grace's spine.

"What's wrong, Millie?"

"Right after we talked this afternoon, I headed downstairs to check on Lori Logan, like you asked me to. One of the kids had left a book bag at the top of the stairs. I was preoccupied and didn't see it. I tripped over the darn thing, tumbled all the way down.''

''Are you okay?''

''Broke my arm in two places. It took a couple of hours at the clinic to get me patched up. But that's not why I'm calling. It's about Lori.''

''What about Lori?'' Grace looked up, met Mark's waiting gaze.

''I was in so much pain after I fell that I forgot about her for a while. When we got back to the shelter from the clinic, I didn't see Lori with the other kids. Turns out, no one has seen her.''

Grace's felt her throat close. ''Since when? When's the last time anyone remembers seeing her?''

''Right after lunch. Just before she slipped away in the van to drive to Winding Rock to see Mr. Harmon.''

''She made it back, right? You saw the van in the parking lot.''

''Yes, the van's still here. All of our vans are. But none of the kids remember seeing Lori after the van came back. Sergeant McCall, we've looked everywhere for her. Scoured the neighborhood. My assistant director drove to all the places we thought Lori might have gone, just to hang out. Nothing.''

''It's possible she went into labor.''

''We called every clinic and hospital in the city with no luck.''

''Have you reported her missing?''

''When I couldn't get you right off, I called 911. A patrol officer came and took a report.''

''Did you give him a picture of Lori?''

''Yes. He said he would make sure it got distributed.''

Concern for the young mother-to-be settled on Grace's shoulders, leaden and oppressive. "You've done everything you can right now, Millie. Call me if Lori shows up or you hear from her. I'll contact you if we find her."

"This isn't good," Mark stated when Grace ended the call. "Our cover gets blown. One of our suspects drops Lori's name to draw us into an ambush. Now she's missing. No way we're dealing with any kind of coincidence."

"Mark, we need to interview both Harmons," Grace said as dread curled in her stomach. "If Iris was murdered, if they took Lori…" She shook her head, not wanting to think about the prospect of Lori and her unborn baby having met the same fate as Iris.

Five minutes later Mark nodded to the uniformed cop guarding a room down the hallway from the E.R. The cop opened the door, then led the way inside. Grace followed; Mark brought up the rear.

Mark took in the room, which was a small rectangle with gray walls and white vinyl flooring. The air reeked of hospital disinfectant. A single table was positioned in the center, with four gunmetal-gray straight-backed chairs gathered around it. Their prisoner sat in one of the chairs, his wrists handcuffed behind him.

Although still wearing his gray cashmere T-shirt and black slacks, Stuart Harmon, Jr. barely resembled the man they'd met earlier that day. His narrow face looked pale and gaunt. His small wire-rim glasses were missing; his coal-black hair was disheveled. Just above his heavy dark brows, a line of stitches and a jagged bruise mottled his forehead. While the uniformed cop uncuffed Harmon's wrists, Mark paid particular attention to the scratches on the man's right cheek that looked livid against his bone-white skin.

"Cops." Harmon regarded Grace and Mark as they settled into the chairs on the side of the table opposite him. "Never would have guessed. When it comes to two people acting like they're in love, you guys take first place."

Mark kept his expression unreadable. Seeing Grace bruised and battered had shaken him from the inside out. He'd almost lost her again. Forever. Knowing that had put things into perspective.

Grace gave Harmon a sedate smile. "How and when did you find out we were police officers, Mr. Harmon?"

"Just now. When you walked in the door." His mouth curved. "It's the badges and guns clipped to your belts that gave you away."

Mark recited Harmon's Miranda rights, then asked if he understood them.

"I'm a lawyer," Harmon said, massaging his wrists where the cuffs had been. "I know my rights. You need to tell me why you're harassing an innocent citizen."

Grace arched a brow. "You're not a lawyer, nor are you innocent, Mr. Harmon. You've never passed the bar exam and you attempted to kill me and Agent Santini tonight."

Harmon lazed back in his chair. "Don't know where you got the idea I tried to kill you. My brakes failed and my van hit you from behind. It was an accident on a dark, rain-slick road. Nothing personal."

"*Your* van?" Mark asked. "That wasn't your van, was it, Stu? Belongs to a friend of yours."

"Yeah." Harmon shrugged. "Next time I see Iris, I'll mention how she ought to keep her brakes maintained."

"Iris," Grace murmured. "Why don't you tell us about Iris?"

"Sure. I met her nearly two years ago when she was a hospice nurse. My mother was dying, and Iris worked the night shift at our house. She and I would sit around and shoot the breeze.''

''And after your mother's death, you and Iris continued your friendship.''

''The fact she let me borrow her van tonight ought to tell you that much.''

''Why?'' Mark asked. ''Why did you borrow her van?''

''The engine on my car started pinging. I didn't want to be late for my meeting with *the Calhouns,* so I borrowed Iris's van. Simple as that.''

''And you left your Porsche in Iris's garage.''

Mark spotted a flicker of emotion in Harmon's eyes. Grace's comment was his first indication the police had been to Iris's house and knew she was dead.

''Yeah. Because it was raining, Iris suggested I pull the Porsche inside. Nice of her.''

''It was,'' Grace agreed. ''Less chance of someone breaking into your car and stealing your coke out of the glove box.''

''Coke?'' Harmon shook his head. ''Don't know anything about that. You might want to check with Iris, since she's the last person to have possession of the vehicle.''

''Let's get back to the meeting you set up with the Calhouns,'' Grace said. ''Where is Lori Logan?''

Harmon wiped the back of his hand under his nose while giving them an incurious look. ''You tell me. When she called and told me she wanted to meet the Calhouns, she said she would hitch a ride to the café. Maybe she's still there?''

''She's not,'' Mark said. ''So, she called you and said she wanted the meeting. Meaning, there should be a record of that call coming in to your phone.''

''Actually, I called her. Dad said she'd gone to see him this afternoon and was upset. I had to come to Oklahoma

City on business, so I decided to call her while I was here.''

''What sort of business?''

Although Grace asked the question, Harmon shifted his gaze to Mark and gave him a knowing look. ''I told Dad I had a date. Actually, I had some bar hopping on my agenda. Planned to pick up a friendly female, have a night of fun. You know how it is.''

''Did you use your cell to call Lori?'' Mark asked.

''Tried. I couldn't get good reception—must have been the storm. So I stopped at a pay phone and called Usher House.''

''What pay phone?'' Mark asked.

''Outside some convenience store. Hard to say which one.'' Harmon scratched his chin. ''I live in Winding Rock, not Oklahoma City. I'm not real familiar with the streets here, so I can't give you the phone's specific location.'' He pursed his mouth. ''You could check the phone record for Usher House.''

''We will,'' Mark said evenly, although he suspected doing so would be futile. Harmon obviously knew that the homeless kids who stayed at Usher House didn't have money for their own cell phones and pagers. Anytime they needed to call the shelter, they used a pay phone. Chances were, there'd be calls made most nights from various pay phones to Usher House.

Grace leaned in. ''Lori is due to give birth at any minute. We need to find her.''

''I can't help you.''

''How about trying to help yourself?'' Grace shot back. ''We already have you for overcharging fees for an adoption. A felony. Then there's the two homicides Iris committed. DeeDee Wyman and Andrea Grayson are dead because your pal, Iris, injected them with an anticoagulant drug after they gave birth. Then Iris kidnapped their infants and gave them to you to sell. That makes you an accessory all the way around. Where are those two babies?''

''Ask Iris. I don't know anything about any murders or kidnappings. And I don't overcharge anybody. I collect substantial fees for arranging private, upscale adoptions. Period.''

''I'm not finished outlining your problems, Mr. Harmon,'' Grace continued. ''You now have counts of assault and the attempted murder of two law enforcement officers hanging over your head. My partner is an FBI agent, meaning one of those charges is federal. That alone will get you a life sentence in a federal trial. Then you'll be remanded back to state custody and tried again.''

''That won't be a walk in the park,'' Mark observed. ''Oklahoma juries don't like scum who murder young women, kidnap their babies and try to kill cops.'' He paused, then looked at Grace. ''Don't forget the possession of cocaine charge.''

''Right. There're so many that one must have slipped my mind.''

Mark noted Harmon's red-rimmed eyes now tracked between Grace and him like a spectator at a tennis match.

Grace tapped a fingernail on the table, pulling Harmon's gaze back to her. ''Andrea *Grayson*,'' she said. ''Mr. Harmon, did you pick up on the last name of one of the girls Iris murdered?''

''I don't know anything—''

''Maybe you've heard of U.S. Senator Landon Grayson?'' Grace persisted. ''Andrea was his daughter. Iris killed her, then *you* sold his granddaughter. The senator is a powerful man, used to getting what he wants. Right now he wants his grandbaby.''

Mark gave Harmon a scalpel-sharp smile. ''Let's cut to

the chase here, Stu. Grayson's involvement makes this whole case political. You're smart. You know what that means. Everybody's got to look good, and the only way that happens is if someone pays the big price. Right now, that someone is you.''

Harmon's mouth compressed. "I *told* you, I don't know jack about what Iris has done. As for tonight, the brakes on the van went out. It was raining. The road was slick. I lost control of a vehicle I'm not used to driving. What happened was an *accident*.''

"It's no accident Lori Logan is missing," Mark said. "Tell us where she is. We find her alive, I'll work with you on this. See you get a deal.''

"I don't need a deal," Harmon shot back. "Logan told me she was going to hitch a ride and meet us at that café.'' He clenched his hands on the edge of the table. "The girl is a runaway, known to hitchhike. Maybe her luck ran out tonight. Could be she stuck her thumb out and some pervert picked her up. Did something awful to her. Who knows? We might never hear from her again.''

"Bastard's lying," Grace said after she and Mark finished with Junior. As they walked along the hallway back toward the E.R. where they'd left their coats, she flexed her fingers, unflexed them. Anxiety over the young girl's welfare curled in the center of her chest. "He knows where Lori Logan is. I can *feel* it.''

"Yeah, he knows," Mark agreed. "He's just never going to tell us.''

When they rounded a corner, Grace spotted Harmon Senior and another man, standing at the nurses' station, waiting to be helped.

"There's Senior," Grace said. "Is the guy with him the FBI agent who picked him up?''

"Yes." Mark slid her a look. "Ready to conduct another interview, Sergeant McCall?"

"Ready, Agent Santini."

After a brief private meeting between father and son, the uniformed OCPD cop put Junior in a scout car and headed for the Oklahoma County jail. Grace and Mark resumed their seats at the table in the hospital's interview room, this time with the elder Harmon seated across the table.

"I understand your reasons for obtaining a warrant to search our home and office," Harmon, Sr. told them after Grace and Mark advised him of his rights, then ran down the evidence they had. "And a subpoena to view our records. You don't need those documents to gain my cooperation, however. I will tell you what I know. Try to help you in any way I can."

Grace studied the silver-haired man, clad in an impeccably tailored suit. Although he sat in the chair ramrod straight, she sensed an air of defeat around him. Sadness. It took her a second to realize it wasn't the attorney she was seeing, but the father whose child was in desperate trouble.

"We appreciate your cooperation," Mark said. "We've already explained the fees your son planned to collect from the Calhouns in order to adopt Lori Logan's baby. We need more than just your word you were unaware of that amount. We need proof."

"All I have is my word, Agent Santini. I've been semi-retired for several years. I deal with the people part of the adoption process—meeting the birth mothers, the adoptive parents. I've left the legalities and paperwork to my son. From what you've told me tonight, that was a mistake." Harmon lifted a hand speckled with liver spots. "To say that Stuart has been a disappointment to me would put it mildly. I've bailed him out of trouble all his life. Another mistake on my part. He's my child, and I'll continue to stand by his side. But it's time for him to answer for his own actions.''

Grace's cop's sixth sense told her the man was telling the truth. That he was just another victim on a growing list. ''Mr. Harmon, while you were meeting with your son, Agent Santini and I received a phone call from the OCPD lab. Lori Logan's fingerprints were found in Stuart's Porsche. Lori is missing. She's due to have her baby any minute. Do you have a lake house Stuart might have taken her to? A vacation place? A relative or friend who owns a house or some other structure Stuart has access to? Something private.''

''No. I'm sorry.'' Harmon closed his eyes. ''She's a sweet girl. Told me I remind her of her grandfather. If I could help you find her, I would.''

Half an hour later Mark and Grace stepped onto an elevator at OCPD headquarters. Grace stabbed the button for the third floor where the juvie division was located. She felt as if it had been a hundred years since the day Mark showed up in her lieutenant's office. For a moment her heart ached for the man she loved. The man whose life simply would not meld with hers.

With regret washing over her for what they would never have, never share, she glanced across the elevator. Mark was shuffling again through the photos taken earlier at Iris Davenport's house.

''Something just hit me,'' he said, his eyes sharpening on one of the photos.

Putting a choke hold on her emotions, Grace stepped beside him, saw the photo was of Junior's Porsche, parked in Iris's garage. "What just hit you?" she asked, looking up.

"It's a long shot."

"Right now we don't have any shots."

"Okay, go with me here. Senior told us he and Junior talked after we left the law firm. At that point, Junior still believed we were the Calhouns."

"Right."

"So, Senior tells Junior that Lori Logan drove there in one of Usher House's vans to tell him she's having second thoughts about giving up her baby. Senior tells Junior to hold up on the adoption. He doesn't want to do that because he needs the money. My guess is for cocaine. He asks Senior how long it'd been since Lori left to drive back to the city. Junior then claims he has a date and rushes out."

"Junior lets the Porsche's engine out of the box," Grace says, picking up Mark's thread. "He gets to Oklahoma City in time to waylay Lori. Since the van she drove was back at the shelter, he must have gotten to her there, in the parking lot."

"She knows him by sight. Wouldn't think twice about getting into the Porsche with him. So she goes willingly, doesn't make a scene that would draw anyone's attention."

Grace nodded. "Junior takes her to some out-of-the-way place where he can lock her up. Keep her there until she gives birth."

"He needs Iris to deliver the baby."

"He goes to her house," Grace said. "For some reason they fight, which is probably when he got those scratches on his cheek." Grace frowned when her thinking hit a snag. "Iris would have gone along with the plan so she could collect her part of the fee they'd get for selling Lori's baby. Iris has killed twice already. Why should delivering Lori's baby, then killing Lori matter?''

''Shouldn't.'' Mark scrubbed a hand over his jaw. ''We'll figure that out later.''

Grace looked back down at the photo of the Porsche. The sleek, silver body was streaked with dirt, the expensive wheels caked with mud. She thought about it, then realization hit her. ''You're thinking about the mud, right?''

''Right. Senior said Junior is a stickler about keeping his car clean. That he washes the Porsche weekly, more often if it needs it. Senior thinks he glanced at the car this morning when he got to the office and didn't see any mud.''

''That might mean Junior picked up the mud when he drove Lori to wherever he has her stashed.''

''Let's hope to hell that's what happened.'' Mark pulled out his phone, stabbed a button. ''And that a forensic geologist can analyze the mud and give us an idea where it came from.''

Chapter 16

For Grace, the following hours sped by in a blur of activity.

Luck smiled on the investigation in the form of the FBI forensic geologist who had been in Dallas, winding up his testimony in a criminal trial. With thoughts of Senator Landon Grayson watching over the Bureau's shoulder, the FBI director dispatched his jet to pick up the geologist for transport to Oklahoma City. Upon examination of the mud on Junior's Porsche, the geologist determined the soil contained traces of paint, bits of concrete and asphalt, and a chemical used exclusively in the tanning of hides.

Grace's thoughts instantly shot to a hulking warehouse once used as a tanning factory. Abandoned years ago, the structure was a dilapidated, rundown eyesore where drug dealers conducted business.

Dark, dangerous and forbidding, the warehouse was the perfect place to imprison a kidnap victim.

Grace, Mark and a team of heavily armed cops descended on the dank, rodent-infested warehouse. Minutes later they found Lori Logan. Her ankle was chained to a heavy metal table, and she was in the throes of labor. Grace gripped the teenager's hand, whispering encouraging words while two EMT's delivered a healthy, wailing baby girl.

Huddled with her baby on an ambulance stretcher, Lori identified Stuart Harmon, Jr. as her kidnapper.

"That's all the evidence we need to nail Junior," Mark said, small rocks from the warehouse's crumbling parking lot crunching under his feet as he moved to Grace's side.

Shoulders hunched beneath her heavy coat, she stood in the freezing wind that carried the smell of snow. Shadows oozing from the abandoned, hulking warehouse made the night seem even darker. Metal grated as the EMTs quickly loaded Lori's stretcher into the ambulance.

"Yes," Grace agreed. "We've got Junior."

"You and I make a good team, McCall."

A short-lived one, she thought. The ambulance's siren whooped to life and the red-white light bar flashing from its roof performed a dazzling show across the faces of the cops who'd taken part in the teenager's rescue.

Grace met Mark's gaze, not wanting to think about how few hours remained until he walked out of her life forever. If she remained aloof, she could cope. Get through it. Survive.

"Time for us to pay Junior a visit," she said levelly. "Maybe he'll be more willing to talk when he hears we've got him cold on the kidnap."

Emotion flared in Mark's eyes, then was gone. "Our early Christmas present to him."

Upon hearing Lori Logan had been found alive, Junior began cooperating in hopes of avoiding a cell on death row. He admitted working in tandem with Iris Davenport.

Her job at the clinic had been the perfect setting to meet pregnant girls wanting to give up their babies. Iris had collected a fee from Junior for each of the mothers she'd referred to the Harmon law firm.

Things had run smoothly until DeeDee Wyman had gone into labor and changed her mind about giving up her child. Iris, desperately needing money to pay off heart-stopping gambling debts, had killed the girl and kidnapped her baby. Six months later Andrea Grayson had become Iris's second victim.

Acknowledging he'd been at Iris's house when she fell, Junior insisted her death was an accident—she'd panicked after spotting FBI Special Agent Mark Santini on television. Junior then revealed the location of hidden files on the adoptions of the two kidnapped infants.

Senator Landon Grayson had wasted no time in dispatching his attorney to begin proceedings to obtain custody of his granddaughter.

Now, with the investigation wrapped and her final report written, Grace shut down her computer. With the squad room nearly deserted, she glanced at the clock on the wall. It was nearly noon on a snowy Christmas Eve.

She'd missed a night's sleep, skipped a few meals, and her system was buzzed on cop-shop caffeine.

On top of it all, she felt like a coward.

Too bad, she thought as she pulled on her coat and grabbed her purse. Mark was in an office down the hall on a conference call with the FBI director and Senator Grayson's top aide. The director's jet was waiting at the airport to whisk Mark to Anchorage so he could take up where he'd left off, tracking Alaska's current serial killer.

Grace headed out the door and down the stairs. Nothing between her and Santini had changed. For all intents and purposes, they had already said goodbye. She couldn't hang around this time and watch him walk away forever.

You can run, but you can't hide, Mark thought an hour later when he wheeled a loaner FBI cruiser into the driveway behind Grace's car.

He hadn't been surprised when he finished his conference call and walked into the juvie division to find her gone. After all, she'd expected him to leave town and had opted to pass on saying goodbye.

Mark set his jaw. If things turned out the way he hoped, he was never going to say goodbye again.

He shouldered open the car door against the wind and stepped out into snow falling in white, wild, wicked sheets. Popping the trunk, he pulled out Grace's suitcase and debated whether to leave his own behind. Deciding to go for broke, he snagged it, then headed up the porch steps.

He rang the bell. Standing there, he felt as if a lifetime had passed since he'd last seen the evergreen wreath adorned with a gigantic plaid bow and loaded with shiny red balls that hung on the front door.

He heard muted footsteps approaching the door. In the seconds that followed, instinct told him he was being observed through the peephole. Another second passed, then the door opened slowly.

"Grace."

"Mark."

She stood in the doorway between the wind and the warmth, unmoving. He lifted a brow. "It's freezing out here. How about inviting me in?"

"Fine," she said dully, then stepped back.

Her dark hair was damp and slicked back from her face, the deep-purple bruise on her cheek a stark contrast to her pale skin. She wore a long red sweater and black leggings, and she was the best thing he had ever seen.

He followed her gaze to the suitcases he'd settled just inside the door. "We left all our clothes in the suite in Winding Rock," he said. "I had everything packed and brought to the Oklahoma City office."

"Thanks." Her gaze lifted slowly to meet his. "Only one of those suitcases is mine."

"I know." Not waiting for an invitation to stay, he pulled off his coat, draped it over the suitcases. "I told you at the hospital there were things I need to say to you. That hasn't changed."

"*Nothing's* changed, Mark."

"Wrong." He shoved up the sleeves on his sweater. "If you had waited at your office for me, we would already have this settled."

"Settled," she repeated, temper sparking in her eyes. "We've already *settled* things, Santini. I understand why you do what you do. Why you can't give up your job. I accept that. What you need to accept is that I won't settle for just the scraps and pieces of your life."

"I know that."

"Then what the hell are you doing here?"

Without waiting for his answer, she turned and moved down the hallway. She paused at the entrance to the living room. "You have a plane to catch," she said without sparing him a look. "Do me a favor, Santini, and just go," she added, then stepped out of sight.

He fisted his hands. "You're damn well going to listen to what I've got to say, McCall."

Fueled by rock-hard determination, he tracked her down the hallway. He would beg, he would fight, do whatever was necessary. But he wasn't going to lose her again.

Pausing beneath the arched entrance, he swept his gaze

around the living room. Its neutral-toned furniture, dark wood and lush green plants were made even more cozy by the flames dancing in the brick fireplace.

Grace stood with her back to him, her arms wrapped around her waist, her gaze centered on the towering Christmas tree with its twinkling white lights and tinsel. An ocean of packages covered the floor.

"My mother never bothered with a Christmas tree," he said, stepping into the room. "Or decorations." He paused inches behind her. "No presents. Buying them would have cut into the money she spent on booze."

Grace turned. The temper was gone from her eyes; they were now dark, unreadable pools. "Mark—"

He held up a hand. "I need you to listen, Grace. Just listen. Please."

She stepped past him, moving across the room to stand in front of the fireplace. "I'm too tired to haul you down the hallway and toss you out the front door."

He felt a small seed of relief that he'd gotten over the first hurdle. Shifting his gaze back to the tree, he tucked his fingers into the back pocket of his jeans. "Even after I bought my condo in Virginia, I never once considered putting up a tree. No reason to, since I spent most Christmases at crime scenes. Most holidays."

He looked back at her. She stood before the fire, a gorgeous, sexy woman with flames dancing gold behind her. "I've been doing that for six years. Giving everything I had to the job. I had nothing else in my life. When you decided not to move to Virginia with me, when you cut all ties, you left a hole."

"A hole?" she repeated incredulously. "You didn't try to change my mind about staying here and moving with you. Not once."

"I thought staying in the same city with your family,

keeping your job on the OCPD was what you wanted. Needed. I dulled the pain by burying myself in the job, tried to fill the hole with work. Work I told myself I *had* to do. Kids were being abused, murdered. No way could I look the other way like an entire town did while my mother spent thirteen years beating the hell out of me.''

He walked toward Grace, his thoughts circling in his head. He had so much he wanted to say to her. *Needed* to say. ''Over time, the work just made the hole bigger. I tried to fill it with more work. The past year, maybe longer, I've felt like there's nothing left of me. I didn't know who I was anymore, and I blamed it on the job. Then I came here and found you again. And myself. I opened up to you, and that hollow spot inside me started to fill. Last night when I saw you hurt, unconscious, I realized it wasn't the job that had made me feel so empty for so long. It's because six years ago I gave a part of myself to you. A part of my heart. You still have it, Grace. All of it. I love you.''

''Don't.'' When tears welled in her eyes, his gut tightened. ''Don't say that. Don't come here and tell me you love me, not when you're leaving.''

When she started to turn away, he caught her wrists. ''I'm not going anywhere.''

''For how long? A day? A week? You can't do your job and stay here.''

''I can't do my job anymore, period. Not the way I've been doing it.'' He thumbed away a stray tear that slid down her uninjured cheek. ''I've learned I can't slay all the dragons, no matter how hard I try. That's basically what I told the FBI director this afternoon when I turned in my resignation.''

Beneath his hands, he felt her go still. ''You quit the Bureau?''

"I tried. He wouldn't accept my resignation. So we worked a deal."

Grace gave him a wary look. "What deal?"

"First, I'm taking some of the mountain of leave time I've accrued. After that, I report to the Bureau's Oklahoma City office. I'll lend my expertise via fax, phone and video conference to field agents handling high-profile cases. There may be some travel involved, but it'll be rare."

"A desk job?" She eyed him with the same suspicious intensity as she would a prime suspect in a murder. "Not your style, Santini. What makes you think you can all of a sudden handle staying grounded in one spot?"

"Because this particular grounding comes with unique benefits." He angled his chin, studying her face. "At least I hope it does."

"What benefits?"

"You. A life with you." Afraid she might slip away, he slid his arms around her waist, tugged her close. "I want a chance for a new beginning with you, Grace. I want to make a home with you. A family. I want to give you the life you need. The life *I* need. Let me do that, Grace." He closed his eyes, opened them. "Please let me."

She said nothing, just stared up at him, her eyes searching his face.

A column of fear wafted up his spine like smoke at the thought she might say no. He tightened his arms around her. "Aren't you going to say anything?"

"If you gave me a piece of your heart six years ago, how come I didn't know about it?"

"Because I didn't know it myself. I grew up hating the people I was supposed to love. Who were supposed to love me. I walled off my emotions and focused on my career. I wouldn't even let myself examine my feelings for you. Turns out, it wasn't just a piece of my heart that I gave you." He feathered kisses along her jaw. "I gave you all of it, Grace. You've had my heart all this time."

His kisses traced a trail to her throat. When she shuddered and leaned into him, his mouth curved against her soft flesh. "Got anything to say now, McCall?"

"Two things," she murmured. "I love you, Santini."

He buried his face in her damp hair, drew in her seductive scent and sank into her like a parched man into calm, restful water. "What's the second?"

Her hand slid beneath his sweater, her palm pressing against the center of his chest. "Now that I know your heart's mine, you're not getting it back. Ever."

* * * * *

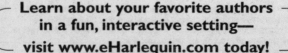

Silhouette®

COMING NEXT MONTH

#1279 THE RIGHT STUFF—Merline Lovelace
To Protect and Defend

Major Russ McIver had strict rules against dating other military personnel—that was, until a mercy mission stranded him in the jungle with independent Lieutenant Caroline Dunn. Would their heated encounters and the threat of death from rebel forces make him reevaluate his ironclad position on love?

#1280 ONE TRUE THING—Marilyn Pappano
Heartbreak Canyon

Retired police officer Jace Barnett's instincts told him that Cassidy Rae was hiding something. Jace felt compelled to protect his attractive new neighbor, liar or not, from the man she claimed had murdered her husband. But with no way of knowing the truth, was he conspiring in a crime…of the heart?

#1281 DOWN TO THE WIRE—Lyn Stone
Special Ops

DEA agent Joe Corda took the missions that scared everyone else away. That was what led him to rescue emissary Martine Duquesne from a brutal Colombian drug lord. They'd sent Joe to get her out alive—but the problem was, saving her life was only the beginning.…

#1282 EXTREME MEASURES—Brenda Harlen

With a potential murderer on his trail, Colin McIver took refuge in the hometown he'd never forgotten—even though that meant facing the woman he'd never stopped loving: his ex-wife, Nikki. Stunned when she revealed she'd given birth to his child, he was suddenly ready to risk everything to keep danger from his family's doorstep.

#1283 DARKNESS CALLS—Caridad Piñeiro

Powerful, dangerous and the key to catching a psychotic killer, Ryder Latimer was everything FBI agent Diana Reyes couldn't have—and everything she wanted. But once she learned his secret, would his sensual promises of eternal love be enough to garner her forgiveness? For Ryder was more than a lover of the night…he was a vampire.

#1284 BULLETPROOF BRIDE—Diana Duncan

Gabe Colton had been on the verge of telling Tessa Beaumont who he really was—until his accidental hostage distracted him with her intense response to his bad-boy bank robber image. Now, on the run from the authorities, and with the *real* criminals chasing them, he must use all his skills to protect her…and his true identity.

INTIMATE MOMENTS